S0-CQR-491

CRITIC'S
CHOICE
fiction

Also by John Halkin

SLITHER
SLIME

Squelch

JOHN HALKIN

A Critic's Choice paperback
from Lorevan Publishing, Inc.
New York, New York

ISBN: 1-55547-135-8

First Critic's Choice edition: 1986

From LOREVAN PUBLISHING, INC.

Critic's Choice Paperbacks
31 E. 28th St.
New York, New York 10016

Manufactured in the United States of America

Squelch

PROLOGUE

Kit gasped aloud when he spotted it. Not from fear; not at that stage. Fear came later.

The caterpillar was the most gorgeous he had ever seen. It was also the largest, measuring at least six inches from tip to tail. Possibly more. Kit stood on tiptoe to examine it closely through the glass wall of the tank and it rewarded him by rearing up to stare back with dark, baleful eyes. It was plump and hairy, too; a brilliant green with diagonal purple markings along its sides and a distinctive yellow stripe down the full length of its belly.

He was fascinated by it. 'Real beauty, y'are!' he murmured, unable to drag himself away.

The glass tanks, around a dozen of them, were set out in line along the high laboratory bench. They were clearly incubators of some kind. Each contained a different breed of caterpillar, but not one in the same class as this beauty. He had to have it for himself. No way was he going to leave this place without it.

Anyway, that would be his proof that he had been inside the 'Research'. None of the kids in the village would doubt him once he produced that caterpillar.

But first he needed something to stand on.

Kit was small for his age. Always had been, and the others had never let him forget it. But sometimes — as today — it had its advantages. Had they known where to find the gap under the high security fence, one or two of them might have been able to worm their way through. Jacko perhaps, though not Lenny. Lenny was far too big, most of it muscle too. Then, he was almost thirteen.

Once inside the fence, only Kit was small enough to squeeze between the bars over the open basement window and get into the building. That was worth some credit.

No use going back without evidence, though. They'd never believe him just on his say-so. He struggled over to the bench carrying a high lab-stool which he positioned carefully, trying not to make a noise.

'Out of the way, cat!' he breathed in annoyance.

Ever since he'd climbed in, that black cat had followed him around, rubbing itself against his legs to demand attention. Now it decided to sit and lick itself just where he needed to place the stool. He steered it away with the side of his foot. The building was quiet. No sound even of distant voices, though he knew there must be people about somewhere.

Standing precariously on the stool he slowly shifted the tank's close-fitting plastic cover to one side. Filling much of the space in the tank was a potato plant, its roots in a thick layer of soil at the bottom; among its profuse leaves he now saw several caterpillars of the same type, though none quite as big as the first. The emerald green of their long-haired fur coats stood out against the darker background.

It eased Kit's troubled conscience a little to know there were more. With all those to play with, the scientists weren't going to miss just one. From his jeans pocket he produced the empty cassette box he'd found one day in the high grass near the village bus-stop. A bit small perhaps for the very big caterpillar, but it would do till he got home.

He leaned over the tank, his left arm inside up to the elbow, and gently grasped his prize between finger and thumb.

6

'Jesus!'

The pain was like hot, sharp needles plunging into him, forcing him to drop the caterpillar. In a reflex action his hand jerked upwards towards his mouth, but before he could suck the agony out of his fingers his weight shifted and the stool on which he was standing began to tip over. To steady himself he clung to the tank, only to bring the whole thing down with him as he fell. It shattered on the hard floor.

Half-stunned, he must have lain there for quite a few seconds before recovering his wits sufficiently to realise that he had to make his escape before someone came to investigate. That crash must have been heard all over the building.

What was worse, the cat suddenly started dashing zanily round the lab like some mad creature in a horror movie, letting out strangled screams of terror as it skidded along the benches knocking over the racks of test-tubes, beakers, pipettes, flasks and all the other various apparatus.

'Must get out,' Kit was muttering to himself, his finger and thumb smarting viciously as if they were on fire. Strands of pain spread up his hand, too, as far as his wrist. 'Must move. Now. Stand up first . . . careful . . . careful . . .'

On the floor beside him he noticed the caterpillar, swaying as though hypnotised by some Indian snake-charmer's music, inviting him to touch it again.

To stretch out his hand and stroke it.

On his knees – preparing to get up – he hesitated, spotting the empty cassette box among the splinters of broken glass. He reached out with his good hand to pick it up. Then, in one quick movement, he scooped the caterpillar into it and snapped it shut.

'Gotcha!' he grinned in triumph. 'I bloody gotcha!'

7

Through the scratched perspex he could see the long green caterpillar curled up inside making no effort to escape.

Pushing the box into his jeans pocket, Kit scrambled to his feet and ran to the door, almost colliding with that crazy cat as he reached the corridor. Somewhere in the background he thought he heard a woman calling, but he neither paused nor looked back. He took the steps two at a time down to the basement boiler room which was the way he'd come in. The window was still open. With difficulty he climbed on to the sill.

Irrationally, the bars of that steel grille seemed set much closer together than before. First his hips stuck; then his shoulders refused to go through. He knocked his injured left hand; the pain was so intense he almost fainted. But at last, somehow, he found himself on the outside, sprinting towards the fence.

To worm his way under the wire he had to lie flat on his back and push with his feet to propel himself along that shallow rain gully he'd discovered less than an hour earlier. By the time he emerged on the far side he definitely heard voices from the building he'd just left. But he didn't wait to see what was going on. He plunged into the thick undergrowth which at that point grew right up to the fence.

Within seconds he had reached the protection of the trees. He had made it! He'd succeeded in penetrating the 'Research' and he now knew what went on there, which no one else did. Now Lenny and the rest of the gang would have to treat him with some respect. They'd be green!

He pressed on through the woods, pushing through patches of high fern, stepping over thick, gnarled roots, and from time to time fingering that plastic cassette box in his jeans pocket. Just wait till he showed them the caterpillar.

8

That King Caterpillar!

That Super-caterpillar, the greatest yet!

That Superpillar!

At last he stopped for breath. He was deep in the woods now, well clear of the 'Research'. The only sounds were a vague rustling among the leaves and the sudden buzz of an insect close to his ear. His fingers had settled to a sort of raw numbness; so long as he didn't bend them the pain was bearable.

It was then he became aware of an odd tickling sensation against his thigh as though something were scratching about inside his pocket. His *left* pocket, the same side as his injured hand.

The caterpillar?

The thought flashed through his mind. To make certain, he retrieved the cassette box from his right-hand pocket but the captive was still visible inside, curled up contentedly. So what could it be?

It bit into him sharply, a quick pin-point of pain at the very top of his leg which caused him to stagger back, dropping the cassette box.

'Bloody hell!' he swore as the pain continued, growing in intensity. He doubled up, gasping.

His left hand was useless, but with his right he managed to hold the pocket open so that he could at least see what was going on. Despite the fact that he was damp with sweat a cold shiver ran through his whole body as he realised he was looking at another of the bright green caterpillars. Its tail was undulating gently as if in sensual delight as its powerful jaws worked into his flesh.

He gazed down at it, paralysed with horror at what was happening to him. Ever since he had once seen living tapeworms on TV he'd had nightmares about terrifying creatures burrowing through his intestines. He wanted to scream out *Stop it! Stop it!* but somehow couldn't; he could imagine the other kids laughing at him, jeering, calling him chicken, finger-lickin' chicken.

Biting his lip in an effort to keep his self-control, Kit slapped his hand firmly over the spot where the caterpillar was at work, aiming to squeeze it to extinction through the fabric of his jeans and carry on squeezing until it was no more than a mess of juice and pulp.

Before he could get a grip on it, another charge of savage pain shot through him, travelling up the full length of his leg which began jerking convulsively, beyond his control. He fell sprawling, unable to hold back his screams of agony any longer.

Two of them now.

Three.

Jesus, how many caterpillars were there?

Rolling over in a desperate attempt to escape, to crush them, *anything*, he found himself slipping into a deep hollow beneath the giant tentacle-root of one of the older trees. As he slithered into it they attacked again, gnawing into fresh areas of his flesh. Into his stomach . . . through his navel . . .

'No . . . please . . . NO!' he sobbed and yelled as they gorged themselves on him. 'Oh Mummy, stop them! *Mummy!*'

He was no longer twelve. He was a baby once more, reaching out to be comforted, to be petted and told everything was all right, that there was nothing to be afraid of, nothing at all, nothing but . . .

Oh Jesus, that cassette box was lying open on the ground, level with his eyes. The king caterpillar was coming towards him, looping its back as it moved, ripples spreading down its long furry body, its eyes fixed on his.

Incoherently he yelled at it to leave him alone, what harm had he ever done to it? Why him?

He tried to retreat farther into that hollow among the tree-roots, that womb in the earth which enclosed him lovingly. The caterpillar came nearer. He felt a slight

10

prickling as its precise little legs touched his cheek. Then –

'Mummy? Oh Mummy . . . '

The staff at the University of Lingford Research Institute were completely foxed by the accident. No one felt totally convinced that the cat was responsible, least of all Dr Sophie Greenberg whose research project it was. Dark-haired and slim, she had a touch of Lady Macbeth about her pale, intense face, and ambition to match. If this project succeeded, it might well mean a Nobel prize. Now months of work were down the drain.

Returning after lunch with her colleagues – they always used the top floor canteen as there was nowhere close enough to the Institute to make it worthwhile going out – she found the place a shambles.

Apparatus lay smashed on the floor, including an expensive microscope which was her personal property. Glass everywhere. Nitric acid eating into the parquet blocks. One caterpillar 'cage' knocked down, scattering soil and debris. Its plastic cover dangled from the high bench, suspended from the tubes and cables which had helped control atmosphere and temperature in the experiment.

Her cry of dismay brought Adrian running.

'What the hell happened?' he demanded, staring at the mess.

'You tell me!' she countered grimly. 'Someone got in here, obviously. But why cause this damage? And none of us heard anything!'

'I thought I heard something but took it to be a radio. You've noticed the door to the back stairs is open?'

She nodded. A clear trail of soil crumbs led over to it. 'Whoever they are, they're still here,' she said, picking up the long window-pole. 'Come on.'

On their way down the concrete steps they became

11

aware of odd noises coming from the boiler room at the bottom: an unusual high-pitched screaming sound followed by a series of bumps. Sophie felt Adrian's hand on her arm.

'Should I go first?' he whispered.

'Don't be daft!'

Gripping the window-pole firmly, she rushed down the remaining steps and into the boiler room, determined to catch red-handed the person who had destroyed her lab *and* all her work into the bargain. Baggy, the lab cat, shot past her legs and hurled itself against the steel bars over the open window, bouncing back off them like a rubber toy, rolling over and over, then scrambling to its feet again, emitting a sequence of pathetic screams as it dashed hysterically between the boilers.

'Oh, my God!' Sophie exclaimed in distress. 'Oh, the poor thing!'

'Here she comes!' Adrian announced, squatting down like a wicket-keeper, ready to grab the cat as it passed. 'Hell!'

It dodged between his legs. Once again it threw itself at the steel bars. Once again it bounced back. This time – hitting the floor – it lay still, though whether dead or merely stunned Sophie could not yet tell. Around its neck was a long, bright green caterpillar. She recognised it immediately as coming from the destroyed 'cage'.

'Don't touch it!' she snapped, grabbing Adrian's arm as he bent low for a closer look. 'Unless you fancy a week's sick leave.'

A couple of their colleagues trooped in from the other labs. 'Anything wrong? That was an awful row! Poor old Baggy have a fit, or what?'

The cat was dead, its skull cracked by the impact with the bars. It had definitely caused the damage in the lab, there could be no question about that, though it remained a mystery how it had managed to topple the 'cage' down

12

from the bench. Those glass tanks were heavy.

The security men did a thorough check of the building but drew a blank. No one had passed through the entrance hall which had electrically-controlled doors which only the man on duty could open. All other doors were locked and bolted in accordance with normal procedure for a high-risk laboratory of this type. Every window was barred; no sign anyone had tampered with them.

In Sophie's lab itself they conducted a perfunctory search for footprints, but so many of the staff had trampled through there during the excitement, it would have been a hopeless task even if there *had* been anything to find. The paw-marks on the benches were evidence enough as to what must have happened.

'Then I suppose we'd better start clearing up,' Sophie commented wearily when it was all over. She had already hunted down some of the escaped caterpillars, though six were still missing. 'Thank God it wasn't worse. Must be grateful for that.'

In the village some eight miles away from the Research Institute, Kit's absence was not noticed for several hours. His mother came home from work expecting to find the kettle on but the house was empty. No eggs even, though she'd asked him to go to the farm for them. They were at least fresh from the farm which was more than she could say for Jackson's in the village. Supermarket rejects he sold, she could swear. Oh, it was too bad of Kit not to get them. She'd put the money out; it was there under the vase still. He hadn't eaten his dinner either. Those two bacon sandwiches hadn't been touched.

She ate them herself with a cup of tea, glad to get the weight off her legs after standing all day plucking factory chickens. The line never stopped. It was as if they couldn't wait to get deep-frozen, and by the end of the shift she knew exactly what they felt like.

Though she was no chicken herself; no longer. Thirty-five she was and she'd already found a grey hair in her comb. She'd held it up to the window to make sure. It was grey all right. Or white. Her tits were sagging too, she could swear.

Where the hell was Kit? Should have been home an hour ago. With those kids probably, and up to no good. The *gang*, he called it; well, that was his age. Could do with a man's hand, that was the truth of the matter. Come to think of it, so could she.

She yawned. A tired, long-to-sleep yawn. Then she switched on the telly and transferred to the armchair, kicking off her shoes to make herself comfy.

Just forty winks, then.

Two hours later when she woke up Kit was still not home. 'Kit?' She went up to his bed to make sure, but he wasn't there, nor was he out in the shed at the back. Swearing she'd have his hide off, she would, when she got hold of him, she ran down the lane to Lenny's Mum. He was always on about Lenny.

Lenny hadn't seen him since early that morning, nor had the rest of the gang.

There remained the police.

The next few days were a nightmare. Two brusque young detective-constables searched the cottage as if they were hunting for stolen bullion, raising floor boards, examining the water tank in the loft, even lifting the lid of the lavatory cistern. On Sunday morning the uniformed men assembled a team to trample through the ditches and beat the copse bordering the motorway. As one pointed out, they were hampered by the fact that there had been a heavy thunderstorm on the night of Kit's disappearance. It would have wiped out any traces.

Kit had run away from home once before, the local policeman reminded her. On that occasion he had hidden

14

beneath the tarpaulin of a fairground trailer. It had taken a week to track him down and by then he'd been more than fifty miles away.

But although they issued pictures and appealed on television, this time all leads proved fruitless.

1

When she was first visited by the moths, Ginny misinterpreted the signs. She had moved into her new cottage that same day. At dusk they crowded the sky like a flight of starlings, hundreds of them alighting briefly in her garden.

As if to welcome her, or so it seemed at the time. Later on, she was to remember them with increasing bitterness.

It was late October when she made the move down from London and so warm, it might have been the height of summer. The leaves were still a luscious green and the garden was alive with the murmur of late insects. As she unpacked her crockery from the tea chest, piling it up on the old dresser which had been included, part-and-parcel, with the cottage, she noticed a drowsy wasp brushing against the window pane. Normally she hated wasps and would kill them on sight, or call Jack to do it, but this time she even felt sorry for it. She tugged the window open to let it out.

Ginny was twenty-six, though some mornings that felt like a hundred, specially when she looked in the mirror. What she saw was a less-than-attractive blonde, tired-looking, dark around the eyes, sour lips, and unfashionably short. Stumpy, she'd overheard someone call her. Unemployed, too – though that was her own fault rather than anyone else's. She'd walked out on a job other girls were queuing up for. Director on a well-known TV series: she knew a dozen people prepared to offer up their virtue on lesser altars than that, yet *she* had to throw it up!

Her mind had been in turmoil ever since. Of course there were still days when she was convinced she'd been right. She couldn't have done anything else: it was a question of self-respect. Integrity. But on other days she knew she'd been a fool.

Now she was in the cottage she'd have to sort herself out. Already she felt better, just being there. It was a dream cottage: two rooms – one up, one down – with a lean-to kitchen, adjoining loo, and a mass of flowering creeper around the front door. Off the main road, too; tucked away down a meandering lane bordered by high hedges. Here, at last, she could be alone.

'Ginny, I've fixed the bed!' Jack's voice boomed out in triumph from upstairs.

'Great!' she called back. She had left him the double bed and bought herself a new single which had been delivered in sections, ideal for manoeuvring up awkward stairs but hell to assemble. 'What was the secret?'

'What?' His jeans-clad legs appeared at the top of the narrow, creaking staircase; then a hand, still clutching the spanner. 'Oh, the bed? It was just a question of working out the underlying principle. Not really as complicated as it seemed.'

That answer was so typical of Jack, she almost threw a plate at him. Gadgets or people, it was always the same with him; just press the hidden spring, and he thought he could do whatever he liked with them. Well, this was one situation she intended to keep firmly under control. He came down, ducking his head to avoid the low rafter, and she recognised from the expression on his face that he was just longing to rough-house with her as a prelude to trying out the new bed. She was determined *that* was not going to happen. Not this time.

'You'd better have a wash before you go,' she suggested coolly. Too coolly, considering all he'd done to help her with the move. 'I'll get you a towel.'

'You're sure there's nothing else I can do?'

'I can manage now, thanks.'

'You're quite certain? If there *is* anything . . . Well, now I'm here I may as well . . . '

'Jack . . . please . . . ' She could have screamed at him, but she held on. 'Don't make things more difficult than they are.'

His T-shirt was damp with sweat and clung to his skin as he peeled it off, tugging it over his head. Fragments of cobweb stuck to his sandy hair, cropped short for the latest television epic in which they had cast him. He had a swimmer's shoulders with Olympic-class muscles; watching them, she felt the usual unease stirring inside her. Abruptly, she turned her back on him and fetched a couple of towels from the drawer.

The little kitchen had only one tap which was set high over a low, shallow stone sink. He bent down to hold his head underneath it, then turned it on, grunting as the full force of cold water hit him. Three years they had lived together, Ginny marvelled; three years in a strange, blind dreamland until one morning she woke up and realised that she'd fallen out of love with him.

It had come to her in a flash, quite unexpectedly. Like a blown fuse.

Months ago, now. Hateful months during which he'd refused to believe it, pleaded with her, quarrelled, demanded to know whom she'd been seeing, who had turned her against him, too hurt to accept that he had no rival. Love – if that's what it had been – had simply died in her, leaving nothing.

'Towel?'

Dripping with water, he reached back for it. She put it into his hand. Then, out of habit, she took the second towel to dry his back. While he rubbed his head

19

vigorously, she ran her forefinger slowly down the hollows around his shoulder blade. Oh Christ, why did he have to be so bloody physical?

'Thank you for helping with the move,' she said quietly, moving farther away from him.

'Couldn't let you struggle on your own. Least I could do.'

'Hiring that van was brilliant,' she went on. 'Can you imagine a pantechnicon getting down that lane?'

'There's always a bed for you when you come to London.'

'I'm sure!' she laughed. 'You'll find somebody else.'

'It's not that simple.' He draped his wet towel over the back of the kitchen chair, then picked up his T-shirt without bothering to put it on. 'By the way, I meant to tell you. You've got cockroaches in this kitchen. And ants.'

'I'll get some insecticide in the morning.'

The hired van was parked in front of the cottage next to her own 'battered baby', as they had once dubbed her small Renault. Ginny helped him shut the rear doors, slipping the bar across to secure them. Before he climbed in he reached out to kiss her lips, but she turned her head, offering only a cheek. The hurt look on his face made her regret it immediately but by then it was too late.

'You are going to be okay by yourself?' he asked awkwardly. 'I mean, I'll stay if you want me to. Just for your first night.'

'Jack – *please*? You promised you'd not make it difficult.'

'We both promised a lot of things.' He started the engine. 'I'll come down next week to see how you're getting on.'

'You're filming next week!' she shouted above the noisy revving and grinding as he tried to engage reverse.

'Monday, Tuesday, Wednesday!' he called out. She was forced to jump back to safety as he went into his clumsy three-point turn over the rough ground. 'Make it Thursday, shall we?'

'That's too soon!' she yelled after him. How could she make him understand she wanted to be on her own? 'I need time to settle in!'

In reply, he merely waved his hand. 'I love you, Virginia Andrewes! Don't forget!' he sang out, then immediately roared off down the twisting lane, leaving her laughing in spite of herself.

She went back inside and began to gather up the torn pages of the *Telegraph* in which she'd wrapped her plates and cups for the move. A couple of months and Jack would probably have some new dolly girl twined about his neck. Some fresh young actress fishing for introductions to the right producers. When it came to re-casting, actors like Jack never had any problem.

But that was no longer any of her business. She had cut herself free from all of it – from Jack, from that whole world of television, and their friends. Killed off a way of life.

For three years Ginny had done her stint as a director on that plodding tea-time soap opera. Then – at last – she'd been offered the first play in a brand-new drama series. A really great chance it had been and she'd given it all she'd got. Lived it. Dreamed it – well, Jack could bear witness to that. And that gas chamber sequence! Everyone was impressed: at last here was something to grab the audience where it hurt. Till the producer got cold feet and brought in the Head of Drama who tutted like some demented school-marm and insisted the footage had to come out. Ginny stood on her rights and appealed to the Head of Programmes, woman to woman. The ruling was not only upheld; the sourpuss demanded an additional cut as well. 'Then it'll go out without my name on it!' Ginny had stormed at them furiously. They welcomed that suggestion so warmly, she felt she'd no alternative

21

but to put in her letter of resignation the same afternoon.

Her blood still boiled when she thought about it. That had been the best scene in the play, for Chrissake! The key to the whole lousy plot!

She sat at the little round table by the cottage window and went over it all yet again in her mind. What he said . . . what she said . . . 'Keep your head down,' the producer had warned her before that final meeting. 'You don't think they worry if the scene's good or not? They're scared of the pressure groups: I know the signs. It's my guess they've had a nod and a wink from Downing Street.'

But she hadn't listened. God, how *could* she have been so stupid?

She could hold it back no longer. Her head sank forward on to her arms and her shoulders heaved as she sobbed out her unhappiness. In a fit of pique she'd ruined her career. Destroyed everything. If only she'd knuckled under she'd still be working in television, on the *inside*, with more chances still to come. But she'd blown all that.

After a while she blew her nose, dried her eyes and told herself not to be so futile, but that only brought the tears back again. Who cared, anyway? She was alone here in her own cottage: no need to put on a brave face any longer. No need to hide anything.

With Jack gone, there was no one to hide it from, was there?

It was almost dark when she stirred herself at last. This wouldn't do. Time to pull herself together and get organised. She began to hunt around for the matches. After inspecting the cottage, the Electricity Board had refused to reconnect the supply until she had it completely rewired and it might take weeks before someone was free to do it. Her sister Lesley who lived on the far side of the village had come to the rescue with a couple of oil lamps she'd bought during the last miners' strike.

Ginny found the matches and lit one of the lamps, placing it on the round table where she had been sitting. It made the room look quite cosy. Still sniffing – on her third hanky – she was starting to range the plates along the dresser shelves when she became aware of a wild squeaking sound coming from outside.

Bats?

She shuddered, visualising dark, menacing shapes swooping down to claw at her hair.

But then the squeaking came closer, until finally it seemed to enter the room itself. She pressed back against the dresser, biting her lip as she stared around apprehensively, trying to see what it could be. Quietly putting down the plate she was holding, she reached for the large wooden spoon which was the only weapon to hand.

The creature – whatever it was – flew about the room in great uneven circles. Its shadow danced around the walls, now as small as a dinner plate, now suddenly expanded like some demon magician's cloak.

Then it stopped and hovered near the lamp as if preening itself. It was a large moth, almost the size of a blackbird. In that soft gentle light, the intricate pattern on its wings seemed like rich velvet, with varying hues of brown shading into each other and curling around brilliant pools of red and purple.

How gorgeous, she thought. How fascinating!

She returned the wooden spoon to the dresser and tiptoed to the table, not wanting to disturb it.

It began to fly again, fluttering around the lamp until she was afraid it might burn itself in the up-draught of heat from that tall glass funnel. She had a vision of those fragile wings bursting into a puff of flame, destroying it.

She reached forward and turned down the wick. For a second or two a tiny blue flame remained, dancing and spluttering; then that went out too. The room darkened, though it was still possible to see. Outside, the sky was a dull grey from which the last tinges of the sunset had already disappeared.

'Out you go!'

She attempted to shoo the moth towards the open window, cupping her hands. It flew upwards, escaping towards the ceiling, only to reappear a moment later and sweep majestically around the room. In the gloom it had become a huge, shadowy being like – she could not repress the thought – like some disembodied soul. Ridiculous idea of course; she knew that. After all, it was only a moth: wasn't it?

Several times it collided with the glass of the little sash window, attracted by what remained of the daylight. Then it settled on the ledge where it seemed determined to stay.

'Okay, have it your own way,' she shrugged. 'If that's what you want.'

As if in reply, a full Hallelujah chorus of squeaks came from the garden and she realised the air outside was thick with giant moths, wheeling and fluttering like bluebottles over a dung heap. Should she close the window? But then three or four of them were inside already. One flew close to her face, its wings lightly brushing her cheek in a passing caress. She wasn't afraid, that was the remarkable thing about it. Normally she didn't like creepie-crawlies, yet here she was now – completely calm, for all the world as though she were receiving visitors.

The shrill squealing stopped, leaving behind a death-like silence, tense with unspoken threat.

Nervously she stared out through the window but nothing was visible, only the dark silhouettes of tall trees against the dusk sky. She could swear they were still in the garden: yet where?

24

Moving as quietly as she could, she crept up the narrow, creaking staircase to her bedroom, where she leaned out. Beneath the trees everything seemed to be in deep shadow. Then from all sides of the cottage came a faint sighing on the air, like someone breathing, and the shadows began to change shape as a dense swarm of giant moths rose from the garden and appeared to hover for a time before heading south over the tree-tops.

Disembodied souls? The idea came back to her insistently. Hadn't she once read in a book somewhere of a peasant community which believed just that? That night moths were nothing other than the dead returning to keep an eye on the living?

Or to warn of impending disaster.

That first moth she'd saved from the flame: might it not, in reality, have been the restless soul of the old woman who had died in the cottage not many weeks earlier? The woman whose death she'd so callously welcomed because it meant the cottage was available at last. Freehold. With vacant possession.

The mere thought set her flesh tingling. She clattered down the bare wooden stairs, deliberately making as much noise as she could. Lighting both oil lamps, she searched the living room and the lean-to kitchen to satisfy herself that the last moth had left. Visitation from the 'other side' or not, she did not want them fluttering around her in the night.

But there was no sign of them anywhere. They might never have been there at all.

Through the open window came the busy murmur of other insects, grating on her nerves. To blot out the sound, she switched on her radio and filled the cottage with the jungle beat of the week's new Number One which she hated. At least it chased the ghosts away.

Jack found driving that van more cumbersome than he

25

had anticipated when hiring it. For one thing, the gears were not arranged in the familiar order of his own red Ferrari; for another, the steering was heavy, slow to respond, while the turning circle was so cramping, it was practically arthritic. As for acceleration, that word had been erased from the instruction manual, and with reason.

All this added up to a slow drive back, as he realised only too well before he left the cottage. It probably also saved his life.

Thinking it over as he turned into the main road which led through the village, he felt pleased Ginny had at least accepted his help with the move. She'd been in an odd mood all year. Post-termination depression syndrome, their platinum blonde doctor had called it when Jack — behind Ginny's back — had decided to consult her. As a diagnosis it stank. Ginny had been behaving that way since long before the abortion; since before they knew she was pregnant, in fact. But before he had a chance to argue the point, the doctor was already conveying him to the door.

Jack hadn't approved of the abortion either, which naturally led to a quarrel. He'd pleaded with her that a baby needn't mess up anyone's career if they were sensible about it. As an actor, he frequently spent long weeks at home waiting for the phone to ring, so most of the time he could look after it. Having at least one parent available all day long was more than many babies enjoyed.

'I'd be tied to you!' she'd objected vehemently. 'I don't intend being tied to anyone. I want to be free. I must be.'

He remembered it as clearly as if it were yesterday — a straight-from-the-shoulder, brutal declaration, muffled by the towel as she dried herself after washing her hair. She probably did not even realise the effect it had on him. Water trickled down over her breasts, gleaming in the yellow light of their dingy bathroom, and he'd wanted

26

her more than ever. His whole body yearned for her.

Oh shit!

Pulling off the road into a service station on the far edge of the village, he bought petrol, checked the oil and tyres, and spent some minutes testing the plugs, suspecting he might have been driving on three cylinders only, though he found nothing obviously wrong. The lad behind the counter was reading *New Musical Express*. He didn't even look up when Jack went to pay.

Once he'd left the village, the A-road became a simple, twisting tarmac strip with an intermittent white line painted down the centre and high hedges on either side blocking the view. He drove slowly; not that he had much choice with the van in the state it was.

Ginny had gone, he told himself, though his mind seemed too dull to take it in. After more than three years together with eyes for no one else, resenting every minute they had to be apart, after all that they had split up. Of course the real break had happened weeks earlier, but until today at least she'd stayed on in the flat; now even that was over.

He could almost pinpoint the day. It was soon after she started work on that big drama production. It all followed from that, he thought bitterly, working at the wheel as the road took an unexpected sharp turn. She had plunged into it so wholeheartedly, she'd never come back. Location shooting, outside rehearsal, long days in the studio: he might have been living with a stranger during those weeks. The quickie abortion was slipped in between recording and editing; only she'd been kept in hospital a few days longer than she'd reckoned, which messed up her timetable.

Then she blew it.

Her own fault too. She'd been too intense over the whole thing, and he'd told her as much. All right, so her TV bosses had wanted to cut a scene! Don't they always? Of course she was furious, understandably, but that was

27

no reason to throw up her job. Work wasn't that easy to come by. Ask any actor.

Another bend in the road and suddenly the trees were higher, blocking out much of the remaining daylight. The gloom matched his mood so exactly, he switched on his headlights only reluctantly. Something touched his cheek. Just a slight irritation: a midge perhaps, or a hair, even. He brushed it away with the side of his hand, hardly thinking.

It fluttered close to his ear, then settled on his neck.

'Oh hell!' he exclaimed, annoyed. 'Bloody insect!'

He slapped his hand over it, merely wanting to get rid of the thing, whatever it was. It was only when he felt it struggle to get free that he realised the size of it. A bird – was it?

No, it couldn't be. His fingers closed over its wafer-thin wings: no feathers there. No bones. Just a thin, pulsating membrane which left dust on his fingertips.

A moth?

He almost laughed, relieved that at least it wasn't dangerous. In the next second he saw the swarm in the headlights; so many, they obscured the road ahead. They massed over the van, bouncing and skimming against the windscreen, dropping back on to the short bonnet, and some – a dozen at least –penetrating the cab itself to flutter crazily about his head as they persistently attempted to settle on his face.

Over his eyes, even.

Swearing, he tried to brush them aside with his left hand while steering with his right, bullying the reluctant accelerator in the hope of driving straight through the swarm. Suddenly he was blinded when a moth on his face succeeded in blotting out everything with its spreading wings. And squealing in triumph.

In a panic he seized it, crumpling it up in his fist and throwing it aside. Straight ahead was another of those unexpected bends. He jammed his foot on the brake.

The van went into a skid. He could sense how the tyres were crunching the life juice out of those moths' fat, slug-like bodies. It was like waltzing on thick slime until — jolting — it mounted the soft verge and embraced the nearest tree. His head hit the side of the door.

The impact must have knocked him unconscious. He'd not heard the police car approaching, yet there it was when the mist cleared from his eyes. One of those pale blue panda jobs.

'You all right?'

A burly police constable gazed in at him. Jack gazed back. Obviously a wow with the old ladies, this one. He wore a solid reliable air as if it was part of his uniform.

'Passed out, did you?'

'Banged my head.' He winced as his fingers found the swelling on his right temple. 'Where are all the moths?'

'Moths, sir?'

'Cab was full of moths. Couldn't see where I was going.'

'That so?' His tone indicated that he had heard it all before. 'You do have your driving licence with you?'

'Yes.'

'Then perhaps you might let me see it. Sir.'

To extract his wallet from the back pocket of his jeans Jack had to pull himself out of the cab. No bones broken, it seemed, though his head spun unpleasantly. He steadied himself against the side of the van, watching the policeman's every move. It was a scene he'd played a dozen times in one TV series or another.

After examining the licence, checking its details conscientiously against the Contract of Hire for the van, the constable began to enter it all up in his notebook. He took his time over it too, asking a few routine questions along the way, but showed no interest in the moths.

'Now let's get this straight, sir. You helped your friend move house.'

'Yes.'

'Lugging furniture about can be thirsty work, specially on a warm day. She must have offered you a drink. Hit the vodka bottle, did you? A house-warming libation, you might say?'

'I don't drink vodka.'

'Oh? I'd have taken you for a vodka-and-tonic type.'

'No.'

'That shows how wrong one can be. But we'll just check if you don't mind. Sir.' He fetched his breathalyser kit from the panda and instructed Jack to blow into the little tube. 'A long steady breath. I'll tell you when to stop.'

The result was negative. Obviously. His tongue had been hanging out all day but all Ginny had offered was tea, brewed on her camping stove.

The policeman seemed disconcerted, to say the least. Muttering under his breath about having the machine overhauled the moment he got back, he packed it away, then enquired if Jack felt up to driving after that knock on the head.

'I feel fine. But you haven't asked about the moths.'

'Ah, the moths!'

'You can see on the road where the tyres ran over them. Look here . . . and here . . . '

He pointed to what remained of their fat, sausage-like bodies, squashed flat against the tar together with fragments of their wings, as delicate as ash, which disintegrated at a touch. The policeman squatted down to examine them.

'Must be the weather,' he mused philosophically when he stood up again. 'Brings out a lot of insects, this weather. They like the warmth, d'you see?'

'I think I heard one squealing like a bat.' Jack tried to recall those last seconds before the crash.

'Could have been your brakes.'

'I remember them coming at me, trying to settle over my eyes, almost as though they deliberately wanted to blind me. It was an odd experience, I can tell you.'

The policeman shook his head doubtfully. 'Can't say it would stand up in court, not that story. Not as a defence for losing control of the vehicle. Wasps might, but moths? Never.'

'Court? Is there any question of – ?'

'You can set your mind at ease, sir. Nobody was hurt. Nothing on the breath. The landowner might claim something for damage to his tree, but otherwise . . . ' He shrugged, then turned his attention to the van. 'Body-work's taken some punishment. Couple of bad dents here. But you should be able to get home all right. You've been lucky.'

'That's one way of looking at it.'

Something in his voice must have alerted the police-man's sense of duty. 'If you'd like someone to give you the once-over our nearest hospital is fifteen miles from here in Lingford, but we've a doctor in the village who may be able to help.'

That would be Ginny's brother-in-law, Jack thought. He said he was okay. A couple of paracetamol before creeping into his lonely bed, that's all he needed. Certainly no doctor. But those moths –

'The size of them,' he persisted. 'Surely you don't often get them that big?'

'Discover something new every day, that's the country-side for you. Not like London down here. Now that cottage your friend's bought – that would be straight through the village, third lane on the left after you pass the Plough?'

'Let me guess. You've got second sight.'

'Not many cottages changing hands these days. Old Mrs Beerston lived there – oh, as long as anyone can remember. Died a couple o' months back. She'll get a lot more insects round that cottage than up on the hill.'

'Better her than me, then.'

Jack got back into the van. The engine groaned into

31

life, sounding much the same as before the accident. His headlights illuminated the damage to the thick tree-bole, but where the hell were the moths?

'Thanks for your help!' he called out as he reversed on to the road.

The breeze through the open window as he drove should have worked wonders for his aching head but it didn't. All the way back to Chiswick the pain over his eyes nagged him relentlessly.

Then — once back at the flat — the unaccustomed silence scratched at his nerves. Even when Ginny had taken to sleeping in the next room there had always been some sound to remind him she was still about. A creaking board. A tap turned on, or left dripping. A cupboard opened.

Now there was nothing.

Emptiness.

He hunted for the paracetamol, couldn't find it, assumed she must have packed it with her things, so poured himself a large Scotch instead. Ice from the fridge. Two lumps in his glass. The rest he wrapped in a shower cap she'd left behind. Sinking back into an armchair, he balanced it over the swelling on his temple.

Bloody moths.

It was a rum story all right. Constable Chivers sat on the edge of his bed the following morning, lacing up his shoe and thinking it over. The evidence was there on the road too. After the man had gone he'd scraped up the remains of one moth and popped it in a transparent plastic bag for examination. But then actors could spin a few when they were in the mood!

'George! Your breakfast is getting cold!'

'Ay, all right!' he called back, reaching for the other shoe.

He was about to put it on when he spotted the cater-

32

pillar: a hairy green thing, five or six inches at least. With the shoe in his hand he clumped downstairs.

'Here, Sue – take a look at this!'

'Urgh, how did that get in the bedroom? I only cleaned there yesterday. You'd better kill it.'

'It's not harming anyone.'

Placing his shoe on the tiled kitchen window ledge where he could keep an eye on it, he sat down first to eat his bacon and fried bread. When he'd finished, he pulled on his gumboots and took the shoe out through the garden gate into the field beyond where he tipped the caterpillar out into a nettle patch.

2

A fortnight or more passed before Ginny plucked up enough courage to discuss the moths with her sister Lesley. She tried explaining how a visitation like that had to be a good omen.

'A visitation? *Moths*?' Lesley snorted, her laughter erupting uncontrollably. 'Oh Ginny, you're not serious?'

Lesley had that impulsive way of blurting out whatever came into her head, sweeping across other people's sensitivities like a gust of cold wind. Not that anyone took offence, ever. She was completely frank and open, and had a generous, warm laugh. It was impossible not to like her. Three years older than Ginny, too. Taller – and louder – she was endowed with beautiful auburn tresses which she left to tumble freely over her freckled shoulders, though sometimes she'd put them up for formal occasions.

In reality they were only half-sisters, but as children they had been so close, it was unbelievable. Their mother had been twice married: first to Lesley's father who was killed in a climbing accident a few months after the wedding, then to a faintly-remembered solicitor who lasted just long enough to sire Ginny before being discarded. His considerable trust fund had made it possible for her to buy the cottage, but the man himself had died of lung cancer years earlier. Ginny had never met him. Now her mother had moved to Australia, she scarcely ever saw her either.

'I'm not saying I believe it but – '

'I should hope not!' Lesley retorted.

' – that's just the effect those moths had on me. You didn't see them.'

'I wish I had.'

'They were really massive. I never thought moths existed that size. And so many! You know how small the garden is – well, there must have been a hundred at least crowded in there. Great shadowy forms fluttering about in the dark. And that squealing! I thought at first they were bats.'

'It's understandable you were scared,' her sister conceded.

'But I wasn't, that's what is so strange. Then I remembered old Mrs Beerston had died only a few weeks ago and it *was* her cottage. That made some sort of sense. The souls of the dead – why not? A village is a community after all, and here am I, the intruder . . . '

'Moths are arthropods, Ginny,' Lesley instructed her in a flat, down to earth manner. 'Not spirits or ghosts or devils out of hell. Simply arthropods.'

Ginny laughed. 'I don't even know what that means.'

'It means they are living animals. Oh – like lobsters or prawns, with a hard skeleton on the outside. But *alive*. Can you imagine old Mrs Beerston coming back as a flying prawn?'

'I never met her. And a lot of people do believe in reincarnation. Buddhists do.'

34

'Old Mrs Beerston didn't, you can be sure of that. Ask the vicar, he knew her better than anyone. In her young days she used to go stomping around the country preaching atheism and the like. One of Bertrand Russell's early lays, he says, though I think that's just his dirty mind. Anyway, she'd be the last to want to come back haunting people.'

'Oh, you're obviously right,' Ginny admitted, tiring of the argument. 'It's common sense. But can't you feel the mystery of it? No, I don't suppose you can.'

'You were hungry, that's all. You hadn't eaten anything all day, I'll bet.'

'I had!'

'What? Two nuts and a yoghurt? You picked up some lousy habits in that television job. Don't think I don't know, sister mine.' She shook her head, disapproving. 'Now Ginny, if I bring some books of pictures, d'you think you could remember the markings on the wings well enough to identify those moths? Because they do sound unusual.'

'Isn't that what I was trying to tell you?'

A peal of laughter. 'Ginny, you're impossible! Can't you be serious even for one minute?'

Perhaps she should never have brought the subject up, Ginny thought ruefully. The experience of watching those moths from her bedroom window on that first evening in the cottage now seemed like a moment of sheer poetry which she had no wish to destroy. Lesley would trample over it if Ginny let her, and not even understand what she was doing.

And it was odd how Jack had also encountered the moths on his drive back. 'Obviously seeing you off the premises,' she had teased when he described it to her. Much to her annoyance he had turned up on her doorstep days before she'd expected him. 'I think they're watching over me,' she'd added. 'Protecting me from predatory

35

males.'

In a strange way she had meant it, too.

With her sister Lesley creepie-crawlies had always been something of a passion. As a girl – much to Ginny's horror – she had collected caterpillars in empty matchboxes. Later, at London University, she had chosen to study zoology, aiming for a career in science until the day came when she found herself pregnant and gave it all up to marry the medical research student responsible.

Of course everybody told her she was stupid to throw away her career like that, but the truth was – she'd confessed to Ginny – she had begun to hate the whole business of slicing up living creatures to discover how they functioned. What she loved was observing them alive, unharmed, in natural surroundings.

She was also in love.

Head-over-heels.

So hopelessly in love, it was impossible to get any sense out of her.

After the wedding, her husband Bernie left his university research project and took over his father's general practice in the village. Old Mrs Beerston had been one of his patients: well over ninety and seemingly destined to live for ever. She might have succeeded too if one day, some six years later, she hadn't developed bronchitis after pottering in her garden too long in the rain. Within twenty-four hours Lesley was phoning Ginny to say the cottage could be hers if she moved fast.

Which she did.

Before the local estate agent had even realised what was going on, she had spoken to the old woman's solicitor – he played golf with Bernie – and clinched the deal, cash on the table.

'I'll hunt out a couple of books then,' Lesley said, preparing to leave. 'Moths have never really been my subject, but it would be interesting to know what you've seen. This squealing you mentioned should narrow down the possibilities.'

'I never knew before that moths could make that kind of sound.'

'Some do. The Death's Head Hawk moth for one – though they are very rare. Oh, don't worry!' she laughed, obviously seeing the dismay on Ginny's face. 'They're quite harmless! I know who you should talk to – the Reverend Davidson! Why didn't I think of him? He's scatty about moths.'

'Who is he?'

'Vicar of St Botolph's – that's about fifteen miles away. Not far to drive. They say he even preaches moths in his sermons. Not that his congregation objects. I'm told he only ever gets two old ladies and they're both deaf. That's one thing about being a doctor's wife in the country – you do learn what goes on!'

'But does he really know anything about them?'

'Moths? He breeds them! Anyway, I've got to rush to collect Frankie from school. Why don't you drop in for Sunday lunch? The children would love to see you.'

'I might.' She accompanied Lesley out to her Mini.

'It'll be roast lamb with potatoes and veg from our own garden. Apple pie to follow. *Our* apples. You look like you need feeding up!'

Ginny found St Botolph's on the map and drove there that same afternoon. The church was tucked away among the trees, a simple barn-like structure with a square tower and a remarkable Norman doorway. The community it served was not so much a village as a scattering of isolated houses, the most impressive of them being the vicarage, a mature Georgian building in brick. She rang the bell but there was no answer, so she investigated the back of the house and found the vicar working in the garden.

He was a thin, frail man of medium height with a scholarly stoop and an untidy fringe of grey hair around his otherwise bald head. Well over seventy, Ginny judged.

'Ah yes, I know Dr Rendell!' he exclaimed enthusiastically when she had introduced herself. 'And his lovely wife! So you are her sister? Well, well. You'd like to see the church, I expect. A fine building!'

'I've really come to ask about some moths I saw.' She tried briefly to describe them. 'Nobody else seems to know what they are.'

'Are you sure about the size?'

'Oh yes. The first one that came into the room was as close as I am to you. And they whistled like bats.'

'And they weren't frightened? Some species do that as a sign of fear. It's the expulsion of air through the proboscis. I think we'd better go into the house and I'll take some notes. Perhaps you'd care for a cup of tea?'

Sipping her tea, she had to admit her total ignorance of the subject of moths or butterflies or any other insects, but she tried her best to answer his questions. No, unfortunately she hadn't noticed the antennae; nor had she actually *seen* any curled-up proboscis.

'It's a tube-like tongue used for sucking up nectar out of flowers,' he explained, taking pity on her. 'Not all lepidoptera are equipped with one.'

'D'you have at least some idea what my moths were?'

'Not native to this country, I imagine. But so many species are imported these days for study, or for zoos, some are bound to escape. Moths of that size are not impossible, specially in very hot countries.' He thought for a moment, sucking irritatingly at his teeth. 'This could be very interesting. You saw a swarm of them in your garden, you say? Some could have been laying eggs. You may find caterpillars in the spring.'

'I never thought of that.' She grinned shamefacedly. 'I

really don't know anything, do I?'

'The moths you saw would include both male and female. They copulate much as we do.' He paused, then added with a slight laugh: 'Though I'm afraid that doesn't apply to me any longer. Too old, more's the pity!'

'Never say die!' she retorted.

He smiled regretfully. 'Then the female lays her fertilised eggs on some suitable food plant where they'll have a chance of survival when they hatch out. Of course they have natural enemies. If they hadn't – most people don't realise this – a single pair might produce as many as three million caterpillars in one season.'

Ginny was fascinated. 'Then if they *are* new to this country – ?'

'In the right circumstances they could soon be as commonplace – and as numerous – as bees. I don't actually think that will happen, of course. Not in our climate.' He stood up and shut his notebook. 'Now let me show you where I breed.'

He took her into what had once been the vicarage dining room, but was now, he said, his 'work station'. It contained a laboratory bench with a microscope and other items of equipment, together with three Victorian-looking cabinets whose tray-like drawers were filled with carefully classified specimens. On rough shelving along one wall were several rows of transparent plastic cylinders containing varying types of vegetation: his 'cages', he explained, in which he was breeding caterpillars which would eventually become moths.

'Best way to study them,' he commented, holding one up for her to see the little brown larvae inside. 'You know, my dear, when I was first appointed to a country living, I thought – what luck! I saw myself as a famous naturalist like Gilbert White of Selborne. Instead, here I am, a moth-eaten lepidopterist. Of course I've parish duties, but not onerous. More funerals than christenings these days. The souls in these parts are so set in their ways, they'll go straight to heaven or the other place regardless of what I say.'

'How can I find out more about my moths?' Ginny interrupted his musings. 'If I want to write a script about them, for instance?'

'Tell you what – I'll set a trap tonight, just in case there are any more about.'

'A trap?'

'Yes, a mercury vapour trap. The night is full of insects, far more than we imagine. The mercury vapour lamp attracts them and they get caught in the trap. Specially moths. You'll see in the morning.'

'So if I come back tomorrow?'

'First thing. I'll be waiting for you.' He went with her to her car, then gently put a hand on her arm as if trying to tell her something. 'Stay the night if you can't face the drive. Plenty of room.'

'That's very sweet of you, but I have to get back.' The randy old goat, she thought as she put the key in the ignition. But then she looked up and caught the look of haunted loneliness on his face. 'See you in the morning!' she called out.

In the morning she telephoned from the call box instead of driving back there, telling him – a white lie – that she had some trouble with her car. Any news about her moths? As she half-expected, he explained that the haul was excellent – one of the most varied yet, not merely Broad-Bordered Yellow Underwing as was so often the case recently – but unfortunately they had caught none of her beautiful, ethereal giants. Perhaps she could drop by again when her car had been fixed? She'd be welcome any time.

The warm weather gave way to long bouts of cold rain and high gales which brought down the leaves in a rush and made the country lanes treacherous to drive along. Ginny found it oddly exhilarating after all the tensions of her old life in London. At last she felt truly free of it all!

Of course sooner or later she would get back into television, that was obvious. She began to work on an idea, something that would get the companies excited. *City girl goes to live in country cottage previously occupied by old woman with supernatural powers – pact between them – girl returns to London now able to influence events to her own advantage . . .*

Ginny cleared the oil lamp from her round table, took some A4 typing paper and sat down to scribble her random thoughts. She had written one sentence, crossed it out, and was starting again when she heard a car drawing up outside.

She went to the door, expecting to find Lesley; to her surprise, it was a mud-spattered Rover 3500 in front of the cottage. Bernie's car. He hurried the few steps through the pouring rain to the shelter of her porch.

'Hoping I'd find you in. Not disturbing you, am I?'

'Come in,' she invited, not unwillingly.

Bernie had changed since the days when Lesley had brazenly introduced him to all their relations as the putative father of her unborn child, declaring that they had not yet decided whether to marry or not: before making up their minds they intended to inspect each other's families. At that time he'd been a tall, gauche, slightly bewildered student dressed, typically, in faded jeans, sweater and CND badge. Now he was crisply-spoken, with sympathetic blue eyes and a doctor-patient manner to inspire confidence. With the years, plus Lesley's cooking, he'd filled out a little too, and his face was weather-tanned from the regular weekends and holidays he and the family spent sailing at Chichester. The jeans now appeared only for gardening or tinkering with the car; his normal dress when calling on patients was a light tweed suit.

'You've certainly altered this place!' he commented approvingly, glancing around her living room. 'Mrs Beerston would never recognise it.'

'D'you think she'd approve?'

'Oh, I think so. She had a very young mind in that poor old body of hers. She hated old age, you know.' His eyes fell on the sheets of A4 and the felt-tip. 'Oh, I'm sorry. You're working.'

'You're welcome any time, Bernie.'

'I really wanted a word about your moths. How are you getting on with identifying them?'

'Well, I went to see the Reverend Davidson, then Lesley brought me these two books which I'm working through. No luck yet though. But she said she'd try to get hold of something more comprehensive if there is such a thing.'

'I said nothing when you came to lunch on Sunday, but I've a patient in Lingford Hospital who claims she was attacked by giant moths. About the same time you saw them.'

'D'you mean they stung her, or what?'

'It may be just in her mind, you understand. History of depression and quite a heavy drinker. She was found unconscious on the road. Fractured leg, bruises, ribs damaged. If you could have a talk with her it might help.'

'Are you sure she wasn't knocked down by a car?'

'The bike wasn't damaged. We think she simply lost her balance. There was some roadwork going on and she fell awkwardly across a pile of kerbstones with one leg twisted through the frame. Must have been lying there in the dark for an hour before they found her.'

'Naturally I'll talk to her if you think it'll do any good,' Ginny said doubtfully.

'Shall we say four o'clock at the hospital?' He got up, glancing at his watch. 'Ask for me at Reception. And don't look so nervous! I think your visit will cheer her up.'

At the door he kissed her on the side of the mouth and said he was grateful she'd agreed to help. Was he merely trying to involve her in good works, she wondered. Well, she'd soon put a stop to that. She waited as he made a dash for his car, then waved and closed the door, glad to shut the weather out.

By afternoon the rain had blown over, leaving sodden roads. Diversion signs indicated that her usual route was closed because of flooding; as a result, she arrived in Lingford late.

The hospital consisted of a network of one-storey wards radiating like spokes from an elegant country house which accommodated the administration and out-patient departments. Ginny parked at the side on the patch marked 'Doctors Only' and went in. Bernie was waiting in the entrance hall, talking to a white-coated young man whom he introduced as Dr Sanderson.

'Afraid I have to rush, Ginny, but Dr Sanderson will look after you,' he said. 'I'll drop by the cottage later.'

Dr Sanderson had that sanitised look about him, familiar from American TV hospital series. He wore his white coat buttoned high at the neck, plus frameless glasses. Ginny disliked him immediately. He said very little to her, but walked slightly ahead as he guided her through the maze of corridors linking the wards; though he did suggest she should not raise the subject of moths herself, but wait for Mrs Kinley to bring it up. It was obvious he thought her some sort of mental case. Or lying.

When they reached the ward, she was not in the main room where a lively conversation was going on, but by herself in one of the alcoves near the entrance.

'You've a visitor, Mrs Kinley!' he announced from the foot of the bed. 'Someone to see you. All right now?'

Without waiting for an answer, he turned and

43

departed, leaving Ginny face to face with the patient. She was a woman in her late fifties with greying hair which had once been black, and dark, scowling eyes. Her right leg – in plaster – was held up two or three feet above the bed by means of a sling around her ankle.

'Who are you? From the Welfare?'

'No.' Ginny fetched herself a chair.

'They said to expect someone from the Welfare.'

'My name's Ginny,' she explained, sitting down. 'Dr Rendell asked me to drop by. He's my brother-in-law.'

'He's a gentleman, is Dr Rendell,' the woman said. 'Listens to you, he does. He's what I call a *real* doctor, not like that bugger who brought you here, with his fancy glasses and his silly coat. I told the nurse, he's a gelding if I ever saw one. Know what I mean? Doctor?' Her voice spat scorn. 'He's the one who's been doctored, ask me.'

'D'you like grapes?' Ginny fished in her shopping bag. She'd felt she ought to bring something. 'Got 'em cheap at the supermarket. I suppose we ought to wash 'em first. Should I ask the nurse?'

'I'd leave her. She's having her tea.'

'Okay. Have some.'

'It's all clean dirt, innit?' She separated a couple from their stalks and put them in her mouth. They were large, purple, and bursting with juice which spurted on to her nightie as she bit into them. 'Years since I last tasted grapes. Seems you've gotta come in here before anyone gives you grapes. Did Dr Rendell explain what happened to me? You wouldn't credit it.'

'He said you'd had an accident on your bike,' Ginny answered cautiously, taking another grape for herself.

'An accident? This was no bloody accident. It was deliberate, I can swear to that. I was riding me bike, not doing any harm to anyone, when all of a sudden they just come at me.'

'Who did?'

'Bloody moths.'

'Moths? You're sure?'

'Big bastards, like I've never seen before, and I've lived all my life in these parts. Thought they was bats at first, but I know bats. These was moths all right. Vicious buggers.'

'What kind of sound did they make?'

'What d'you mean – sound?' Mrs Kinley stopped chewing and stared at Ginny suspiciously. 'Why have you come here?'

'I told you, Dr Rendell asked me to drop in,' Ginny repeated calmly. 'So what kind of sound did they make? Why did you think they were bats?'

'That squeaking noise. And if you want to know, they was attacking me – in me hair, flying into me face, me eyes, everywhere. I was on the bike, you see, trying to keep me balance, but I got into such a tizzy with these things, over I went. Which is why I'm in here, innit?'

She stopped and eyed Ginny cunningly. 'Didn't tell them nothin'. Not about the squeakin'.'

'The doctors?'

'Them bloody doctors. That gelding thinks I'm mental. I heard him. It's all fantasy in her head, he said. From the drink.' Unexpectedly the tears began to roll down her strained cheeks. 'I dunno. Sometimes I saw them moths, sometimes I think I'm making it up. Maybe I really am going off me rocker, then they'll keep me locked up, won't they? That's what they do, you know, to the likes o' me.'

'I'm going to talk to Dr Rendell, so don't you worry,' Ginny stated firmly. 'You did see the moths.'

'You're just saying that.'

'Oh, I don't accept that they attacked you, but you certainly saw them.' Briefly, Ginny tried to describe her own experience of them on that first evening, stressing how beautiful they were, and how gentle. 'So you under-

45

stand, I saw them too. They do exist. When you rode into them in the dark like that, they were probably just as frightened as you were.'

'They didn't have a go at you though, did they?' Mrs Kinley sniffed. She groped under her pillow and produced a grubby handkerchief with which she dried her eyes. 'Them moths is bloody vicious, so you watch out for 'em. Watch yourself.'

'I'll tell the doctor they're real anyway, not just in your head.'

'They'll be back, young miss. You mark my words.'

Somehow she seemed to have offended the woman rather than reassured her, Ginny thought. She stood up and returned her chair to its allotted place by the wall. Then she paused at the bedside, feeling dissatisfied.

'Can I come again?' she asked.

'You've better things to do than waste your time with me.' Mrs Kinley's dark eyes were suddenly alive with mockery. There was no trace of self-pity. 'You've done your bit o' charity. I'm not saying I'm not grateful.'

'I'd like to bring a friend.' She was thinking of Jack. 'He had a similar experience to yours.'

'You'd be more welcome if you brought a half-bottle of gin. You've got nothing to drink in your shopping bag, have you?'

'Only a carton of milk. Sorry. I should have thought.'

'You just make sure Dr Rendell gets me out of here, that's all I ask. Away from that bloody gelding. It turns my stomach to have him near me.'

Ginny laughed. 'Is he really that bad?'

'Oh, I know I'm not much to look at these days, but when I was younger, he'd never have got near me for the crush, doctor or no doctor. So now you know.'

Ginny found her own way back to the main building. She sought out Dr Sanderson in his office but ignored his invitation to sit down. There was nothing to report really, she informed him coldly. His patient had ridden into a swarm of moths, panicked and fallen off her bike. Why did he think she was making it up?

'Those moths actually exist? That size? In the tropics perhaps – but *here*?'

'They match the ones I saw, so they obviously do exist. She was frightened, don't you understand? Anyway, I must be off now. You're the doctor, so you sort her out.'

Outside, it was raining again.

She had genuinely intended to pay Mrs Kinley a second visit, but what with one thing and another she never got round to it.

Jack, when she rang him from the call box in the village, turned out to be on the point of flying to Spain for a fortnight's filming. Needed the money, he said cheerfully, after that massive penalty he'd had to pay for damaging the van. What about joining him for a few days on the sunny Costa del Sol? No? Well, he'd be in touch when he got back. Missed her though, he added.

When she mentioned it to Bernie, he didn't think Mrs Kinley really expected to see her again. In his view, that one brief chat had amply served its purpose in restoring her self-confidence. Dr Sanderson, he implied – though he voiced no open criticism – had got her into such a state that she'd no longer felt sure whether what she remembered was dream or reality. And not only about the moths, either.

But if Ginny really wanted to go back, he suggested, there was no reason why she shouldn't.

Before she could make up her mind, the man came to rewire the cottage. For the best part of a week she had to endure stale cigarette smoke, non-stop music from his cheap, tinny radio, and several clumsy attempts to chat her up. She was tied to the place, for she was certainly not going to leave him there on his own to poke around

47

among her belongings. She tried to work, but ended up throwing away most of what she'd written on the witchcraft idea. The electrician's undisguised curiosity irritated her.

But at last he finished and power was connected. She celebrated by opening every door and window to give the rooms a thorough airing, then drove into Lingford where she bought a trendy cream-coloured television and ordered some storage heaters. The telephone would take longer, they informed her when she called in to ask why nothing had happened yet. Six months at least, they estimated.

It rained most of the winter, though it was never really cold. She found herself beginning to long for the sun. And, of course, for a decent bathroom. She had to go to Lesley's for a proper bath, which she was forced to share with the assortment of plastic ducks, fishes, submarines and other flotsam belonging to her three nieces. The only alternative was to strip off and wash in her own tiny lean-to kitchen.

One evening during a downpour she tucked her hair under a shower cap, clutched a new bar of soap and ventured out naked into the garden. The rain was bitterly cold and she was soon back in the cottage again, her teeth chattering. It took a good two hours in front of the fire and several large glasses of whisky before she could stop shivering.

But it was that same evening that the Great Idea for her television proposal came to her in a flash: her Road-Back-To-Success, she dubbed it in her own mind.

Moths, of course – why hadn't she thought of it before?

She'd already made copious notes while working her way conscientiously through the fat books Lesley had brought her, and visited the British Museum of Natural History, but all that had been for her own satisfaction.

48

The riddle of what *her* moths really were remained unanswered.

But the Great Idea was something quite different. Not a documentary – that would be too tedious and, in any case, she wasn't a documentary person. No, this would be a six-part drama serial with top casting and centred on a village where on certain evenings the dead rose from the churchyard in the form of giant moths, not to haunt, but actually to take over from the living.

It needed a lot more development, naturally; in the meantime it would be best to keep her thoughts to herself, though she did try it out on Bernie next time she saw him. He was very encouraging.

In fact, during that winter Bernie took to dropping in occasionally on his way home, slipping off his jacket and sitting down for a quiet chat before – as he put it – plunging back into domesticity. And if Ginny didn't mention these visits to Lesley, it was simply because she'd have hated her sister to get the wrong end of the stick.

3

Ginny lay on a rug on that patch of rough grass she called her lawn and browsed through *House and Garden* in search of inspiration. Somewhere beneath the other magazines was her abandoned bikini top. No one could overlook her here. That, she constantly reminded herself, was one of the joys of a country cottage.

The mild winter had given way to an almost tropical spring. A couple of weeks' hot sunshine punctuated by short, heavy rain-showers had brought the whole countryside to life again. Her garden stirred with fresh green shoots and the first exploring insects. Its fruit trees

49

were like brides in their veils of blossom.

She let the magazine slip from her fingers and turned on to her back, luxuriating in a sensation of well-being as the sun's warm rays soaked into her. Her television proposal was ready and she had made an appointment to take it in person to a highly recommended London literary agent she'd met while still working on that tedious tea-time soap opera. On the whole she was satisfied with the way it had turned out. The character sketches were lively, she felt. The plot peaked in the right places. And the whole thing was *visual*, that was the main point.

Mm, it was so lovely lying in the sun after that damp, miserable winter. No wonder Bernie had said rheumatism was the commonest complaint among his patients.

She felt an odd, prickly movement on her tummy but took no notice of it at first. It persisted, as though someone were tickling her with a blade of grass. She opened her eyes, imagining for a second that someone must have crept up on her for a joke, though there had been no sound of a car. No one there. Raising herself on one elbow, she glanced down to see what it was.

'*Urgh!*' A shudder went through her, bringing gooseflesh. '*Oh hell – !*'

A hideous green caterpillar was shuffling slowly across her abdomen just above the line of her bikini briefs. Oh God, she'd always hated caterpillars. Once when they were children Lesley had put a couple in her bed as a joke. Ginny had actually been in bed and had already said goodnight when she discovered them. The shock had been so great, she'd screamed hysterically, locking herself in the bathroom where she'd stayed until the family doctor was called. The sight of that hairy caterpillar on her skin brought it all back.

Now, Ginny Andrewes, be sensible! she told herself

firmly. It can't harm you.

She tried forcing herself to think about it calmly. Phobias took people in different ways. Some couldn't stand spiders but she didn't mind them. It was these long, hairy things she hated, like amputated fingers, but alive, undulating in every joint, able to squirm into any crevice in her body. Such as her navel.

Oh, not her navel, *please*!

The front end of the caterpillar moved around inquisitively while the rear remained stationary. Then it began to crawl forward, its little legs working rapidly as it circled around her navel, heading towards her ribs.

'Oh, go away,' she prayed. 'Please go away.'

Almost as if in response, it turned and went back to its first position on the rounded swell of her abdomen. She should get rid of it, she knew. It needed only a little mental effort to overcome her scruples sufficiently to pick it up and fling it towards the bushes.

But what if it curled around her finger? What if it clung to her?

Rationally, Ginny was disgusted with herself for being such a coward, yet whatever decision she took, she still couldn't bring herself to touch that caterpillar. Her hand . . . her arm . . . they just refused to obey.

Suddenly the caterpillar reared up and looked at her, sphinx-like, with dark eyes which betrayed nothing. It was six inches long at least and had a bright yellow stripe down its underside. On its tail was a little rounded horn which made it seem even more disgusting. It swayed to and fro as she watched it, as though trying to hypnotise her.

No way could she touch it now, yet she had to steel herself to deal with it somehow. Gingerly she began to shift her weight on to her other elbow in order to reach for the magazine she'd been reading, at the same time not daring to take her eyes off the caterpillar. Its body seemed to ripple as it sat there, but that was its only movement.

Oh, she was being such a fool, she despised herself for her own inadequacy. God, if they could only see her now in that TV studio where one of the crew had once referred to her as 'that tough young director'! Tough? She felt as weak as a jelly.

Her fingers recognised the feel of those glossy, printed pages. Slowly, she tried to draw the magazine towards her, intending to fold it over for a firmer grip. Not that she wanted to hurt the caterpillar, merely to brush it away, no more than that, however obscene and disgusting she found it.

Those bulging, dark eyes still regarded her. Did it understand what she was doing? Well, that was a daft idea if ever there was one. Her thoughts were coming feverishly and she realised she'd broken into a sweat. Yet . . . what if it *could* pick up some wavelength from her? Some sense of threat? Many animals had that facility, didn't they? That made it all the more important to remain absolutely still as she gradually took hold of the magazine.

So intense was her concentration, she hardly heard her sister's car arriving in front of the cottage. The engine revved, then died. The door slammed.

'Ginny! Are you home?'

The voice approached, lively and happy as usual. Ginny felt a sudden surge of relief and she must have moved because the caterpillar straightened up, becoming visibly more alert.

'Ginny, what on earth are you doing with a caterpillar on your tummy?' Lesley's voice boomed out, followed by her usual gust of laughter which sounded – oh, so *normal*! 'I thought you couldn't stand them!'

'Les, get it off me,' Ginny begged.

Her sister squatted down, holding back her thick auburn hair from her eyes as she bent forward for a closer look. 'My, aren't you a beauty!' she murmured to it, like talking to her cat. 'A real giant, too. As long as my hand, *and* you've been feeding well, to judge by the size of you. A bit overweight, I'd say. Greedy, that's your problem, my beauty. Just greedy.'

'Lesley! *GET-IT-OFF-ME!*'

'Come on, Ginny. No hysterics,' Lesley scolded her. 'No need for that. They've just as much right to exist as we have. And they can't do you any harm – watch!'

Ginny didn't wait that long. The second her sister had lifted the caterpillar away from her, she rolled over the grass to get well clear, then scrambled to her feet, trembling. Harmless or not, that was the last time she wanted one anywhere near her.

Lesley held up the caterpillar level with her eyes and cooed over it in that silly way she had; then suddenly she yelled out and dropped it, hastily stuffing her fingers into her mouth.

'Hell, that hurt!' she exclaimed as she sucked them. 'That bloody hurt!'

It was Ginny's turn to laugh. 'Harmless?' she mocked, getting her own back for once. 'Serves you right! I only hope that –'

'Bloody hell, it's biting my feet now!' Lesley burst out, but her voice trailed off and became a quick, shuddering gasp of pain. The blood drained from her face. 'Ginny . . . help me . . . '

Before Ginny could reach her, Lesley's knees gave way and she crumpled on to the grass, moaning incoherently. Ginny stared at her, bewildered, unable to see anything wrong. But then – protruding from the space between Lesley's sandal and her bare instep – she noticed the green rump of the caterpillar.

It seemed to be burrowing into her. Actually eating her flesh! Her blood dripped on to the grass, staining it.

Biting her lip, Ginny looked around desperately for

53

some way to help her sister. She mustn't touch that thing with her unprotected fingers, she knew that. If only she had a glove handy, but there was no time to rush into the cottage to get one. She grabbed the nearest magazine, ripped out a page and, using it, tried to get a firm grip on that wriggling tail.

Through the thick, glossy paper she could feel the caterpillar writhing in its attempts to free itself. She squeezed harder, at the same time pulling, aiming to draw the creature out. Its body pulsated violently between her fingers as it resisted her.

Gritting her teeth, she held on despite the fact that she felt nauseated by what she was doing. Her stomach churned sickeningly and she could feel the clammy sweat lying cold on her skin.

Unexpectedly, the caterpillar burst under the pressure, like a fat green sausage grown too tight for itself. The rear end of that hairy body came away in her hand.

'*Urgh!*'

She almost did throw up as she saw the green sap ooze out. It spread over the torn magazine page, coating the eye of an exotic, raven-haired girl modelling underwear. Some got on to Ginny's fingers, leaving a sticky smear when she attempted – almost hysterically – to wipe it off.

But there was no time to stop and think about it. The old, tough Ginny took control. Lesley needed help urgently. She was lying on the grass, hardly moving, though an unnatural, high-pitched mumble came from her parted lips. *That's how she'll look when she's dead!* The thought flashed through Ginny's mind. *Oh please God don't let her die!*

Her hands shook as she fumbled at the ankle straps of Lesley's sandals. Though it probably took less than a minute to get the first knot untied, it seemed like hours. At last she was able to tug the sandal clear. The sole of her sister's foot was a mess of blood and raw flesh with the

54

remains of that hideous caterpillar buried in it. She dashed into the kitchen for the first-aid box, to get some sort of dressing on the foot to staunch the blood before dragging her into the car and going for help.

If only she had a phone, at least she could ring someone, but they still hadn't come to install it.

That wound looked such a mess, she felt quite helpless when she saw it. She fished in it with the tweezers and somehow managed to remove the rest of the caterpillar although there were probably still fragments sticking inside. Then she pressed a generous pad of lint on the foot, sticking it down with Band-Aid. As she straightened up, wondering how she could manage to get Lesley to the car, she saw a second caterpillar.

She gasped.

It was emerging out of the grass and beginning to creep on to Lesley's freckled arm near her shoulder, its body rippling as it climbed. The same kind, too: long, emerald green hairs, and that little horn-like bulge on its tail. Its yellow stripe became momentarily visible when it reared up to survey the soft hill of flesh on which it found itself.

Oh, Jesus . . . What should she do?

Ginny grabbed Lesley's sandal and knocked the caterpillar away. It landed on the rug – *her* rug – next to the magazines and her sunglasses. Still clutching the sandal, she scrambled over and brought it down hard on the caterpillar which twisted under the impact, then curled up, then uncurled again, and was definitely still very much alive.

Desperately she hammered at it, bringing that sandal down again and again, but she could swear it was having no effect. The more she hit it, the more menacing that caterpillar seemed to become. At last, steeling herself, she placed the sandal carefully on top of it, then pressed down with her full weight until she felt the sudden *Squelch!* as she squashed it to death.

Its sticky, green body fluid spread over the sandal, dissolving and mingling with the dull brown stain left by her sister's blood.

That whole afternoon was a nightmare, not least the problem of moving Lesley to a place where she could be looked after. Ginny prayed that Bernie would be at home, not out on his rounds. It would take her no more than three minutes to drive to his surgery, whereas the hospital was fifteen miles away. Lesley could even die before she got there.

She was just conscious, but in a delirium. Her eyes moved wildly though it seemed they saw nothing; her lips scarcely even trembled as she muttered a stream of words which had neither shape nor meaning.

'I'll have to try and lift you,' Ginny told her, bending down to take hold of her arm. Vaguely she remembered the fireman's lift one of her actors had been taught for a soap opera episode. 'I'm not sure I can manage.'

The 'lift' had appeared a lot simpler on the screen. Her sister was heavy; Ginny was scared she might drop her as she attempted to swing her up over her shoulder. She lowered her gently back on the grass, abandoning the idea. Somehow she'd have to bring the car down the side of the cottage.

A section of shaky old fence was the only real obstacle. It had been on the point of falling down; only a few days ago she'd done a temporary repair job, lashing it to the post with a length of twine. Hurriedly she fetched a sharp knife from the kitchen and slashed through the knots. Taking a grip on the loose fence she pulled it back and felt the rotting timber snap free of the few remaining rusty nails. The question now was whether the gap was wide enough to drive through.

Lesley's Mini was the nearer of the two cars and her keys were still in the ignition. Reversing down the path to the broken fence was tricky. Her nearside wheels ploughed through a flower bed, flattening the hyacinths and clusters of daffodils, while on the other side stray branches and twigs from the unkempt hedge scratched along the paintwork. She hit the decaying fence-post as she went through, bringing it down.

Half-lifting, half-dragging her sister across the grass, she somehow managed to get her into the front seat of the Mini, using the seat belt to hold her there. It was then Ginny realised she was still almost naked, wearing only her bikini briefs, just the way she was when that first caterpillar had appeared. Her top was still on the rug, among that mess.

She ran into the cottage to pull on a T-shirt and grab a pair of jeans which she tossed on to the Mini's back seat as she got in. Lesley's head was slumped forward, her chin resting on her chest; she seemed frighteningly quiet.

'Won't be long now,' Ginny tried to reassure her as she turned the key to start the engine. 'I *am* trying to hurry, Les.'

Lesley's silence accused her of every sin in the book. It all crowded back into Ginny's mind as she drove off, scraping against the cottage wall in her haste: the occasions when they had quarrelled, the hard words, the small selfish acts when she could have been more helpful. Oh God, what if she died?

Oh please don't let her die!

Not that Ginny had ever believed in God, not since she was small when she'd imagined Him as a Father Christmas figure with a long beard. In fact, she'd never given it much thought. Until now, which probably meant it was too late.

She took the corner too quickly. Lesley slumped towards her, held back only by the seat belt.

'Oh Les . . . ' Ginny slowed down and tried to push her upright again. 'Les, hold on. We're almost home.'

'Home' was at the far end of the village, a double-

57

fronted Edwardian house with creeper spreading cosily over the stonework around the windows. Bernie had taken it over from his father together with the practice. His surgery and waiting area occupied a self-contained suite on the ground floor with its own separate side entrance, but that still left – as Lesley so often explained – plenty of space for the family. Three large rooms downstairs, five bedrooms – six at a pinch – two of them equipped with their own washbasins. Only one bathroom, though.

The moment she turned into the drive which curved gracefully up to the front of the house she realised Bernie's car was missing. He must be out on call.

Or playing golf, she thought bitterly as she pulled up.

Or was this one of his days in Lingford where he was also a part-time consultant?

Oh hell . . .

The front door was locked and she could hear no sound of voices from inside the house. She rang the bell violently, prolonged. No response. But there must be somebody in – what about the children or Phuong, their nanny? She ran back to the car to sound the horn, holding her finger on it steadily, desperate for someone to hear. In her mind she went feverishly over the alternatives. Phone from the police house? But he was usually out at this time of day. The two or three village shops had early closing. The garage? At least there might be someone there to let her use the phone.

Then Phuong appeared, running towards her around the side of the house. 'I'm sorry. We are at the bottom of the garden. By the summer house.'

'Oh Phuong! I thought no one was in!' The relief was almost too much for Ginny to bear. It was all she could do to hold back her tears. 'There's been an accident. Where's Bernie? I must phone for an ambulance.'

Phuong stooped to take a quick look at Lesley's

huddled figure in the front seat of the Mini, an expression of concern on her pale Vietnamese face. Then she nodded briskly, grasped Ginny's arm and led her into the house.

'You sit down,' she said calmly. 'You want I phone?'

'I'll do it.'

'Okay. You phone. I look after Lesley.' Her attractive, lilting English sounded clipped and prim.

She was so cool-headed and practical, Ginny thought enviously as she fumbled through the dialling. Of course, they must have taught her some nursing when she did her child care course, but that could not be the only reason. It was in her character too. She had been one of the first batch of Vietnamese boat people to settle in Britain. Most of her family had died during the long weeks of drifting in that open boat. When at last a passing freighter picked them up, only she and her brother were still alive. But she seldom talked about those days now she was happily settled with Lesley's family. She seemed to live only for the children; in return, they loved her like a sister.

'Hello?' the operator was repeating patiently. 'Which service do you want, please?'

'Ambulance,' Ginny said.

When she went outside again, she found Phuong holding a basin of warm water and bathing Lesley's face. It was puzzling that she was still not properly conscious. The wound in her foot was deep and she must have lost an awful lot of blood, but would that in itself have caused this delirium? And so quickly?

'She has high fever,' Phuong informed her. 'What cause this? She hurt her foot?'

'An insect bite,' Ginny explained wearily. It was only a half-lie, but would anyone believe the truth? 'An ambulance is on its way. That's something, I suppose.'

'I think we take her inside house,' Phuong announced. She put the basin down on the wall beside the steps. 'Is better she lie down. Can you help?'

59

'Of course.'

Ginny held Lesley by the shoulders, ready to take her weight the moment Phuong released the seat belt. Before she could do so, they heard the crunching of tyres on the drive.

'Bernie! Oh thank God!' Ginny was running towards him even before the car had stopped. 'Bernie – oh, something crazy has happened! It's Les, she's hurt!'

Bernie examined his wife briefly before agreeing that they should move her into the house. He kept very calm, every inch the professional doctor, but Ginny could see that his eyes were troubled. Phuong unfastened the seatbelt, leaning across the driving seat to reach it; then he lifted Lesley up in his arms and carried her in through the front door.

'Ginny, can you fetch my bag? It's on the seat of my car. D'you mind?'

By the time she got back with it, Lesley lay face-down on the surgery couch. Bernie, now alone, was timing her pulse. He opened the bag and took out his stethoscope.

'Phuong has gone back to keep an eye on the children, so you'll have to help if I need it. Suppose you tell me what happened exactly. Did you put the dressing on her foot?'

Somehow, now Bernie was back Ginny felt stronger again. Better able to cope, at any rate. She gave him the bare facts, though it seemed such a bald, unconvincing account after the tension of actually experiencing it all.

'A caterpillar – it's so ridiculous!' she ended.

'I'm afraid it isn't,' Bernie told her grimly as he removed the dressing and began to examine the wound on Lesley's foot. 'One of the apprentices on Bottom Reach Farm was attacked in the same way. A long green caterpillar, was it? About six or eight inches, with a yellow stripe underneath?'

'That's right. And hairy.'

'In the case of this poor lad it wasn't his foot. He was fooling around with the caterpillar, making it walk up his arm. Not a nice business.'

Painstakingly he cleaned the wound as he talked, from time to time glancing up at Lesley's face. Her eyes were closed now and she was breathing regularly.

'What I don't understand is this fever,' he commented, worried. 'And her bloodshot eyes.'

'How bad is the apprentice?'

Instead of answering, Bernie looked pointedly at Ginny's bare legs and at the scanty mules on her feet. 'I'd feel a lot happier if you'd cover yourself up while these things are around.'

'I've got my jeans in the car. I'll put them on. Is the boy all right?'

'He died. Already dead by the time I got there. By all accounts he had the caterpillar on his forearm only inches from his face. His friends were looking on. One took a photograph. Then somehow it moved and landed on his throat. Bit into the jugular. Or chewed into it would be more accurate.'

'He bled to death?' She felt sick in the stomach even thinking about it.

'That's about the size of it. As I said, not a nice business.' He applied a fresh dressing to Lesley's foot, bandaging it clumsily. 'Let's hope that ambulance isn't too long coming. I'm tempted to take Les in the car, but – '

He changed the subject abruptly.

'Ginny, do me another favour. You'll find Phuong by the summer house at the end of the garden. If you could warn her about the caterpillars, I'd be grateful. I don't suppose there are a lot of them about, but she could keep her eyes open. But try not to alarm the children, if possible.'

'I'll go now.'

'And if you could – ' He stopped and regarded her intently. 'I'm afraid I'm being rather selfish, aren't I? How are *you* feeling? Did it do anything to you? No bites?'

'I was lucky. It did nothing, apart from being a bit prickly on my tummy.'

'Let me see.'

She pulled up her T-shirt. There were a few slight marks on her skin where she thought the caterpillar had rested, but they could just as easily have been heat rash.

'Are they itchy?'

'No.'

'Well, let me know if there's any change. Now I think I'll phone the ambulance service to find out what's happening.'

Ginny fetched her jeans from the Mini and also put on some fashion boots of Lesley's before venturing down the garden to find Phuong. The grass was cut very short and the summer house where the children were playing was well clear of the trees. Even so, Ginny could not help feeling uneasy.

When the ambulance came, Ginny's first thought was to accompany her sister to the hospital, but Bernie begged her to stay with Phuong and the children. At the sight of his worried expression she agreed without argument, saying she would do whatever he thought best. She helped him post a notice on the side door cancelling surgery for that evening.

She waited until the ambulance had left before venturing down the garden again to suggest that they might like to play in the house for a change, and in any case wasn't it time for tea? She found them this time inside the summer house. Phuong was entertaining them with a story-cum-game from Vietnam and they protested vigorously at Ginny's interruption.

The truth was, while Ginny was fond of her three nieces she had never felt completely at ease with children. Wendy, the youngest, she found the most difficult to manage; she was a lively, highly intelligent, stubborn two-and-a-half who demanded long explanations before she would consent to do anything. Caroline, aged four, was the dreamy one and easier to control, while six-year-old Frankie listened bright-eyed to Ginny's news that their Mummy had gone away for the night and immediately wanted to know if she was going to get a divorce.

'No, of course not!' Ginny laughed. 'What a ridiculous idea!'

'Susie's Mummy left like that without saying goodbye and she's getting a divorce. Susie told me. Everybody gets a divorce sometimes.'

'What's a divorce?' asked Wendy. 'Can I have one?'

But at last they were all in bed and asleep. Phuong went to her room, while Ginny stayed in the lounge with the television on, though hardly watching it, waiting for a phone call from Bernie.

It was then she found herself thinking about the giant moths once more, wondering uneasily what connection there might be between them and these new killer caterpillars. Those moths – *her* moths – had seemed so elegant and gentle, yet . . .

4

'Killed by what? A caterpillar? You must be joking!' He was standing up against the bar, wide-legged, as though he owned the place. His face was redder than it used to be and he had a bald patch. He turned and saw her. 'D'you hear that, Liz? Eh, Lizzie Kinley! Why are you sitting there in the corner? Come up here an' be sociable.'

She took another sup of Guinness and ignored him. That Harry Smith always did have a loud voice *and* a laugh to match, the noisy bugger. Remembered him from way back when they both went to the same school, only he hadn't got that beer gut then. Had the voice though. When he'd whispered to her that time on the back row, the whole village heard it. But he was a Red Lion man usually, so what was he doing here in the Bull?

'Beer gone off in the Red Lion, then?' She emptied her glass and banged it down on the little round table. 'Can't say you're welcome in here. Keeps a decent house, does Charlie.'

'Did you hear what he just told me?' Another deep laugh rumbled out of him. 'No, Charlie, you're having me on! Go on, pull the other one!'

'Kid o' nineteen,' the landlord confirmed. He was polishing the glasses he'd just washed: a burly, slow-moving man who prided himself on his glasses, which was one reason she always came in here, the other being that the Red Lion refused to serve her these days. 'They've got these agricultural apprentices down that place, an' it was one o' those lads. A caterpillar bite!'

'Sure it wasn't a wasp?'

'No, the other lads saw it. A long green caterpillar, they said. Long as your hand.'

'Must've been an adder then. Who ever heard of a caterpillar biting anybody? Come on, Charlie – have you?'

'They've ruined my lettuce this year. Made a right mess o' the whole bloody garden.'

'Ay, but that's not the same as biting people. What d'you say, Liz? You've had plenty o' little nibbles in your day. Ever had it with a caterpillar?'

'You watch your mouth,' she told him. 'You always did shoot off your mouth, didn't you, Harry Smith?

'Always the big mouth.'

Another laugh exploded out of him, loud enough to rattle the glasses on the shelves.

'Ah, no offence, Liz! Come on. Come up to the bar an' I'll buy you another Guinness. I've only got a minute. Meeting someone.'

'I'll have it here,' she said, not budging.

'It's her leg,' Charlie explained, reaching to the shelf behind him for a bottle of Guinness. 'Months now since she came out of hospital, but it's still not right.'

'Knocked off me bike by a bloody moth, you wouldn't credit it. Now here I am on sticks for the rest o' me bloody life. And I wasn't even drunk.'

'You'd had a few.' Charlie brought her the bottle, taking the empty back to the bar with him. 'You've had more'n you should today as well. That's your last one, Liz.'

'Fuck off!' She concentrated on the Guinness, pouring it in against the side of the glass with a skill born of long practice, her hand as steady as a rock despite everything. That was more than she could say of some. Raising the glass to her lips, she said: 'Here's to you, Harry! Always had a soft spot for your Liz, didn't you?'

'That's right! We had many a good grope, eh Liz?'

'Dirty bugger!' she spat at him.

He sipped his large whisky. 'Ay, but we're no longer as young as we were then, more's the pity. That's life.'

'Young girl came in to see me in hospital,' she told them, remembering. Thinking it over. 'Some relation o' Dr Rendell's, she said. Kept going on about them moths, saying as how they didn't attack me at all, and how nice they were and all that Sunday School stuff. Daft kid.'

They weren't listening. The man Harry Smith was expecting had arrived and they went off into a corner to talk privately. He was a younger man than Harry, in cavalry twill and a flat cap, the kind who'd talk a farmer into mortgaging his last field to pay for a new tractor he didn't need. Ay, she'd seen them all, she had. Slipped upstairs with a few back in her barmaid days. Saved quite a little nest egg. Men? If they want it they'll pay for it, so why give it to 'em free?

'Charlie!' Jesus, those bloody doctors should've patched her up better than this. Getting up was murder, even with her two sticks. That gelding was to blame; she'd told him so, too. 'Charlie, take me drink into the garden, would you, love? It's too stuffy in here. I've got me hot flushes coming on.'

The seats out in the pub garden at the back were a bit on the rough side, not as comfortable as in the bar, but she found one in the long shadow cast by a couple of apple trees and sank gratefully on to it. Charlie put her glass down on the shaky table beside her, and didn't forget the bottle either. Through the open window came Harry's loud voice arguing about delivery dates. She still couldn't fathom why he'd chosen to come in here rather than the Red Lion.

She leaned back on the rough wooden seat humming some tune or other, she couldn't put a name to it. Ten years old she must have been, she and Harry both. Back row of the class, sharing one of those double desks. She'd never forget that look of concentration on his face as he pretended to be interested in the blackboard while all the time his left hand was exploring her leg under that short frock she always wore. Pushed him away that morning, she had – she could no longer remember why – so he'd fumbled with his fly buttons till suddenly he had his thing out. She'd giggled. That was a hot day too, now she thought of it. 'He's come up for air,' he'd whispered so loud, the whole class had heard him. 'Can't breathe in there.' God yes, and she could remember Teacher's words now, clear as yesterday. 'Harry Smith – is that you talking again? Stand up, boy! Stand *up*!' And Harry stood up, stung into quick obedience by her tone of command, not thinking. They all saw him, turning around to stare at his bit o' white meat. Of course they laughed, all but Teacher. 'Kindly adjust your clothing and stand outside the door till I call you.' Her very words.

It had brought everything back, seeing Harry again. After all, what was the harm? It was only a little boy's prick he'd had then, nothing for the lady teacher to get excited about. A giggle, that's all – and here she was, supping her Guinness, still remembering it.

Oh hell, that bloody leg was bothering her again. If it wasn't aching, it was pins-and-needles, this time on the soft flesh above her stocking-top. She tried to scratch it through her skirt, but that only made it worse. A quick, sharp pain cut into her, causing her to swear. Involuntarily her foot jerked forward, kicking the table. Her glass fell, spilling the Guinness over her.

Another sharp bite, and this time she screamed in agony. It just went on and never seemed to end, chewing into her leg like a slow-turning drill. Then a second drill started up – on her left leg now not far from her crotch – and she realised dimly through that excruciating pain that it was not her usual trouble, not this time, but something quite different, as if sharp-toothed ferrets had got under her skirt. Twisting with pain, she fell off the bench, yelling and cursing with all her might as she thrashed about on the grass and tried desperately to end the torment.

It did ease momentarily, long enough for her to get a grip on herself. She pulled up her skirt, now blood-stained, and let out a shriek of terror. Two long, hairy green caterpillars were on her legs: one busily burrowing into her inner thigh which was now almost numb, its tail end shifting backwards and forwards as it fed; the other gradually rippling upwards towards her groin, leaving a wet smear of blood behind it.

Her blood.

But she saw everything in a paralysing slow motion. Get rid of them, her mind insisted urgently; you've only to reach out, take hold of them, fling them away: but she couldn't. Her own dark blood was trickling over her skin, but she could do nothing. She stared as though hypnotised at that second caterpillar which had now almost reached its destination.

'Help me!' Her voice quavered weakly. 'Help!'

The men were running towards her, she could hear them. They had been mentioning caterpillars earlier. Killed a boy, wasn't that it? Killed someone? But they were too late. All too late. She almost welcomed that stab of pain in her groin when it came, knowing the sooner these green caterpillars had their way, the sooner it would all be over. On that tree above her, on those fresh young leaves, that's where they were. She was screaming uncontrollably, she could hear herself, when one dropped down on her face, inserting itself into her wide open mouth.

'Bloody hell!

Men bending over her: that had been so much part of her life, feeding the insatiable hunger between her legs. Her own private curse, even now when men no longer wanted her. Oh God she couldn't breathe. She was choking. Dying. Was this it? Was this how it happened?

Let me breathe . . . please . . . oh let up for a moment, love, just so as I can breathe . . .

A hot knife burned in her throat, the most savage pain she'd known yet. No screams now though, however much she wanted to. Just that red-hot, jagged knife, and the drumming in her ears ever louder.

'Get that bloody thing out of her mouth!' Harry Smith

was roaring. He elbowed his way past, sending Charlie reeling against the overturned table. 'Here, let me, for Chrissake!'

Charlie didn't argue. Already dead, wasn't she? Her body lay twisted unnaturally on the grass with fat green caterpillars – six at least – gorging themselves on her. Jesus, he thought he'd seen a few things in the army, but nothing like this. Turning away, he spewed his guts out over the bench where she'd been happily sitting only a couple of minutes ago.

'All right, Lizzie,' he could hear Harry Smith's voice behind him. 'It's all right, love. I'll get it. Easy does it now. You're going to be all right.'

Was she hell, Charlie thought.

He looked back to find Harry Smith on his knees beside her, slowly drawing the caterpillar out of her mouth. There must have been a couple of inches down her throat at least, judging from the length of it. The cavalry twill slicker stood just behind him, watching with interest, obviously unmoved, though Harry Smith himself sounded unusually tender when he spoke. Not that Liz Kinley would ever hear him again.

'Harry, she's dead,' Charlie tried to tell him as gently as he could.

'Who says so?' Harry Smith's face, flushing even redder than normal, peered up at him angrily. 'You go an' ring the fuckin' ambulance instead o' standin' there like a prick. I'll give her mouth-to-mouth. Let's hope to God it works.'

'Be careful they don't get you while you're at it!'

In her agonising death throes, Liz had ended up directly beneath the old apple tree. As Harry Smith bent forward to try to revive her, something fell from one of the overhanging branches. It might have been a leaf, but then Charlie knew that leaves never plummet straight down; nor, landing on the back of that red bull-neck, would a leaf have immediately uncurled and started crawling.

Charlie dashed forward to help him. 'Come on, get it away from his neck!' he yelled at the slicker who stood there looking on, uselessly.

The caterpillar began to chew into the soft patch beneath Harry Smith's ear. He fell forward, bellowing in anguish. At the same time, more dropped out of the tree. Two of them joined the first, concentratedly penetrating his neck at the base of the skull.

For protection, Charlie wrapped his handkerchief round his fingers. Then he grabbed one of them, tugging it away from its feeding ground, intending to throw it aside; but it wound itself rapidly around his fingers and its head reared up like a snake's.

He didn't pause to discover what it might do next, but squeezed hard, digging his short fingernails into it through the handkerchief until its fat body burst under the pressure. A tacky green slime spread over his hand.

'Urgh . . . A ca-ca-ca- . . . '

The cavalry twill slicker – a fertiliser salesman, wasn't he? – reeled across the garden towards him, holding out his arm, terrified. At first Charlie thought the caterpillar on his wrist must be only a small one; then he realised the greater part of it had already moved into the sleeve of the man's hacking jacket.

'Ca-ca-caterpillar!' he was burbling hysterically.

'Oh, for Chrissake!' Charlie snapped at him.

But it was no use; he had to help him. Charlie hesitated for only a second, uncertain what to do, before grasping the man's forearm with both hands and squeezing hard. Despite the thick tweed of the jacket he could feel the caterpillar squirming as he tightened his grip. He'd always had strong hands – in the army he'd been heavy-weight champion for a year – but it took all his strength to squash the thing to death. He sensed the squelch as its resistance finally gave way.

'Take your jacket off and wash your arm,' he ordered wearily, giving the man a shove to get him moving. 'Not inside, you fool. Use that tap over there by the shed.'

Harry Smith was dead, that was obvious. He lay sprawled across Liz Kinley's body, his leg over hers, as though they had died together while making love on the grass. Which, in a strange, distorted way, they probably had. God alone knew how many caterpillars were still feeding on them. Charlie looked away, too sick to count them.

From beyond the trees came the steady, wasp-like drone of a light aircraft. Crop-spraying. That told him what he had to do, distasteful though it was.

But his wife Mary had the idea before him. She came hurrying out through the back door with those short steps of hers. In her hand she held the old-fashioned pesticide spray she always used.

'I've phoned the constable, and there's an ambulance on the way,' she informed him briskly. She pushed the spray gun at him. 'Here, you deal with that while I look after the customer. Must say you were a bit rough on him. He's bleeding.'

'Didn't know you were back, love,' he said automatically.

He felt so drained out by the shock of what had happened, he was more inclined to walk away from it all than do anything more. Over by the garden tap he could see the fertiliser salesman had collapsed; a patch of blood spread from his arm over the new cavalry twill. Jesus, the place looked worse than a battlefield.

Taking the spray, he went back to the obscene lovers beneath the apple tree. At least it was all over for them, he thought; nothing more could harm them now. He began pumping the chemical spray over their remains, determined to kill every single one of those caterpillars.

5

Ginny was washing up after the children's tea when Bernie came in with the news about Mrs Kinley's death. She stood stock-still, the plate in her hand dripping with the foam-bubbles of the washing up liquid.

'When?' she asked him, stunned.

'Lunchtime today.' He recounted the details in a dry clinical manner which was untypical of him, as though afraid of betraying his true feelings. 'It's getting bad, Ginny. Worse than we feared, even.'

Ginny rinsed the plate and put it in the rack to dry. Then she let out the water and began to clean the sink vigorously. If only she'd kept her promise to visit Mrs Kinley again . . . taken her that half-bottle of gin she'd asked for . . . anything to cheer her up . . . A couple of minutes' conversation at the bedside: it wouldn't have needed more than that. A quarrel, even. It would at least have been a moment's human contact. But no, she'd been too busy, too self-centred, and she blamed herself bitterly for it.

'I never did go back to see her,' she confessed miserably as she peeled off Lesley's pink rubber gloves and draped them over the side of the sink. 'Oh, Bernie, I wish I had.'

'I think you need a drink,' he told her gently. 'And so do I. Come on, there's still another fifteen minutes before surgery.'

The night before, they had neither of them had much sleep. Ginny had sat up in the lounge in front of the flickering television screen until the last of the late-night movies had ended, reluctant to go to bed in case Bernie rang. Twice she had phoned the hospital herself – the first time to pass on a message from a querulous patient, the second because she just couldn't bear waiting any longer – but she'd been unable to speak to Bernie. The girl at the switchboard had taken messages, then transferred her to the night sister's office. No news. Only a kindly reassurance that Lesley was still alive, condition unchanged.

Eventually she'd fetched herself a light blanket and curled up on the sofa to try and get some sleep. The phone was on the small table beside her; she'd only to stretch out her hand to pick it up. But sleep proved impossible. Her mind was too restless, full of thoughts of what might happen if Lesley died. Mother would have to be told, which meant telephoning Australia, only she might not be at home, she seldom was, always travelling.

Then the funeral. She must have dropped off for a second or two, because she saw it all so vividly: the open grave in that little village churchyard, the vicar in his cassock, reading the last words as dozens of huge moths fluttered overhead in a beautiful, eerie tribute.

The phone rang. She sat up, startled, trying to see in the darkness.

'Ginny? It's Bernie. Sorry to ring in the middle of the night, but I know you're anxious to hear the latest.'

'She's dead,' Ginny exclaimed. He sounded so downcast. So utterly exhausted. 'Oh Bernie . . . '

'No! She's going to be all right. She's asleep.'

'Are you sure? Oh, of course you are, or you wouldn't be saying it! Oh, I'm so . . . ' She couldn't finish the sentence. 'I'm crying. I was so convinced that Les . . . Oh, thank God!'

'Ginny, listen.' His voice was calm and patient. 'I shall sleep at the hospital, but I'll be home first thing tomorrow morning as soon as I can get a mini-cab.'

'You need to stay with her?'

73

'No, she's going to get better, Ginny. The worst is over. I'll explain some other time what we found, but she's responding well. And of course Dr Sanderson is here. She's his patient.'

'You *are* telling me the truth?'

'Would I lie to you?' He was infinitely patient, but his voice sounded so metallic on that phone, it was not like talking to the real Bernie at all. 'Look, you'd better get some rest. I'll see you in the morning.'

'No.' She made up her mind suddenly, realising what she had to do for her own sake, if not for his. 'Stay there, I'll come and pick you up. It won't take me long to drive at this time of night.'

Before Bernie could object she had put the receiver down. Then, thinking the children might be disturbed if he rang again after she'd gone, she took it off the hook. The keys to his car were on the hallstand.

It had been an odd drive through those empty country lanes with her headlights throwing surrealistic patterns of light and shade on the moving green foliage. Among those leaves more caterpillars must be lurking, she'd thought. Biting her lip, she had tried to concentrate on the twisting white line down the centre of the tarmac. Tomorrow she'd have to get some really effective pesticide to spray both gardens. Bernie's first, of course, because of the children.

On the way back Bernie took the wheel, tired though he was. It had not been easy, she gathered; her fears that Lesley might die had been only too justifiable. They had taken blood samples and God alone knew what else before finally deciding that they were dealing with two separate factors.

'There's bacterial infection,' Bernie explained tersely as he drove. 'The bacteria are clearly visible under the microscope. Sanderson has put her on antibiotics. Whether there's a link between that and the caterpillar bite is hard to say.'

'That's when she fainted.'

'Not surprising when you see how deep the wound is. Sanderson did some emergency work on the foot but she'll need another operation when she's well enough. There are also traces of something else in the blood, some kind of insect venom, I imagine, but very thinly diluted. It may have no long-term effect. We'll have to wait and see.'

'I think these caterpillars are the larvae stage of my moths.' She had been brooding over it all evening. 'In fact, I'm convinced.'

'What makes you say that?'

'Just a horrible feeling that I'm right.'

They had arrived back at the house. Keeping her voice down in order not to disturb the children she offered to make him something to eat. No, he'd had a bite at the hospital, he told her, adding that they'd both better get to bed. It was three-thirty by the clock in the hall, which meant it was almost certainly even later than that.

As she turned to the stairs, somehow she stumbled against him – certainly not deliberately – and grasped his arm to steady herself. For a few seconds they stood in a close embrace, her head resting against his chest. It was such a comfort having him there; so reassuring after all the tension. He kissed the top of her forehead.

'Go on now, love,' he said gently. 'See you in the morning. Think I'll have a nightcap before I go up.'

Feeling light-headed and slightly guilty towards Lesley, she had gone up to her bed in the spare room to try to sleep. Not that she'd meant anything by that moment of weakness. It was just that . . . well, she was so relieved that everything was going to be all right, it had gone to her head like a shot of LSD. In that mood she'd have hugged anyone who happened to be there, even Dr Sanderson. The gelding, as Mrs Kinley had dubbed him.

As for the caterpillars, she thought as she sank gratefully on to the pillow, a spot of spraying would soon deal with that problem. She'd do both gardens in the morning. They'd been unlucky, that's all. The chances of being so severely attacked by any insect were one in a million. It was not likely to happen again, she had decided, closing her eyes.

But she had been wrong.

Terribly wrong.

She sat in one of Bernie's deep armchairs, trying to come to terms with his news of Mrs Kinley's death. The man with her had died too, he said. It seemed unbelievable.

Bernie poured her a generous dose of his best whisky. She should drink it slowly, he instructed. Doctor's orders. Instead, she gulped it down. It burned in her throat, kicking her back into the present.

'I feel so guilty about her!' she burst out. 'Oh, if only I hadn't promised to go back it wouldn't be so bad. But I did promise.'

'There's nothing to blame yourself for. I'm sure she wasn't really expecting you.'

'I let her down.'

'Mrs Kinley was tougher than you think, Ginny. Believe me.'

'You don't understand, Bernie.' How could she explain, she wondered desperately. She couldn't even put it into words for herself. Not adequately. 'In my TV series – the soap opera – we had characters like her. Alcoholics, shoplifters, people with mental problems. It was a policy decision to include them.'

She spoke bitterly, realising for the first time how they had all been deceiving themselves.

'Oh, we thought we were doing a great job!' she rushed on before he could say anything. 'Giving the series a social conscience. You should have been at those meetings we had about it. You'd have vomited. Then,

76

when you asked me to see Mrs Kinley, I didn't really know what to say to her. I failed.'

'Ginny, you're torturing yourself unnecessarily.'

She stared morosely into the bottom of the cut crystal glass she held cupped in her hands. 'It doesn't help her now, anyway.'

Bernie put his own glass down. 'I'm sorry, love. It's time for surgery. Take another drink, if you want.'

She shook her head.

'No, I said I'd play hide-and-seek with the children and then read them a story. I'd better at least do that.'

'I'll be going to visit Lesley after surgery,' he told her, pausing at the door. 'Like to come along?'

'Please.' She smiled at him ruefully. 'Sorry I've been so silly.'

They talked again about Mrs Kinley as they drove into Lingford in Bernie's car. As far as he knew there was no *Mr* Kinley. She had lived alone – divorced, he imagined; certainly there was no one else of that name on his list. As for her being one of the 'problem' characters Ginny had talked about, he definitely could not agree.

'A sharp tongue, yes,' he conceded, breaking into a laugh. 'I asked her once if she had a drink problem. Well, she had by all normal standards, but she denied it of course. Oh no, doctor, drink's no problem, she said, 'cept for the prices they charge. Her real trouble was she didn't like getting old.'

'Where is she now?'

'The body? In the hospital mortuary. We're doing an autopsy tomorrow morning.'

'D'you think . . . ' Ginny hesitated, uncertain what she herself really wanted. It seemed ridiculous, but Mrs Kinley's death nagged at her conscience. 'Could I see her?'

'Aren't you being a bit morbid?'

'No. A bit old-fashioned if you like. I feel I should pay my last respects. That's the least I can do for her.'

'I'm sure that can be arranged with the undertaker. I'll see if I can find out which one is – '

'No,' she stopped him firmly. 'I'd like to do it today. I don't want any involvement with family, or anything like that. I just want to . . . well, you know. Discreetly.'

'The damage around the mouth and particularly the throat was fairly extensive. It's not an attractive sight, Ginny. I strongly advise you against it.'

'Bernie, please? I'm not squeamish, except for creepie-crawlies and that's only because they move. What I'm trying to say is that I know it's not going to be nice and I hate the thought of it, but I do owe it to her. I'll not stay more than a few seconds. I promise.'

To Ginny's relief, Bernie seemed to give in. At least, he said he'd have a word about it with whoever was in charge. He probably thought she was being hysterical; perhaps she was, although that was not how it felt. The more she went over it in her mind, the more convinced she became that she had to do it. Not only was it a debt she had to settle with the old woman for not going back to visit her again; there was also that story of her having been deliberately attacked by the giant moths. Ginny had not taken that seriously. She'd been as bad as the others.

Everything pointed to there being a link between the moths and these caterpillars. They were numerous, they were both large and they had never been seen before in the area. If Mrs Kinley's account were accurate, both were hostile to human beings. Would it be so surprising to discover that they were in fact identical: two stages in the same life cycle?

It was still daylight when they arrived at Lingford Hospital. As Bernie guided her through the corridors, he explained that he would leave her alone with Lesley after a while in order to find out if it would be possible for her to view Mrs Kinley's body.

'They could well refuse,' he warned her.

They found Lesley propped up on her pillows, looking pale and exhausted but very much alive. Her thick auburn hair lay in profusion around her face like a slightly tarnished halo.

'Hello! Are you two getting on well together?' she joked when they entered her room, but her voice lacked its usual bounce. 'Hope you're keeping him out of mischief, Ginny!'

'Hello, darling! How've you been feeling?' Bernie kissed her. Ginny stood aside as her sister held him close. When she released him, he went to the foot of her bed to glance at her chart. 'Oh, you're doing well!'

'I'm bored,' she said.

'You're obviously on the mend.'

'Paul Sanderson is a very good doctor. You'll have to watch out!'

She gave a brief, tired laugh, then leaned back against the pillows again.

'The children send their love,' Ginny told her. 'Phuong is absolutely wonderful with them, but I'm staying on for the time being. I think they miss their Mummy.'

They chatted generally for three or four minutes before Bernie made his excuse and slipped out. Left alone together, Ginny tried to entertain her sister with the latest gossip from the village, but without mentioning caterpillars, which was just as well. When she began to describe her trip to the Garden Centre that morning for pesticide, Lesley changed the subject right away.

But then she was still very weak. Several times she closed her eyes while Ginny was talking.

'Would you prefer to sleep now?'

Lesley's eyelids flickered open lazily. 'No, go on, please. I like hearing your voice. So what did he say to Mrs Martinson?'

Ginny went on with her story of how the vicar was in deep trouble with the Ladies' Committee who were disgusted that he could even think of accepting that quart bottle of whisky for the All Saints Spring Fête. What if one of those teenagers won it?

But Lesley was already asleep. Ginny sat by her quietly, wondering why it had to happen to her.

When Bernie returned, she put her finger to her lips to warn him, and they both crept quietly out of the room. He took her elbow and steered her a few paces farther away from the door.

'That's the best medicine for her now. Plenty of sleep.' He kept his voice down despite the clatter as a trolley passed them in the corridor. 'I've had a word with Sanderson. She's still responding well, he tells me. If she keeps this up for another twenty-four hours she should be in the clear.'

'It's that bad?'

'It's that *good*,' he corrected her grimly. 'The state she was in when we got her here yesterday, it's a wonder she's still alive. Now — ' he changed tack, 'about this business of yours. Tomorrow won't do, I suppose?'

'I'm going to London tomorrow to see that script agent.'

'I'd forgotten all about that. Very well, then,' he sighed with obvious disapproval, 'if you still insist on going through with it — '

'Which I do.'

'I have obtained permission. I've also asked one of the house doctors to accompany you, so we'd best go along and meet her now. We don't want to waste too much of her time.'

She was left breathless trying to keep up with him as he strode through the corridors. At last he stopped to push open a swing door and she found herself in a common room for medical staff. A young, pretty Indian girl stood

80

up as they entered and came towards them. She hardly looked old enough to be a qualified doctor, Ginny thought; but she carried a stethoscope protruding from the side pocket of her white coat, so that was what she must be.

'This is Dr Roy,' Bernie introduced her briefly. 'My sister-in-law, Ginny Andrewes. I'm extremely grateful to you, Jameela. I hope it's not too much bother.'

'I'm glad to be of help.'

'Now if you'll excuse me. Sanderson has kindly invited me to take a look at one of his patients, the survivor of that last incident. Perhaps I could meet you in the reception area, Ginny.'

She nodded, pressing her lips together. Now it had come to the point of being taken into the mortuary she was beginning to feel apprehensive. Not of the dead bodies. She'd seen bodies before; in the dissecting room too, during her time at university when she'd shared a flat with a girl medical student. But what if she made a fool of herself and fainted?

'We go this way along the corridor,' Dr Roy told her crisply. 'I'm afraid this hospital's a rabbit warren of corridors.'

'Like something out of Kafka.' Ginny grimaced pointedly.

'Oh, you've read Kafka?' Her face lit up with pleasure. 'My favourite. My name's Jameela, by the way. I'm so glad your sister seems to be making progress. She must have a lot of stamina.'

'I think she does.'

The mortuary was a windowless building set a little apart from the hospital. They were met at the door by a Boris Karloff figure in a grey overall coat who grumbled as he put the key in the lock that this wasn't one of his duties and he'd enough to do in his own job without having extra chores put on him. He stood aside to let

81

them through but did not go in himself.

After the warmth of the day, the air-conditioning inside the mortuary made Ginny suddenly shiver and her stomach rebelled against its lingering, stale smell. Three bodies lay on the slabs, shrouded in blue covers. The one farthest from the door, Jameela said, was Mrs Kinley.

'I'm afraid the lower part of her face is – well, really rather horrifying,' she explained as they walked over there. 'But if I can turn down the sheet carefully, you won't have to look at it.'

'Yes.' Oh, why did she feel so nervous?

Jameela folded back the sheet just far enough to reveal the upper section of the dead woman's face. Like a yashmak, Ginny thought as she gazed at her. The dark, lifeless eyes – partly open – returned her stare as though making fun of her.

Oh yes, that was Mrs Kinley all right. Ginny recognised her even from the eyes alone. Well, this was her return visit. Too late, but at least she'd made the effort.

Unexpectedly, Jameela's bleeper sounded.

Ginny was startled. The sound was not so high-pitched as the squealing of those moths, yet it reminded her of them: those same moths which had brought her and Mrs Kinley together in the first place.

'Excuse me a moment,' Jameela said apologetically. 'I must find a phone. Shan't be a second.'

Left by herself, Ginny faced those challenging eyes again. Perhaps a mere visit was not enough, not under the circumstances. Perhaps she should – kiss her? She took a deep breath. Isn't that what people did? She leaned over the half-concealed face, still uncertain, yet feeling she *should* do something more.

A gesture of some kind.

A kiss, then. On the forehead. Then she could draw the blue sheet over those eyes again with a clear conscience and go to rejoin Jameela who was using the wall telephone near the entrance.

Accidentally she must have brushed against the sheet as she bent down. It slipped, uncovering the entire face and throat. Most of the lower lip was missing, together with part of both cheeks and the soft flesh under the chin. White patches of jawbone were visible through the wounds, and there was no sign of a tongue.

The shock at this horrifying sight sent a spasm of revulsion jarring through her whole being, followed by a heartfelt cry of pity.

'Oh, you poor thing!' Ginny's eyes filled with tears. 'Oh, I hope you didn't suffer too much! I should have listened to you.'

'This is what we wanted to avoid.' Jameela reappeared at her shoulder, reprimanding her sharply. 'Come on now. Let's go.'

'It wasn't deliberate!' Ginny straightened up. There was an edge to her own voice too. 'But now I've seen it, I want to know where else they attacked her.'

'Then you must ask your brother-in-law.'

'I'm asking you, Jameela. It's not idle curiosity. These caterpillars will attack again. We've got to know what we're fighting against.'

Jameela softened her approach, as if humouring a fractious patient. 'Please, Ginny, don't make things awkward for me,' she coaxed, taking her arm in an attempt to lead her away from the body. 'I've got to get back. I'm on duty. Can't we leave Mrs Kinley in peace now? You've paid your respects.'

'Peace?' A slight movement beneath the sheet caught her eye. She pointed to it. 'Is that what you call peace?'

It was no more than a faint ripple in one of the folds in the material. If Ginny had not turned to face the doctor she might not have noticed it at all.

'Well, *doctor*?'

Jameela took a step back and an expression of disgust crossed her face.

'I shall report this to the registrar,' she said, obviously upset. 'They've had rats once before in this mortuary, but we were told they'd cleared it up. Apart from anything else, it's a health hazard.'

'Rats?' There was another movement, as if the corpse were flexing its thumb under the blue shroud. 'That's too small for a rat.'

Before Jameela was able to stop her, Ginny had peeled back the sheet. Naked on the slab, Mrs Kinley's body was a pitiful object. The upper sections of her legs, her groin and abdomen were pitted with deep red craters of raw flesh where the caterpillars must have eaten into her. One was still there, emerging slowly from a wound an inch or two above her navel.

Swallowing hard, Ginny somehow managed not to be sick. Jameela clung to her, exclaiming something in her own language which sounded like a prayer. Her eyes were wide with horror as she stared at it weaving malevolently this way and that.

'That's what they look like?' The fear in her voice was undisguised.

'They've been feeding on her!' Ginny cried out harshly, breaking loose from her grip. 'Don't you see? Like so much carrion!'

Her words echoed through the mortuary and the sound must have disturbed the porter who had opened up for them, because he put his head round the door.

'Everything okay in there?'

'No.' Jameela spoke coldly, her emotions now tightly under control again. 'Take a look at this.'

'If anything's wrong it's not my responsibility,' the man grumbled, ambling past the slabs towards them just the same. 'Not the mortuary. That's not one o' my duties.'

He reached them just as the caterpillar decided to make another effort to heave itself out. Under the hard strip lighting the bright green of its long hairs seemed exceptionally brilliant.

'*Jesus!*' the man swore, taken aback. 'That's not good, is it? Never seen anything like that before. Them rats was more'n I could stomach, but they only nibbled at the feet. What d'you think it is?'

'It's a caterpillar,' Ginny told him. As if it wasn't only too obvious!

'Rum sort o' caterpillar, doin' that.'

'Don't touch it!'

He had stretched out his hand, but he jerked it back rapidly at the note of panic in her voice.

The caterpillar was moving again, bunching up its body, then pushing forward over the dead woman's skin. It seemed oddly sluggish, Ginny thought as she remembered the one which had investigated her stomach – God, was it only yesterday? So alert, that one had seemed, but this was dopy in comparison.

Or dying, perhaps.

'There's something wrong with it,' she said.

'Eaten too much!' The ghost of a smile passed over the porter's face and it made him look even more like Boris Karloff in those old black-and-white movies. 'See the size of 'im?'

Slowly it lowered itself on to the slab and without pausing crawled towards the edge. The porter was right about its size. It must be eight inches long, she estimated; in diameter it matched one of those new pound coins that everyone hated. As they watched, it seemed to *flow* head-first over the edge, its body rippling lazily.

'We can't let it get away,' Jameela commented, matter-of-factly. Her keen eyes were following its every move. 'Who knows where it would turn up next. Have we nothing to put it in, if we can catch it?'

'Nothing in here,' said the porter. 'No more than a waiting room, this place, till the undertakers come an' collect what's theirs. Even this one wouldn't be here if the town had its own morgue. Still, the caterpillar's no problem.'

Before Ginny realised what he intended to do, he had whipped a Bic ball-point out of his breast pocket and stood poised over the caterpillar which by now was half-way down one of the slab supports. He gave it a smart tap with the pen. It dropped limply to the floor, not even curling up as she might have expected, and he brought his heel down on top of it to grind it to death. A green smear spread around the edges of his shoe.

'Right, that's your caterpillar!' Ginny recognised the tone of the self-satisfied male who had once more demonstrated his sex's superiority over the mere female. 'Now if you ladies have finished in here, I'll just make the deceased decent again, and I can lock up.'

'Someone had better clean the floor,' Jameela pointed out with a glance at the squashed remains. She wrinkled her nose with distaste.

'I'll pass the message on, doctor. Not one o' my duties, you understand. We've a typed roster settin' out our duties. It's all written down there.' He picked up the sheet and began to draw it over Mrs Kinley's mutilated body. 'Died the hard way, poor love. Though they say she was a right raver when she was young. Not that I knew her then, more's the pity. But it's the way life goes, innit? One thing you can never foretell, that's your own end.'

At last they got away from the hospital, but only after a long delay during which Bernie and Dr Sanderson went to the mortuary themselves to make certain there were no other caterpillars around. Ginny was left to sit on the hard bench in the reception area, and half an hour passed before Bernie returned to collect her. By that time she was more than fed up.

Outside, it was pitch dark. The rain was lashing down and they had to make a dash for his car. As it was, they were pretty well soaked by the time he managed to unlock the doors.

'I'll turn the heating up full,' he said, starting the engine. 'We'll soon dry out.'

'I felt mean, not looking in on Lesley again.'

'Oh, I did put my head round the door. She's still asleep. I checked with the sister too. It's a matter of time now. She's still on antibiotics, of course.' He switched on the headlights and began to drive slowly across the rain-sodden car park. 'I'm sorry you had to go through that experience in the mortuary. It must have been unnerving.'

'Bernie, we have to talk about these caterpillars.' She hesitated, wondering how to put it, afraid that he might think she was being hysterical and fob her off with a Valium. 'People should be warned.'

'I think you're right.'

'Thank God for that!' Perhaps she'd been too tense. Now a sense of relief washed over her like a tidal wave and she threw all caution to the winds. 'It's an epidemic, if that's the right word. We don't know how many there are, or where the next attack will be.'

'Ginny, let's keep it in perspective. We know of only three incidents so far.'

'With three people dead and two in hospital,' Ginny interrupted. 'How many more d'you want before you take it seriously?'

'Believe me, love, I'm taking it seriously.'

He slowed down. Ahead of them, at the side of the dark country road, was a patch of bright light which appeared shapeless and undefined through the rain-drenched windscreen. As they approached it, she recognised the outlines of the area's most exclusive hotel.

'I'd like to invite you to a spot of dinner,' Bernie informed her, turning into the drive. 'If you've no objection.'

'Oh, I couldn't eat dinner!' she exclaimed. Even the very thought of it seemed repulsive. 'Honestly, I just couldn't face it. I'm not hungry.'

'Well, I am,' he said firmly. 'I need to refuel, so could you at least toy with something while I have a meal? Please? It'll save one of us the bother of cooking when we get home.'

She agreed reluctantly. Judging from the number of cars outside, the restaurant was probably full anyway. Expensive cars too, all of them.

Bernie eased into a parking space and they had another dash through the rain to reach the entrance. Once inside, she went in search of the Ladies to tidy herself up. The door was mock-rustic with painted black iron hinges. It was marked, coyly, *Lasses*. Ginny snorted contemptuously when she saw it.

A man on the other side of the corridor, emerging from the corresponding door labelled *Lads*, laughed sympathetically and made some approving remark which she didn't quite catch.

She took her time over tidying up, feeling she should have insisted on Bernie taking her home. There was something indefinably obscene about coming to eat in a place like this directly after that business in the mortuary. It was pagan: a heartless funeral feast with the victims still cold on their slabs, not yet even buried.

In the bar, Bernie handed her the large printed menu and left her to study it while he bought her a drink. Whisky again. Why she was drinking whisky these days, she didn't know; she'd never done so before moving into the cottage. At a table near the bar sat the lean-jawed man from the corridor. Bernie seemed to know him, she

88

noticed; they exchanged a couple of words before he brought the whisky over.

'He was at the hospital visiting our caterpillar patient,' he explained as he sat down. 'Cheers!'

'Cheers,' she responded automatically, but even after the first sip she felt it doing her good already. 'How's the patient? I haven't asked you how he's getting on. He was with Mrs Kinley, wasn't he?'

'He was there with Harry Smith. A Mr Ferguson – a fertiliser salesman, apparently. Quite severe bites on his forearm. In fact he might have bled to death if the constable hadn't applied a tourniquet.'

'And fever, same as Lesley?'

'Not quite so bad. But yes, the same symptoms.'

The head waiter came to take their orders, recommending the specialities of the day. Ginny declared again that she was not hungry. Reluctantly she yielded to his suggestion that she might try the shrimps, just to keep Bernie company. How he could even think of eating after all that had happened she could not understand.

When the head waiter returned to call them into the restaurant she discovered they had been allocated a small table in a corner where they could at least talk privately. Bernie was obviously hungry judging from the way he tucked into his pâté and curly toast. He was accustomed to big meals and probably missed Lesley's cooking.

The shrimps were gathered like pink caterpillars on a pair of large lettuce leaves. She poked at them half-heartedly with her fork, almost expecting them to bite back. They were both arthropods, she remembered Lesley explaining: these shrimps and her moths. She had made some joke about flying prawns. At that time neither of them had suspected how dangerous these creatures could be.

'Aren't you going to eat up?' Bernie enquired, concerned for her.

'Why not?' she declared, plunging her fork into a shrimp. 'They do it to us.'

'Shrimps?' He looked puzzled.

'Caterpillars.' She bit into it.

They tasted good too, she thought as she chewed their firm but delicate flesh. She was hungry after all, she began to realise. Perhaps the wine brought her appetite back. A Sylvaner of Alsace, Bernie informed her as he refilled her glass. Not that the name meant anything to her. Perhaps when all this business was over and she was earning her fortune writing TV scripts she should do some real research on wine. Quite a few wine journalists in the serious papers seemed to be women.

'I've decided I'd like some of that after all,' she announced to the waiter serving Bernie's second course. 'What is it?'

'Breasts of chicken done in lemon sauce, madam.'

'It looks delicious. Sorry to mess you around, but I seem to have worked up an appetite.'

The waiter fetched a second plate and divided Bernie's portion between them, adding that he'd order more right away. Bernie smiled at her.

'Thought you'd approve of this place,' he said, filling her glass again. 'We both needed a break, you know.'

She tasted the chicken. 'Bernie, I think you're seducing me into evil ways. I've hardly touched meat for months, at least at home in the cottage, but tonight I feel positively carnivorous.'

That brought the conversation round to caterpillars again. They reviewed the situation calmly as they ate; to her own amazement she now felt far too hungry to allow the topic to upset her. Many insects were carnivorous, he pointed out. What was unusual about these caterpillars was their manner of burrowing into the flesh. But they should know more about them in a day or two now they had a few specimens for laboratory examination.

'Dead, unfortunately,' he added. 'The landlord of the Bull had the initiative to collect them up after his pesticide spraying, though he told me most of them mysteriously disappeared. They creep away to die, I imagine. It would help if we could get hold of some alive.'

They became so completely immersed in discussing the caterpillars, listing everything they knew about them — which was not a lot — that Ginny hardly noticed the time passing. In the end, they were among the last guests to leave the restaurant.

The rain had stopped, though it was not at all cold. From among the trees and bushes came a whisper of discreet sounds. Water dripping from leaves. A movement among the branches overhead. A sudden rustle.

Ginny slipped quickly into Bernie's car and slammed the door to shut it all out, imagining caterpillars all round her.

During the drive home neither of them spoke. Perhaps they had exhausted everything they wanted to say; or perhaps Bernie, too, could sense the restless activity among those fields and woods.

The house was dark when they arrived. She had her own key and could have gone in to switch on the lights; instead, she chose to stay with him as he retrieved his bag from the back seat, then locked the car. Inside, they paused briefly at the foot of the stairs.

'I feel so much better,' she confessed. 'I was in such a tense mood, I could've snapped.'

'But you didn't.' His eyes wandered over her face; his hand rested on her arm. 'You're really a very strong person, Ginny. And don't imagine I'm not grateful for all your help.'

He leaned forward to kiss her goodnight, his lips aiming for the edge of her mouth; the 'brother-in-law kiss', as someone had once described it. Without thinking, she turned her face to his. Her lips parted. Her

91

arms went around him, holding him tight. She felt a tremor passing through his body and knew he wanted her.

But she broke away. 'Thank you, Bernie, for a lovely evening,' she said softly, almost whispering. 'See you in the morning.'

Bernie nodded, an enigmatic smile crossing his face. 'Goodnight, sister-in-law. Sleep well.'

In her room she undressed quickly, then stood for a few minutes at the window looking out across the dark garden. By now the clouds had gone; the sky was a mass of hard stars. This time she'd no guilty feelings towards Lesley. They had parted virtuously downstairs, hadn't they? Nothing had happened. Almost nothing.

Before getting into bed she raised the sash window a little higher and poked her head out to check yet again that the creeper was not too close. There were more caterpillars out there, she could feel it in her bones. Probably thousands of them. Perhaps they didn't always attack. The one exploring her tummy while she was sunbathing had done her no harm; even the rash was disappearing.

But then she thought of Lesley in hospital, and Mrs Kinley, and the others, and she closed the window firmly despite the warmth of her room. Climbing into that high, creaking bed, she wished Bernie could be with her.

6

Pete Wright stood in front of the tarnished mirror in the men's washroom and pulled a comb through his long hair. Not too long – he kept it cut straight, reaching his neck and partly covering his ears. He was no slob. His fingers still had the letters H-A-T-E tattooed across the knuckles, first done when he was fifteen, and he wondered idly how he could have it removed. It was his birthday today, and at twenty-four years of age he somehow felt he just didn't need that stuff any more.

Like words painted on his leathers, all that old shit – I beg your pardon: 'rubbish'. Nothing wrong with it for kids, but he'd grown out of it by now. *His* black leather jacket was studded, but there was nothing stupid on it. His open-necked black shirt was an expensive, fashionable make and he'd paid the full trade price for it. No cheap tat on his back.

He was on his way.

Up to where the big money was waiting – where else?

The fact that it was his birthday he'd kept secret. No one else's business, was it? If he let it out, the whole crowd would be wanting to drag him down to the pub for a spot of high-speed boozing. That was the last thing he wanted with this new chick in tow ripe for the plucking. Maureen, she called herself. He'd got the van outside, too; everything ready for the sex olympics. Passing his hand over his crotch he hitched himself up before going out into the passage to wait for her. From inside the disco came the amplified voice of the DJ introducing his next choice. Then the deep, heavy beat started, shaking the glass in the window frames.

Maureen came out of the Ladies smelling of eau de cologne. She'd touched up her green lipstick, he noticed; probably added some glitter to her cheeks, too. Sixteen, he guessed; no virgin, though. He hoped not: too much like work. If he had his way, he'd send all virgins to their family doctors to have it fixed before they were let loose on the world. Wash all the stuff off this one and she'd be just your ordinary mousy girl, but she knew how to do herself up a treat with that green punk hairstyle, brown leather mini-skirt and open shortie waistcoat with fringes. Every time she swung around you could see her hardened nipples through the almost-transparent green blouse she had on. Green tights as well, to match.

Dressed up to kill, his old auntie would have said. He grinned at her, passing his tongue over his lips. Wait till he got her in the back of the van; she'd die before he did.

'Yer ready?'

'Yeah.' She snuggled up close to him. 'Come on, let's go before my friend comes out an' sees us. She ain't 'alf nosy, an' it'll be all over the village once she starts talkin'.'

'Who cares?'

'Yeah, who cares? Only you don' come from round 'ere, see.'

'An' that makes a diff'rence?'

'They're funny round 'ere. Funny that way, any road.'

He led the way to where he'd parked his van, stepping carefully around the dark, muddy pools of rainwater left by the storm, holding her hand to guide her so that she didn't get those green tights in a mess. Real bloody gentleman he was, that night. A right git, some of his other girlfriends would've thought. But Mo seemed to like it. She gave a pleased little giggle.

'Think I'll call you Mo,' he said as he unlocked the door and held it open for her. 'Maureen's too long, an' Mo suits you. I once knew a top model called Mo. It's got more class, like.'

'Yeah. Mo. Mo.' She tried it out a few times while he went round to the driver's side and let himself in. 'If yer want. I don' mind.'

He slipped the key into the ignition but before he could turn it she was leaning over, her arms around him, pulling him towards her. Her lips clamped on to his greedily, and her tongue probed, exploring ... inviting ... suggesting ...

'Hey!' he laughed, trying to break away from her. 'Let's get away from this place an' find somewhere quiet.'

94

'I like it 'ere,' she pretended to pout. She took his hand, placing it on her leg beneath that short skirt. 'And 'ere.'

'What if yer friend comes out?'

'Oh, 'er! She's no angel 'erself. Used to play with 'er little brother's willy. Claimed she didn't but everyone knew she did.'

'Bet you did the same!' he teased her as he started the engine.

'Never 'ad a little brother, did I?' she retorted. Then, with a laugh: 'Yer dirty bugger!'

Pete had worked out exactly where to take his new find. About three miles along the main road was a lane leading to the University of Lingford Research Station where he'd sometimes delivered packages in his van. He'd been lucky to get the van, he knew. Bought it off the delivery firm he'd worked for till they went bankrupt. Knew their list of customers by heart, he did, so he picked up a lot of their small business once he struck out on his own. This place was one of them. Not much traffic down that way even in the daytime. Hardly any after dark.

The lane twisted and turned like a restless snake. It was pitch black. Overhanging trees blotted out much of the sky. He found the short rump of track which served a rusting five-barred gate and tucked his van into it, then switched off the lights.

Before he could say anything, her hands were touching his chest and shoulder, tugging him towards her. With her lips she explored his face, brushing his eyelids, his nose, and at last homing in on his mouth.

'We'll be more comfortable in the back,' he suggested when he could breathe again.

He flicked on the interior light to let her see the torn old mattress he used to cushion some of his more fragile deliveries now that the van's springs were no longer up to much.

'Come prepared, didn'yer?' Kicking off her shoes, she

95

braced herself against the seat back, lifted her bottom and peeled down her tights. 'No, leave the light on, else I can't see where I'm at.'

Before he could suggest an easier way, she was crawling back somehow between the two seats. Her tiny mini-skirt covered nothing.

'Come on, Pete!' she cried out impatiently, sitting on the mattress and reaching behind her to undo the back buttons of her blouse. 'Don't be so *slow*!'

It was his birthday, he exulted as he rode above her, supporting himself on rigid arms so that he could look down on her laughing face, her eyes on his, her mouth open with sheer enjoyment. Her hips squirmed beneath him, responding to every little move, and he realised this was the best bloody birthday present he'd ever had in the whole of his life. She was glorying in it, every second.

When at last they rested, she leaned over him, running her fingertips over his skin, moving slowly down towards his soft flesh which was already stirring into life again. But now she was taking her time over it, chatting away as they lay there naked together in the tiny van.

'Girl at school says the Pill makes yer fat,' she said casually as her hand closed on him. 'Not me, though. Feel that, I'm all bones. Yer can count me ribs.'

'Still at school are yer?' *Christ!* he swore to himself. She was under age.

'When I bother to go. Bloody waste o' time.'

She didn't seem worried at all, but then, but then it wouldn't be her they'd slap the handcuffs on, would it? Mustn't let her know what he was thinking, or she'd use it. Turn it all against him, the bitch.

'My birthday today,' he told her.

'Yer birthday? Yer havin' me on! Is it, honest? How old are yer then?'

'Twenty-two,' he lied. 'An' you?'

'Fourteen.' She added cosily, nuzzling against him:

'Fourteen an' twenty-two. That's only eight years dif-
f'rence, innit?'

Eight years in Maidstone Prison, he thought grimly.
Just when he was getting somewhere with the van. His
own business. Oh, Christ, that was just his bloody luck.
Turning away from her, feeling sick in his stomach, he
began to hunt for his clothes.

''Ere, what's the matter?' she demanded sharply.
'What's the 'urry all of a sudden? 'Cos I'm fourteen, is
that it? Yer not the first, yer know, if that's what worries
yer.'

He tried to control his temper. 'Yer really don' understand, do yer?'

'What can they do? Anyway, another year'n a half I'm
sixteen.'

'I'll come back then.'

'Yer'll be wastin' yer time then. Didn't think yer was
fuckin' chicken. 'Ere, what if I tell 'em?'

'Yer wouldn't dare!'

'I will if yer don' come back 'ere,' she taunted him. She
was kneeling, still naked, and grabbing each item of his
clothes as he reached out for it, throwing them behind
her. 'Come on, Pete, let's 'ave another tango, or I swear
I'll tell 'em. An' jus' look at yerself, yer can't say yer don'
want to.'

'Give me those bloody clothes.'

She shook her head, laughing at him with a grim
obstinacy.

Twice he hit her hard across the face. It was not what
he wanted, but what else could he do? The bitch had him
cornered, so he lashed out, then pushed her roughly aside
and collected up his clothes.

'Yer stupid bitch, why did yer make me do that?' he
lectured her as he pulled his things on. 'Get yerself
dressed an' I'll drive yer back. An' listen – jus' try tellin'
the fuzz, that's all. First, I'll deny it. An' second, they'll

97

put yer in care, that's what happens.'

'Shut yer face!' Mo snarled at him in tears. 'Jus' you fuckin' shut yer face!'

They got into the front and he gunned the engine, churning up the mud as he attempted to reverse into the lane. He had to get out and hunt around with a torch for something to put under one of the rear wheels before he could move. A flat slab of stone did the job and he was able to swing around, then drive back in the direction from which they had come.

In the passenger seat beside him, Mo was still sobbing. She dug a handkerchief out of her handbag and blew her nose. 'I've torn me tights,' she accused him. 'An' me blouse is filthy from this rotten van.'

'I'll give yer some money. Yer can buy new.' That was a mistake; he knew it as soon as he spoke, but by then it was too late.

'Yer don' 'ave to pay me!' she yelled at him. 'What d'yer think I am? Keep yer stinkin' money.'

'Right!' He concentrated on the road, taking each bend fiercely, the tyres screeching. 'Right, I will!'

She started to sob again, saying nothing.

'Well, d'yer want the money or don't yer?' he exploded. The van mounted the verge; he almost lost control of it.

''Ow much?' she challenged him.

'Ten. For yer tights an' things, not for payin' yer.'

'Give it 'ere.' She held out her hand.

'When we stop. Oh shit, Mo, yer a bloody brilliant lay, I'll say that. Best I've 'ad, honest. So why d'yer have to be only fourteen?'

Reaching the junction with the main road he kept his foot pressed on the accelerator, making no attempt to slow down as he swung the wheel over. Only as he felt his rear tyres begin to slither over the treacherous surface did he spot the army of green caterpillars on the road, shim-

98

mering in his headlights.

Mo screamed and clutched his arm.

'Oh Pete!'

He might even have succeeded in pulling out of the skid if she hadn't grabbed his arm like that, but it was like driving over sheet ice: he missed the right moment and suddenly they were travelling side-on. Then the tyres gripped – for a second only – and that threw the van into a twisting frenzy.

Again Mo screamed, just before they hit some obstruction at the side of the road – he couldn't see what – and overturned. The impact of the steering wheel in his belly knocked the breath out of him; then a blow fell square on his head and he blacked out.

Silly bitch was lying on him, groaning. Pinning him down with her full weight. Awareness returned to him slowly, like pushing through a mass of grey lace curtains, flimsy as butterflies' wings: push one aside and there's another . . . and another . . .

Accident, wasn't it? Some silly cunt driving into him?

No, that wasn't it. Remembered now – the skid . . . the van spinning round . . . then over . . . Those things on the road had looked like caterpillars: hundreds of the buggers forming a living carpet across the full width of the tar. 'Cept they were moving, he could swear to that.

The van lay on its side now – he managed to work that out, though consciousness came only in waves like that time he'd knocked himself out with a cocaine cocktail. He was in a bad way, he knew that much. Really smashed himself up. That girl on top of him as well – what was her name? Mo? Was that it? He could not remember. Good little fucker, though. Mustn't lose sight o' talent like that. Bloody genius, she was.

Jesus, he was in a bad way. Wheelchairs after this, boy. Really done it this time.

'Pete, stop 'em!' Her shriek was like sharp needles

suddenly piercing his brain, killing every thought and memory. 'They're crawling under my blouse . . . up my sleeves . . . I can feel them — !' Another scream, even more agonised than the first.

Stupid cow, he was thinking.

Stupid bloody cow, screaming like that.

Then something moved across his face. He drew a quick breath. Something prickly it was; a line of tiny pin-pricks. If he could free his arm he'd be able to touch it; but no, there was no feeling in that arm, as if it didn't exist any longer. As if — oh Jesus, how could he even think it — he was already dying limb by limb.

It poked into his nostril; he could feel it like some thick stubby finger. Then the sharp cut through the flesh, into the cavity above his mouth. It was all so terribly clear what it was doing: chewing into him as though he already lay dead under the earth, too greedy to wait.

His yells mingled with hers, though half-strangled in his throat; his mind shaped obscenities which he could no longer voice. She lay on him, a heavy living blanket writhing as if in ecstasy, the sexy bitch, until suddenly she slumped, limp, a dead weight. Vaguely he became aware he was screaming alone.

He wanted to comfort her, to hold her in his arms to make up for — well, whatever it was they'd quarrelled about he could no longer recall. No arms, anyway; just an odd deadness where his body should be and that painful, steady gnawing into his head. Some mad dentist attacking him, that's what it was; drilling through into his skull.

Then the pain stopped unexpectedly in mid-scream, and he crossed the threshold into numbness. Slowly even his awareness dissolved, thinning into void.

Driving his new Range Rover through the night, Jeff Pringle felt reasonably pleased with life. Thanks to this plague of voracious caterpillars his business showed signs of picking up at last. Unlike many larvae, they were not too choosy about their food but nibbled their way through practically anything; not only the usual cabbage or lettuce, but sprouting beans and even – recently – the fresh green leaves of fruit trees. The farmers were desperate.

As a result, his phone never stopped ringing. Already this week he had notched up more than twenty flying hours crop-spraying and there were plenty more bookings in the diary.

It was odd, though, they should be so dangerous where people were concerned, he mused. He changed down on approaching a corner. Once beyond it, he accelerated again and the Range Rover responded like a dream. Still, insects came in all varieties. He thought back to the time when he was flying passengers around West Africa. God, he'd met enough insects then. They'd fed on his blood, jabbed their poison into him, bitten him when they felt threatened and again when they didn't, spread bacteria over his food and set ambushes in his slippers. Destroying crops or bringing a thousand-year-old tree crashing to the ground was nothing compared to what they might achieve if they set their collective mind to the task.

On this planet, insects outnumbered human beings by trillions.

Try slapping your hand over the mosquito on your neck, and you'd be lucky to kill more than one in fifty, if that. Squirt pesticide at them, and within five years they've developed a new strain able to resist it. Not the human beings, though: the poison lingered on the food crop and turned up at the greengrocers.

King Insect always wins.

He'd attempted to explain it earlier that evening to Cousin Jamie in hospital. Both arms in bandages, poor sod. Blood transfusion, antibiotics, the works. Still, his temperature was down a bit and according to the doctor he was expected to be out in a couple of days. The two people with him at the pub were both in the morgue.

Looking like a ferret had been at them, he'd heard someone say. Some huntin', shootin' an' fishin' type.

'Jamie Ferguson,' he spoke aloud, still glorying in the feel of his new car, 'you owe that publican a large drink, and I'm going to make sure you buy it for him, you mean bastard!'

His headlights, on full beam, picked out the wreck of a car on its side across the centre of the carriageway. No – as he approached he could see it more clearly. It was a van, one of those little Ford vans.

'Maggie Thatcher, what a mess!' he swore.

A girl's head protruded through the smashed windscreen. Her shock of bright green hair and staring eyes gave her a grotesque, nightmarish appearance in death.

On the roadway the skid marks were clearly visible, smeared with green slime and caterpillar remains: evidence as to what must have happened. Then he realised that many of those caterpillars around the van were alive.

On applying his brakes, he felt the rear of his car suddenly gliding to the right like a temperamental woman kicking a long skirt aside, but they quickly gripped again and he came to a halt. Taking his torch, he opened the door to examine the ground. They were the first he'd seen; he whistled through his teeth in amazement at the sight of them. As big as anything he'd come across in Africa. Their long-haired bodies shone like shot silk as the light caught them, even those he had squashed to death when his tyres had crunched over them.

Someone in that van might be still alive, though with all those hungry caterpillars milling around he doubted it. Still, he'd better take a look, he thought reluctantly. He glanced down apprehensively at his shoes which left his ankles unprotected and vulnerable. If only he'd brought riding boots in the car with him.

He touched the button which closed all the windows, cocooning him safely inside, and then called up Police Sergeant Roberts on the car phone. Briefly, he explained what he'd found.

'There may be someone else in the van with her, I can't be sure yet,' he went on. 'I'll try to get closer but the road is crawling with these caterpillars. Your people had better bring their wellies.'

'Hang on there, will you, Mr Pringle?' the phone crackled in his ear. 'An' you'd best stay in your car till we arrive.'

He hung up again, feeling vaguely satisfied that at least the police would soon be on their way. At first, he'd been hesitant about installing a car phone in the Range Rover – the turnover in his business certainly didn't justify the cost, not yet – but in the upper segment of the charter flying market which he was attempting to reach it was vital to be able to stay in touch. Not that he intended to give up crop-spraying, however successful his plans; it was good bread-and-butter work which he could fit in whatever else was happening.

Out on the road dozens of caterpillars were clearly visible in his headlights and more emerged out of the shadows. Some were still heading towards the van. What the others had in mind he couldn't imagine. No food for them on that tarred surface, unless . . .

Leaning forward, he gazed around carefully on each side of the car, then lowered a window and shone the torch out once more. He had an uncomfortable feeling they were waiting for him. They were grouped together in platoons at every point of the compass.

'Right, my beauties!' he murmured aloud, stung into action by their obvious threat. 'On behalf of Cousin Jamie!'

103

He touched the starter. The engine purred and he eased the clutch, letting the car roll forward; then, slipping into reverse, he repeated the process, leaving a trail of dead where his heavy tyres had driven over them.

But simple genocide was not his purpose, however rewarding that might have been in itself. He swung the Range Rover around, manoeuvring until he could stop alongside the dented roof of the van, leaving just enough space to be able to open his own door. Before he risked getting out, he unclipped his fire extinguisher and sprayed the area between the two vehicles.

It seemed to have an effect, temporarily at least. Two or three of the caterpillars managed to get away, but the rest curled up, twitched convulsively, then lay still. Carefully Jeff opened the car door and, with one hand on the van, tried to look inside.

He was right. Someone else *was* in there: a young man in a black leather jacket. Obviously dead.

Jeff jumped down on to the road and went around to shine his torch through the jagged hole in the windscreen, but immediately wished that he hadn't.

'Urgh! My God!'

The dead green-haired girl, her head through the glass, was half-kneeling on the man's body. On both of them, wherever there was exposed flesh, caterpillars were feeding. In several places they had eaten through his shirt, and bitten into her legs through her tights. A dozen or more horned green rumps wriggled busily as the hideous insects gorged their fill.

Turning away, the bile rising in his throat, Jeff was on the point of being sick when he noticed another caterpillar on the ground rapidly approaching his shoe. The shock brought him back to his senses. Once it reached him, he knew it would go directly for his ankle. He stamped on it – not once, but several times in a mounting fury, determined to squash the life juice out of it.

When at last its fat body broke under the hammering he gave it, he saw that the green slime oozing out of it was streaked with red.

Blood, he realised dully, his temper subsiding.

Blood which earlier today had been pulsing through some poor sod's veins.

He got back into the car, tore a page out of his log book and cleaned up his shoe as best he could before slamming the door shut. Gripping the steering wheel, he stared out at the wrecked van, his heart thumping violently in his chest as he tried to come to terms with what he'd seen.

A slight fluttering sound behind him was the first evidence he had that something was in the car with him. Then he felt a tickling sensation on the back of his neck. He raised his head, hearing another movement, this time seeming to be immediately behind his ear.

No more than a vague *whoosh* of air, like a lightly blown curtain.

And that tickling again.

Cautiously he reached up, his whole body tense at the thought that somehow a caterpillar must have got on to his clothes, creeping over the sleeve of his tweed jacket, then on to his collar . . . He braced himself for the inevitable stab of pain, remembering all Jamie had told him in hospital.

But he was bitter, too. Christ, had he survived that 707 crash for this? To be killed by – what? A caterpillar?

Whatever it was, he grabbed it. Instead of pain, he experienced the strange sensation of palpitating wings against his cupped hand, like a small bird's panic at being trapped. Instinctively he released it and switched on the interior light. In the car was a large moth wheeling desperately this way and that in the confined space, from

105

time to time flying head-on against the window glass in its attempts to escape.

'Oh, Jesus!' Jeff laughed, so relieved that it was not a caterpillar after all that it made him feel light-headed. 'Here, let's have a look at you!'

For a moment the moth settled on the head-rest of the passenger seat beside him, its wings still spread. It was a giant specimen, as big as any he'd ever seen in the tropical rain forests of West Africa; in fact, larger than most. Its wings seemed to contain every imaginable shade of brown, with purple and red markings like eyes. He bent closer to examine it in more detail but it took off again, flying past his head, then around, uttering a little squeaking noise like a mouse.

Finally, returning from the opposite direction – and when he least expected any attack from it – it spat at him.

Only just in time he managed to jerk his head aside. Had his reflexes been any slower the saliva – if that's what it was – would have gone straight into his eyes. But it missed him, landing on the shoulder of his jacket.

'Bloody hell!' he bellowed at it. 'There was no cause for that!'

A defence mechanism, obviously – but he wasn't even attacking the thing!

Furiously he tried to snatch at the moth but it evaded him easily, swooping down between the front and rear seats, eventually fluttering in vain against the back window. Then he felt sorry for it. After all, what wouldn't a man give to be able to fly like that? He touched the button which opened all the Range Rover's windows and allowed the moth to escape.

The next morning he regretted it. He should have found some way of trapping that moth. Its size alone made it worth a closer look. As for those caterpillars – well, he was a pilot, not a scientist.

He had already made a statement to the police the previous night but that had been concerned only with the bare events. Taking a pot of coffee into his study, he spent the next couple of hours tapping a more detailed version into his home word processor.

When he had finished and read it through once more, he hunted in the desk drawer for his old address book, remembering something Sophie Greenberg had told him last time they met. Eight months ago that must have been at least: some work she was doing which involved caterpillars. She'd be interested, he was sure.

He found her number, only to get a stranger's voice at the other end. Dr Greenberg had been in the United States since the autumn and it was not known when – or even if – she would return. No address, not over the phone, sorry. Dropping the receiver back on to its cradle he turned to the work he should have been doing. An African agency wanted to fly a clapped-out passenger jet back to Britain for overhaul: could he find a qualified crew?

7

The news of these latest deaths caused Ginny to telephone the literary agent in London and put off their appointment for another week.

While Lesley was still in hospital it would be irresponsible to be too far away. Even the short trip into Lingford to visit her sister meant leaving Phuong on her own to look after three lively small girls. It was hardly fair on her, however competent she was proving herself to be. They refused to play indoors all day – naturally, considering the warm weather – but at least with Phuong's backing Ginny managed to persuade them to stay in the centre of the lawn, well away from any of the plants likely to attract caterpillars. Phuong spread a groundsheet on the short grass and invented several new games to keep them occupied.

'When's Mummy coming home?' Wendy would ask gravely from time to time. 'Is she coming home at tea-time?'

'Soon,' Ginny always promised.

And then – what?

For long hours every night Ginny lay awake turning it all over in her mind. Nothing had happened between her and Bernie despite them sleeping in the same house, their bedroom doors hardly a yard apart. Only once had they properly kissed – with a lovers' kiss, that is – for that first occasion after dinner at the hotel was not repeated.

Because there had been no need to repeat it. They had both recognised what was happening. She glimpsed a look in his eyes – oh, a dozen times a day! She would turn around suddenly and a quick signal of understanding would pass between them. A bond which surprised and delighted her, yet at the same time filled her with dismay. She could see Lesley's face, pale against those white hospital pillows, and hated this betrayal which she was unable to control.

Which she didn't want to control. They could each have their part of him, couldn't they? She'd not ask for more than that.

Of course, it had been building up through the past winter, she could see that now, though at the time neither of them would have been honest enough to admit it. Unwittingly, she'd even encouraged him by being always ready with a welcome when he'd dropped in for a quiet moment or two before returning home to the warm-hearted chaos of Lesley and the girls. Not that she regretted it. No, she was much too deeply in love with him to regret it.

Her heart beat faster with a rush of mixed emotions when she heard that Lesley was about to be discharged from hospital. She was genuinely overjoyed for Lesley's sake; impulsively, she ran out to gather the children around her and give them the news, only to be brought up short when Wendy said in her two-year-old innocence:

'Did she get a divorce in hospital?'

It was like a cold slap in the face. Even when Frankie screamed with laughter and with all the wisdom of her six years made fun of her sister for not knowing what a divorce was, even then Ginny still felt humiliated. Had the children noticed already?

But they had kept deliberately apart, she and Bernie: an unspoken agreement between them that nothing must happen – *nothing* – while Lesley was still in hospital. Occasionally his hand had brushed against her arm accidentally and she'd seen from his face how he too experienced that strange, disturbing thrill of desire and apprehension at their touch. The knowledge that Lesley was at a disadvantage acted as a protective barrier for both of them. Now that she was coming out – however much they wanted her home and longed to see her well again – they felt the rules were changing.

He's just as scared as I am, Ginny thought as she gazed up at his face. She loved him even more for it.

They were standing on the driveway in front of the house and he was about to get into his gleaming white Rover 3500 which he'd washed and polished in celebration of the homecoming. Instead, they lingered for a few moments longer. This would probably be their last moment alone together for some days at least.

'I'll have a meal ready when she gets here,' Ginny was saying. 'Something light. Then after we've eaten I think

109

I'll go back to the cottage.'

'No need to move out, love. Not tonight, anyway.'

'Oh yes, there is!' she retorted uncompromisingly. 'I'm a working girl, remember? I've been neglecting things.'

'I wish you *would* stay, at least till tomorrow. Move back in when it's light. Insects have some sense that tells them when a house is empty. You come back and discover they've taken over.'

'Nobody's seen any caterpillars for a week.'

'There've been no more reports,' he agreed. His hand rested on her wrist as he spoke, his thumb caressing her. 'That could mean they've entered the chrysalis stage.'

'All of them? Simultaneously?'

'I don't know,' he admitted. 'But there's no point in taking unnecessary risks. As caterpillars they're obviously at their most vicious because that's when they do their feeding, as I think you know.'

'I've read the books,' she mocked him drily, but she looked up at his smile and was conscious of the emptiness of parting. 'You'd better go, darling. Lesley will be waiting.'

He gave her one more brother-in-law kiss on the corner of her mouth, then got into the car. 'You'll move into the cottage tomorrow morning then?'

She shook her head. 'I went there this morning to clean the place up. It'll be all right. In any case, it's my day for visiting the agent tomorrow. I'm off to the station first thing.'

His mouth twitched with amusement through the open window, acknowledging that whatever he – or any man – might suggest, she'd always do the opposite out of sheer obstinacy. And he was right, she thought: give a man an inch, as the old saying went . . .

She watched as he drove off, then went back into the house to tidy things up a little ready for Lesley.

Bernie was right in saying that they had to think of the

110

life cycle of these insects, she decided as she steered the vacuum cleaner around the lounge carpet. As caterpillars the dangers were only too obvious. They spent day and night gorging themselves until they literally burst out of their skins. But then came the metamorphosis. After a couple of weeks as chrysalids they emerged in all their beauty as butterflies or moths, and it was in this final stage that they were really most dangerous, for it was now that they sought out a suitable food plant on which to lay their eggs. It needed only a couple of generations – a single summer in fact if the weather was warm – to increase the population of these creatures many times over.

No one believed it would happen, that was the problem. Not even Bernie who took the caterpillars seriously enough in every other way, but refused to accept that the attacks were more than isolated incidents. 'It's been a freak spring,' he always insisted when she brought the subject up. 'Wait till the weather changes. They're forecasting a cold summer, so you won't be seeing many caterpillars then.'

But he was wrong, she could swear to it.

Lesley's homecoming was a success. Her loud, joyful laugh rang through the house from the moment she set foot inside the front door. The children plied her with their eager questions and demands, competing with each other to be heard, until at last she collapsed laughing into a chair and kissed each of them in turn. Bernie looked on, beaming with a quiet, self-confident air of happiness that his family was complete again.

Ginny felt she was very much the outsider. With Phuong's help she finished setting the large kitchen table and served the meal. It wasn't much – cold ham and pickles with mashed potatoes and a bit of salad – but she'd bought a variety of scones and cakes from the village baker to follow.

'I've found a caterpillar on my lettuce!' Caroline announced in a highly satisfied tone of voice. 'Ooh, it's wiggling about on the leaf. Bet you haven't got one, Frankie.'

The reaction was electric. Lesley's chair crashed down behind her as she stood up despite her bandaged foot, but Bernie was quicker. He grabbed the plate away from her while Ginny lifted her off her seat and retreated to the far side of the room.

'It's a tiny one,' Bernie said with an unmistakable note of relief in his voice. 'And it's brown, not green.'

'Not one of ours then.' To reassure the children, Ginny tried to speak lightly, but the shock still showed on their faces. Caroline was crying quietly to herself. 'Come on, let's all sit down again! I've got some jelly over here. Anybody want jelly?'

Lesley let out one of her laughs and said she was sure they would all prefer jelly after that, but it was obvious she was shaken. Bernie put an arm around her and kissed her cheek. Ten minutes later the incident might never have happened.

The longer she stayed, the harder Ginny found it to make her excuses and slip away. It was eight o'clock before she stood up and said she had quite a bit to do in preparation for her trip to London the next day. Bernie made no further attempt to persuade her to stay. Lesley even smiled gratefully, obviously wanting to be alone with her family on her first night back from hospital.

They had been deceiving themselves, she and Bernie – that much was obvious, she realised bitterly as she drove back to her dark, lonely cottage. Conned themselves into imagining he was free, when clearly he was not. She should have seen that from the beginning: she *had* seen it, but ignored it. And where did that leave her?

She parked the car on its usual spot and went inside.

Instinctively she checked the room for caterpillars, even lifting her potted plants' leaves with a Chinese chopstick just to make sure. In the middle of her round table to her surprise was a large vase of the most exquisite tulips she had ever seen. Two dozen of them at least, with elegantly striped petals in mauve, black and ochre.

With them was a fold of paper bearing a message tapped out, she suspected, on her own typewriter. It read simply, *Tried to get red roses but the shop hadn't any*.

It would have to stop, she told herself firmly.

Now – before it went too far.

The last thing she wanted was to destroy Lesley's happiness. She would rather suffer herself than risk doing that. Somehow she'd have to make Bernie understand that the flirtation was over. That's all it had been really: a mild flirtation. Under any other circumstances she would not even have let it get that far.

She allowed herself to read his note once more before crumpling it up and throwing it away. Then she moved the tulips to the sideboard, rearranging them a little, and sat down to do some sensible work. Two newspapers had so far reported the caterpillar attacks, the local weekly which carried an item headed DOCTOR'S WIFE BITTEN and *The Times* which mentioned the deaths at the Bull in a single column inch. There would be more, she was convinced. She cut them out and pasted them on to separate sheets of A4.

Her TV proposal kept her up late into the night. She had already talked over her doubts with Bernie who had said it would be a pity to abandon it after all that effort. Yet it seemed wrong to be devising an entertainment about giant moths after all that had happened. Of course she couldn't be sure there was any connection between her moths and these caterpillars. Not yet.

'Why worry?' Bernie had commented cheerfully. 'Most television is about other people's misfortunes, isn't

113

it? That's why it's so popular.'

In the end she decided to follow his advice and at least let the agent see the material. She secured the loose sheets into a neat little folder and dropped it into her briefcase. Before going to bed, she raised her bedroom window and looked out. The countryside was never silent. There was always that faint sighing among the trees, the indistinct movements and muffled calls. No moths, though from this window she had watched them assemble on her first evening.

But they would return in their own time. She was beginning to understand – and she must explain this to the agent – that it was the insects who held the winning cards, not humankind after all.

She drove into Lingford and parked at the station in time for the ten o'clock train, the first after the daily commuter rush. Her compartment was full of Lingford University lecturers – so she gathered from their conversation – on their way to lobby their MPs at the House of Commons about the latest round of Government cuts. At first she ignored them and stared out at the passing fields, but soon she grew tired of hearing their soap-box arguments and went into the corridor for a bit of quiet.

'Hello!'

'Oh!' She was startled, not having noticed the man approach. 'Oh, it's you!'

'Lads an' lasses, remember? You were with Dr Rendell, weren't you?'

Now she looked at him closely, she realised this lean-jawed man she'd first encountered at the hotel was not unattractive. He did not have Bernie's height, nor any of his charm, but that rugged set of his face bespoke the man of action rather than an academic. Fairly muscular too, she judged from the cut of his tropical business suit. That must have cost several hundred pounds.

'Is this your usual train?'

'Heaven forbid!' he laughed deprecatingly. 'No, I have to go up to London for a meeting today. And you?'

'The same.'

'My name's Jeff Pringle, by the way,' he introduced himself. 'And you must be Ginny Andrewes. Oh, after that evening at the hotel I made a few enquiries about you.'

'So it seems.'

'Nothing sinister!' Another laugh: easy and confident. 'We have a mutual friend in the lovely Dr Jameela Roy. Look, what about a coffee? I think we've one or two things to talk about, you and I.'

'Such as?' she asked coolly. She'd always disliked men who tried to sweep her off her feet at their first meeting.

'Caterpillars.'

'What about them?'

'I'll tell you over coffee. It *is* important.'

Ginny retrieved her briefcase from the compartment in which a lively political debate now appeared to be in progress, and followed Jeff Pringle along the swaying corridor towards the buffet car. She tried to remember where she had heard his name before. Not from Bernie, she was sure of that. Nor from Jameela whom she'd only met that once.

The coffee came in paper cups which they had to fetch themselves from the bar. There was nowhere to sit down, so he suggested going back to his compartment. She agreed, and led the way.

'D'you always travel First Class?' she asked, choosing a place by the window and dropping her briefcase on to the empty seat beside her.

'When I can.' He sipped his coffee, pulled a face, and then leaned back comfortably. 'It was a lucky accident meeting on the train like this. I wanted to get in touch with you, and with anyone else who has experienced

115

these caterpillars. You remember the evening we first met?'

'How can I forget it? She gulped her coffee to avoid his quick glance.

'Well, later that evening I was driving home when I came across an overturned van on the road. The two people inside were dead. Caterpillars all over them.'

'That must be why I know your name,' she said, nodding. 'I heard about it, though I didn't associate it with you. It gets nastier every time.'

'You probably don't know the full story. I kept most of it to myself because I wanted to check a few things out first.' Briefly he outlined the sequence of events, describing how the caterpillars had been swarming across that road like a column of driver ants. 'Then, when I got back into the car I discovered a moth inside with me.'

'A moth?' She tried to make the question sound casual, but failed. 'You mean just an ordinary . . . ?'

'A massive thing as big as my two hands put together. You'd expect that sort of moth in the tropics, not here.'

Ginny questioned him eagerly about the markings on its wings. It had been dark of course, but he'd switched on the interior light so he must have been able to pick out the main features. From what he said it was identical with those she had seen.

'A pity you didn't catch it. Then we'd really know.'

'Didn't think. Not then.' Ruefully, he took another mouthful of coffee. 'God, this stuff's awful, isn't it? Sorry there's nothing better. Now one other thing may interest you. By the time the police had arrived, those caterpillars had gone. Disappeared without trace, and taken some of their dead with them.'

'How?'

'Oh, I watched it happen! A couple of live ones pushed and dragged this dead caterpillar over to the ditch at the side of the road. Just the way ants might behave. You may not believe that, but it's true.'

'I think I'm ready to believe anything.' Ginny was shaken by what he'd told her which fitted in so completely with everything else she had learned about these caterpillars. 'So what can we do about them?'

He ignored the question.

'I'm a pilot by profession. These days I run a charter flying business – moving freight, providing executive jets, you name it. If it's to do with flying, I can fix it. That's the slogan. In practice, work is . . . well, intermittent.'

'Hard to get,' she said.

'You've put your finger on the right spot. So to boost turnover I run a tidy little sideline in crop spraying. Do the flying myself. Low overheads. Healthy profit margin. See that?'

With a wave towards the compartment window he indicated an extensive apple orchard stretching over several acres. The trees were still in blossom, like a rich lace veil draped over the branches.

'I've been spraying quite a few orchards from the air. Farmers are worried about caterpillars feeding on the young leaves. The same kind: big hairy green ones with a yellow stripe down their bellies. They eat other crops too, but they've a special liking for fruit trees, pears as well as apples. The geographical spread is patchy, but increasing. To judge from the bookings, that is.'

'So it's not only people they attack?'

'Mostly vegetation. People are an exception.'

'For how long?'

'That's the question,' he agreed seriously. 'Up till now I suspect only very few have become maneaters. That doesn't mean there won't be more. The species is obviously new to this country and in the process of adapting to ensure its own survival. I reckon there are already enough in existence to wipe out the population of Lingford if they set their minds to it. One more gener-

117

ation – another six to eight weeks, perhaps – and they could decimate the whole of Greater London.'

The ticket collector pulled back the sliding door and Ginny welcomed his appearance with relief. Jeff had been doing no more than putting her own fears into words, but it was a shattering experience listening to them confirmed by him.

'I'm sorry it's my fault this lady's in here!' he explained when she proffered her second class ticket. 'I'll pay the difference.'

'You will not!' she snapped at him, annoyed. She fished in her purse for some money. 'From what you were saying about the state of business, you need it more than I do!'

'Touché!' he laughed, his eyes never leaving her face. His gaze was so tactile, it felt almost as if his fingertips were wandering over her skin.

'So what do we do about it?' she asked when the ticket collector had left.

Bernie had already been in touch with the University of Lingford Department of Agriculture, she explained, though with no positive result yet. In collaboration with the police warning posters were to be issued that weekend. More, too, was known of the bacterial infection which was passed on through contact with the caterpillars, at least insofar as it had been successfully treated.

'Yes, and I have my own contacts in other departments of the University,' Jeff told her, 'so between us all we should be getting a fuller picture. What I suggest is that we two meet in a couple of days' time to draft a preliminary report which we can then take along together to the Chief Constable.'

'Very well. That sounds better than doing nothing.'

'What alternative do you suggest?'

'Television.'

'And risk causing a panic? Let's try the Chief Constable

118

as a first step, anyway. He will have a direct line to the Home Office.'

The track had widened to include several different lines running parallel into London and it was now bordered by a patchwork of playing fields and housing estates. Once again in a silent moment she wondered about the morality of suggesting moths as a subject for television entertainment. But then Bernie was right, wasn't he? There had already been drama series on nuclear war, and the holocaust. No subject was taboo, so why not moths?

'I wish you'd managed to trap that moth,' she said as the train swung across the network of points approaching the station. 'We could really do with some living specimens.'

There should have been a DANGER warning on the office door. Joan, the chain-smoking literary agent whom she'd met only once before in her soap opera days, was a fat bullet-headed woman characterised by folds of excess flesh which she attempted neither to conceal nor reduce. When Ginny went in she was telephoning, gripping the receiver with a bunched-up left shoulder which made her look like the hunchback of Notre-Dame, Charles Laughton version.

With one hand she riffled through the pages of a contract; with the other she tapped out figures on her electronic calculator. Waving Ginny to a seat, she announced to the poor devil on the far end of the line that she couldn't agree anything without consulting her client and she'd call him back. She slammed the phone down.

'Sods,' she announced, fumbling in her handbag for a cigarette. 'But they'll not get away with it. Let the buggers sweat for a bit.'

Ginny nodded, impressed. With this agent she could go right to the top. The big league. Confidently she launched into her spiel about the moths proposal, how the technical problems might be handled and which star names might be the most suitable to approach.

After a few minutes the agent interrupted to send her secretary for more cigarettes. What about this tea-time soap opera Ginny used to work on, she wanted to know. For starters, she might be able to land a couple of scripts on that. Had she met the new producer?

Yes, Ginny had met the new producer, a notorious pillar of the Gay Mafia whose tentacles reached into the farthest corners of the TV industry. On those rare occasions when he bothered to greet the cast he offered friendly nods to the women and kisses all round for the men.

But she fell in with the suggestion that it *might* be useful to talk script with him.

'I'll fix the appointment for you,' the agent said breezily, scribbling a note. Standing up, she led Ginny to the door. 'If you leave your folder with the other idea I'll mull it over. Not that I can promise anything. From what you say, you have rather stacked the cards against yourself.'

Depressed, Ginny made a beeline for their old pub, hoping for company, but none of the television crowd were in that day. She rang Jack, but he was out. She tried three or four other numbers: people had moved or were tied up. In the end she sat alone over a ham sandwich and a lager, brooding about the irony of having to return cap-in-hand to the very programme she'd been so happy to escape from only a few months earlier.

Because of the heat, most customers had taken their drinks outside where they stood in huddled groups on the narrow pavement. Christ, there were times she hated London! Best catch an earlier train back, she decided. No point in hanging around.

She finished her sandwich though it tasted like stale cotton wool, left half the warm lager undrunk and was about to leave when Jack appeared framed in the doorway — the same old sandy-haired Jack in a T-shirt and tatty jeans with his key-ring hooked on to his belt. He spotted her right away.

'Ginny! Oh, that's great!' He whirled around to the others following him in – Bill and Margie and Dan. 'Hey, guess who's here! It's Ginny!'

His arms were around her in a strong, actors' bear-hug and the others crowded forward to kiss her, to question her eagerly, making her feel she'd suddenly been brought back to life again. The intensity of those last few days with their caterpillar attacks and that tangled relationship with Bernie: it all fell away from her. This was her own warm, familiar world again, and she'd not been forgotten.

Dan organised the drinks. He was a dark-eyed, innocent-looking young actor with a special gift for playing really vicious thugs. A potential superstar, she'd always thought.

'What's it to be, Ginny?' He glanced at her drink pityingly. 'Not that draught lager? That's cat's piss gone flat.'

'He knows!' Margie mocked, meaningfully.

'I keep on telling them, but they do nothing about it.'

'I'll have a whisky.'

'Oh, it's whisky these days? All right for some! How's the country house then? Any trouble with the peasants, just call me!'

God, it felt so good being back with them! She had not realised how tense she'd become living down in that village cut off from everyone. But now it all seemed miles away. She listened enthralled to the latest gossip, drinking it in like water in a desert. Even the jokes sounded new.

Suddenly it was closing time. She and Jack were left alone together, the others discreetly going their own ways. On the pavement outside Jack paused, as so often.

'Curry?'

The Indian restaurant was next door to the pub, a shabby place with bare, plastic-topped tables and a take-away counter. It was open all day, imposing no rules about eating hours. She must have hesitated, because he added:

'Or there's a new Chinese opened just up the road. Deep-fried caterpillars and chopsticks.'

'Jack!' Shocked, she swung on him furiously; but then she remembered he didn't know yet. She'd tried to ring him but he'd never been at home. 'Sorry. Let's go in here.'

They were the only customers, which made it easier for her to talk openly. She chose a table next to the window protected from the public gaze by a grubby lace curtain and ordered Tandoori chicken with rice and chutney. Jack took the same. While they waited she told him what had been happening since they had last been in touch – Lesley in hospital, then Mrs Kinley and her friend both killed, and that teenage girl with the van driver.

'I'd no idea! Oh, darling!' Across the table he took her hands in his. 'But why didn't you call me? If there was anything I could've done to help . . . Well, you know that, don't you?'

She smiled at him. 'Of course I know it.' Old reliable Jack!

The food came. Jack pressed questions on her as he ate, wanting to hear every detail, bewildered that 'attractive little caterpillars' – as he called them – could actually kill people.

'Wasps do,' she reminded him drily. 'And snakes. And you're obviously enjoying that chicken.'

'That's hardly the same thing,' he protested.

'I think it is. The caterpillars are feeding, not waging war.'

'Can you be sure?'

122

Ginny pushed her plate to one side, hardly touched. The chicken was stringy and the rice not hot enough. Over in the corner, an electric fan chuntered steadily but hardly disturbed the stale, warm air.

'The coffee's always lousy here,' she said, making up her mind. It was the throw of a dice; she still felt uncertain about it. 'Let's have coffee at the flat.'

Never go back, some sage had once pontificated. Yet here she was, sitting beside Jack in his red Ferrari, driving through the old welcoming streets. The heavy London traffic opened up to allow them quickly through, as though part of a conspiracy to draw her into the web. Lights turned green as they approached.

Then Jack was putting his key in the lock, standing aside to let her go in first.

'The flat's in a bit of a mess, I'm afraid.'

She put down her briefcase and turned to him, placing her forefinger over his lips. 'Say nothing.'

That first kiss lifted her over the edge. She felt her whole body yielding to him, like a plant unfolding to drink in the day's warmth. Her mind was still alert, conscious of what was happening to her physically, observing her own weakness with a resigned cynicism. But it wasn't weakness, of course.

Need was never weakness.

His arms were around her; his body hard and firm. She rested her head against his chest, knowing she could only find herself again through surrendering to that need. He tried to say something but again she stopped him, her hand on his mouth.

The bedroom was stifling hot and she raised the sash window to its full extent, then partly closed the curtains before stripping off her clothes. He was slower, still in his underwear while she was already naked.

'Forgotten me already?' she teased softly, going over to him. 'I'll have to give you a hand.'

123

Which she did, slipping her fingers beneath the elastic waistband to find him.

Then it was like recalling all the lovemaking they had ever shared together, rediscovering everything they had known, running their fingers lightly over each others' bodies, renewing old familiarities. At last he towered above her, a great thrusting, sweating chunk of maleness serving her, doing her will, until she could bear it no longer. Her nails dug into his back, her eyes closed and she saw Bernie's face. She moaned and her mind shaped Bernie's name. The spasm that shuddered through her was Bernie's doing.

It did not end there. For a time they lay fulfilled, naked next to each other, but then she got up and padded through the flat to get ice from the fridge while he rooted in the cupboard for his last remaining duty-free bottle of whisky. She sprawled in an armchair to drink, still not bothering to dress.

'You staying tonight?' he asked.

'Of course. Don't think I've finished with you yet.' He was standing beside her and she reached out to lay her hand flat over the firm muscles of his belly. 'Though I imagine you've been kept busy since I left.'

'Missed you.'

'That's reassuring.'

She pulled him down to his knees and he fell across her, his mouth nuzzling her breast. He shifted in an attempt to keep his balance but she held on to him, causing him to fall, crushing her with his full weight.

'God, you're heavy!' she panted, the breath squeezed out of her.

Immediately he moved and she twisted, laughing, from under him. They rolled over the carpet, mock-wrestling until suddenly he yielded, flat on his back, his arms outstretched. She stood astride the fallen male who had not yet fallen, looking down at his grinning face, mischievous with unspoken suggestion, and gradually, teasingly, with swaying, wriggling hips, lowered herself over him.

Less urgent this time, but all the more sensuous, playfully exploring every possibility. For all that, the image of Bernie was still there to fondle her with that steady gaze, to stay with her until at last she and Jack fell apart again, bathed in sweat, and triumphant.

Yet she *would* exorcise him, she swore to herself. Whatever it took.

The usual crowd assembled at the local pub that evening – *their* old local, not far from the flat – although there were some faces Ginny hadn't seen before. One or two people asked if she'd been away on holiday, but most seemed not even to have noticed her absence. Typically London, she thought ruefully.

The odd thing was, even in that crush which spilled out on to the pavement she still felt tempted to come back. Since that afternoon, she mused, watching Jack battling his way through with the lager she'd ordered but didn't really want. Since, in fact, she'd met up with all the old crowd again.

'They were out of Tuborg,' he said, reaching her. 'Is Carlsberg all right?'

Her answer was drowned by a shout of disbelief from the people just behind her. She glanced back to see what was going on.

'No, look, look, look!' a man was protesting – a large, red-faced man in a flowered Hawaiian shirt which looked incongruous on him. 'I've got here a small piece of beef – never you mind where I got it! – and I'm ready to bet you five pounds that if I put it down on this ledge, and take the lid off this jar, the caterpillar will come out and start eating the meat.'

'No!'

125

Ginny couldn't help herself. She screamed the word out. Everyone turned to stare at her. She recognised the man of course. He ran a junk stall in the street market and was often in this pub with some under-the-counter deal or other.

'Oh yes, lady!' He held the jar up – an ordinary pickles jar with a couple of holes punched in the lid. Inside was a large curled-up caterpillar, its yellow under-stripe easily visible through the plain glass. 'See that? No common-or-daily caterpillar, that one! Bite you soon as look at you, he would. Any lady feel like giving him a little tickle just to test him?'

'Don't be stupid, man!' she told him sharply. 'You don't realise how dangerous these things are!'

'How dangerous?' somebody called out.

'They're killers.'

'Oh, that's not fair!' a slim, grey-faced man joined in, full of concern. 'I mean, aren't we all? Homo sapiens now – we're life's greatest murderers. I mean, look at the Bomb!'

'Come on, now – place your bets! Five pounds that this caterpillar will make straight for the raw meat the moment I take the lid off the jar!'

Ginny pushed forward, facing him. 'If anyone gets hurt, you'll be held responsible. I'll see to that.'

'Lady, what do *you* know about 'em?' His voice was patient.

'I know several people are dead already.'

'That's true,' Jack supported her. 'There's a bit of a panic going on down where she lives.'

'Yeah, but –'

The landlord came over, threading his way through the crush. 'Not in here, George,' he said in that world-weary, old-boy manner he adopted whenever there was trouble. 'A quiet wager between friends, okay. But no one's going to run a book in my pub. An' you'd better get that thing

126

out of here just in case there *is* an accident. Never could stand 'em myself.'

The man glanced at Ginny with as much venom as if he'd like to slip the caterpillar down her V-neck. She pressed back as he passed her with the jar clutched in his hand. The caterpillar was moving inside the glass, uncoiling itself.

In the doorway he collided with a couple of teenagers in motorcycling gear. As they entered they were looking back towards the road, yelling out some joking remark to one of their friends, and didn't see 'George' until it was too late. The impact knocked the jar out of his hand and it smashed on the step.

'Bloody hell! That thing cost me money!'

'Should look where you're going, Dad,' one of them taunted.

The crush around the door scattered. Then curiosity got the better of people and they began to drift back to join in the search for the caterpillar. Sharply-pointed fragments of glass lay around the worn step but there was no trace of the green monster itself.

'Jack, let's go somewhere else,' Ginny muttered uneasily.

That afternoon she'd slipped out to buy a simple long frock in Indian cotton, having nothing to change into because she'd never intended to stay the night, but now with that caterpillar around it made her nervous every time the hem brushed across her feet.

In London at least she'd felt she'd be safe from them; now even that illusion had gone.

She allowed Jack to take her arm and steer her out through a side door. Crossing the street, she could still hear the excited chatter of those who were hunting for it. For everyone's sake she hoped they'd find it, yet she hated the thought of what might happen when they did.

127

8

The morning of the All Saints Spring Fête started with a thunder storm. Lesley woke up at about five o'clock, disturbed by the window rattling in the spare room. The rubber wedge must have become dislodged again. As she swung her legs out of bed and felt around for her slippers, a flash of lightning briefly illuminated the bedroom, followed by a close, growling rumble. The storm could not be far away, she thought, though Bernie still lay there dead-out, too deeply asleep to hear anything.

As usual in the morning her foot was numb. She almost fell when she put her weight on it, but with the help of the stick she steadied herself and managed to hobble out into the corridor. The wind was gusty, raising the lino and moaning in the old chimneys, yet not at all cold. An odd spring it had been. More like a hot, humid summer. Everything a lush green, flowers a feast of colour, and fat, lazy insects crawling everywhere.

In the spare room she found the rubber wedge and pressed it in again between the window and the frame, banging it home with the edge of her hand. Another flash of lightning and this time the thunder was closer, more urgent. She dragged a chair across and sat down to watch.

This room would be the best for what she had in mind, she decided. It already had a washbasin, which meant the extra plumbing would not cost too much, and power was no problem. It would make a good little laboratory, if only she could keep the children out.

That stay in hospital had given her time to think. She'd thrown away a career, they had told her when she'd dropped out of university to marry Bernie. Well, that didn't worry her, not when she saw what careers were doing to some of her friends. But she *would* like to get down to some real study, for her own sake. If she could get hold of some of these caterpillars . . .

Do some work on them, perhaps.

Publish a paper: it would be a start.

The next crash of thunder was immediately overhead, as if the house roof were being ripped off. It left her trembling, much as she was fascinated by thunder storms. Heavy rain started simultaneously, pebble-dashing the window panes. And her injured foot had to choose that moment to resume its aching.

'*Mu . . . mmy . . . !*'

Frankie was awake. Of course.

Lesley grasped her walking stick and with difficulty pulled herself up to go along the corridor to the children's room. There'd be no getting back to sleep for anybody now.

By six o'clock the rain had stopped; by eight the flooding on the drive had drained away and the gravel surface was dry. It was going to be a gorgeous day after all. If anything, too hot. The girls were dashing about the house, excited by the prospect of the fête. Frankie's infant school class had been rehearsing their Sherwood Forest play for the past month; now the day had come she was constantly dragging the others into Phuong's room to admire her Maid Marion dress on its hanger.

Immediately after breakfast, the big kitchen table was cleared ready for sandwich cutting. Lesley had undertaken to run the tea stall long before her 'accident' with the caterpillar, and she saw no reason to go back on her word now she was out of hospital. Phuong was there to give her a hand, and Ginny dropped in shortly after nine.

'Oh, you've finished most of them already!' Her tousled blonde head appeared around the door and she gazed, astonished, at the piles of quartered brown bread sandwiches on their trays. 'Cheese and chutney ... cress ... egg ... What else d'you need?'

'That's only half,' Lesley informed her cheerfully. 'Get yourself a knife out of the drawer and start buttering that pile. Oh, it's a lot of work, but I do enjoy these days!'

'How's the foot?' Ginny asked.

'A bloody nuisance!' she declared. 'You've no idea how much slower it is having to do these sandwiches sitting down.'

Ginny was looking better than she'd seen her for weeks, Lesley thought as they worked. A bit more colour in her cheeks since that trip to London. There were times she could be really beautiful – a delicate, petite beauty which she ruined by slopping around in jeans and dark T-shirts. Bernie noticed it too, as she'd observed only yesterday, catching the way he glanced at her. It was high time Ginny made an honest man of Jack, she thought but refrained from commenting.

'Any coffee going?' Bernie called out, coming into the kitchen from surgery. 'Oh hello, Ginny! Had a phone call for you. Jeff Pringle.'

'There'll be coffee as soon as you make it,' Lesley said, pausing to count the sandwiches she'd just completed. 'And keep your fingers away from those. They're for the fête.'

'You've got jam on your nose, Les,' he retorted. 'Ginny, I told him about the fête. He says he'll try to come over this afternoon and meet you there.'

Lesley rubbed her nose with the back of her hand. 'Do we know Jeff Pringle?'

'That pilot who crashed the holiday jet, or so they all said at the time. All the evidence pointed to pilot error,

130

though the final report exonerated him. The newspapers had a field day.' As he talked he spooned the coffee powder into the cups. 'Then you remember that scandal about a cargo of zoo animals from Africa. When the crates were opened, half of them were dead.'

'That was hardly his fault,' she recalled, doing one more jam sandwich to make the numbers even. 'Wasn't he held up by some military coup, or something? I didn't know his name was Pringle. Where did you meet him?'

'His cousin was the other caterpillar victim in hospital.' He began to pour on the hot water, stirring as the cups filled. 'You keep an eye on him, Ginny. He's had a few brushes with Customs and Excise from what I hear. Gets his money from somewhere.'

Ginny looked up from her buttering and pulled a face at Bernie, letting the tip of her tongue appear. 'Jealous?'

Lesley laughed, watching them both affectionately. It felt so wonderful to be home again. Only now since she was back had she really begun to grasp that she might have been killed. She tried to imagine what it would be like. Would they be cutting sandwiches without her? What would they be saying to each other? *Yea, though I walk through the valley of the shadow of death* . . .

'Mummy!'

In the doorway, giggling shyly, stood Caroline and little Wendy dressed already in the white frocks the parents had made for the play school group exhibition of dancing.

'Oh, aren't you pretty!' she exclaimed happily yet with tears in her eyes at the thought of what might have been. She longed to hug them, but it would never do to get jam on those clothes. 'I think it's almost time to go, don't you?'

Police Constable Chivers strolled along to the field next to the church where the All Saints Spring Fête was

131

held every year without fail. This would be his fifteenth, he mused – a longer stint than anyone had ever expected. But then he knew everyone in the neighbourhood by now, ran the boys' club and the football team, and felt no inclination to move. By his age in a big city force he'd have been retired, a prospect he certainly didn't relish.

No, he thought as he approached the field, the longer he could still do the job, the better.

It was a good show this year too, by the look of it. An ornamental gateway had been constructed, bedecked with flags, and people were already queuing up to buy their tickets. *One, two, three . . . One, two, three, testing!* He recognised the vicar's voice. Around the field were a good variety of decorated stalls including – the star attraction, as usual – the Church Tower Tombola which this year offered a quart bottle of whisky as first prize. Mrs Martinson had twice been along to the police house to complain about it. Then, a little away from the main field – the routes marked out by means of cardboard arrows pinned to the trees – he picked out the St John's Ambulance tent, the Teas marquee and – one of the vicar's innovations – the mobile toilets.

'Guess how many sweets in the bottle!' a wheezy male voice accosted him. 'Come along, constable – ten p for one guess, twenty for three! Guess how many sweets in the bottle!'

'Later, Jim. Later. We're going to do well this year by the look of it. Remember last year's rain?'

'I'll never forget that. Took me till Christmas to dry out.'

By eleven o'clock when the vicar took possession of the loudspeaker again to announce the play school group dancing there were more people on that field than he could ever remember. They must have come from villages and hamlets for miles around, some even from Lingford maybe. The neighbouring meadow set aside for parking was rapidly filling up. Perhaps in a couple of minutes he should go over there to take a look.

But first he stayed to watch the dancing. Knew all these, he did, as though they were his own, and they'd be disappointed if they didn't see him there. He stood on the edge of the crowd nodding to Mrs Rendell the doctor's wife, and to that young sister of hers who'd moved into old Mrs Beerston's cottage.

Near the trees the little girls in their white dresses formed a ragged line, each faced by a boy in a dark waistcoat. They started a clapping dance, encouraged by the lady playgroup leader.

'It's on her dress, look! On that little girl's dress! A caterpillar! Oh God, it's one of those big caterpillars!'

Someone in the crowd screamed, he couldn't see who; nor could he spot which girl they were talking about, but the dancing stopped in confusion.

'Now calm down everyone!' He pushed forward to gain control, using his best reassuring tone. 'Nothing to get excited about. Now let's have a look at the little girls.'

'It's on Caroline! The doctor's girl!'

Mothers were already surging past him to rescue their children. He tried to keep them clear, but it was hopeless. While he begged them to hold back, a young man dodged around his outspread arm, knocked a couple of women aside, and somehow got to Caroline. *Never touch them with your bare hands*, the police instruction had come through earlier that same week, but the young man knew nothing about that.

Grasping the caterpillar between finger and thumb, he peeled it off Caroline's white dress – it attempted to cling to the material – and carried it away. The crowd parted to let him through. He held the insect out in front of him, his face distorted with pain, until he reached the fence where he deliberately rubbed it hard against the creosoted slats until it disintegrated. Then he collapsed.

133

Someone started clapping, then others joined in until there was general applause. Not that the lad was aware of it, the constable thought grimly as he bent down to examine him. His fingers were swollen with red blotches where the sharp, defensive hairs had injected their poison, and there were raw patches too on the palm where the mandibles had bitten.

He signalled to the couple of St John's Ambulance men who had come running up with a stretcher. They'd need to get him to hospital, and quickly.

'Caterpillar bites,' he started to explain briefly as they set the stretcher down, but he was stopped by an ear-piercing shriek from a group of three or four women standing near the secondhand book stall by the beeches.

Leaving the St John's Ambulance men to get on with their own job, he sprinted over towards the women, only to hear more screaming from a different part of the field. He hesitated, puzzled as to what was happening. Then he saw them.

Thick, hairy green caterpillars were deliberately dropping from the overhanging branches on to the people below. Like pussy willow tails, only many times larger.

For a second he stared around, stupefied. Only a couple of minutes before this had been the scene of a happy, relaxed Spring Fête, people enjoying themselves, trying their luck at the stalls, 10p on the spin of a wheel, tossing a metal ring to win a can of hair spray, buying a home-made cake or a hot-dog; but now there was chaos and there was no one here to help him deal with it. People rushing for the exit clashed with others who wanted to get back in to avoid the thick belt of horsechestnuts lining that side of the field. Women thrashed about on the grass in agony as caterpillars crawled over them leaving trails of blood. A man charged through the crowd bellowing out his pain, his hands held high with clenched

134

fists, until he collided with one of the stalls, bringing it down on top of him.

As an experienced police officer he was only too aware of what he had to do; as a man, he knew he could do nothing.

Staying clear of the trees, he clasped his personal radio in his hand and called up the sergeant in Lingford to give as clear and concise a report of the situation as he could manage with those panic-stricken people shouldering him out of their way every few seconds.

Then he made a start on attempting to get some order into the situation, hoping at least to get them to calm down and move off in a more reasonable fashion, or else stay to help with the casualties. It was useless from the word go.

'Everybody in the middle of the field!' he bawled out in his most stentorian manner, putting on a show of confidence he did not feel. 'Everyone in the middle!'

But they simply brushed him aside.

Mrs Dorothy Martinson, JP, Colonel Martinson's widow, an imposing woman even at sixty-nine, was coming out of the vestry when she heard yelling and screaming from the field. Alcohol was her first thought. She had told the vicar that he was asking for trouble permitting drink on the stalls, even as prizes. For as long as anyone could remember there had been a total ban on alcohol at the Fête.

She was half-way across the churchyard before she realised just how bad things were. Under the old beeches two women were actually rolling on the grass; nearby, some sort of fight seemed to be going on. Well, she'd soon put a stop to that!

'Mrs Jones!' she called out sharply as she hurried across. For months now she had suspected Mrs Jones of over-indulging her weakness for gin. 'Stand up this

135

moment! I want you on your feet right away!'

Her words had no effect, but it was not until she had reached the women that Mrs Martinson understood why. A fat, green caterpillar was creeping purposefully over Mrs Jones's scrawny neck; another had already penetrated the solf pulp-flesh of her breast and only a gross, stubby tail was now visible. The second woman was in an even worse condition, with four or five of those hideous caterpillars burrowing into her exposed midriff.

Mrs Martinson stared at them horrified, her mouth dry, her stomach rising in protest.

A girl in jeans and a halter top reeled crazily in front of her, her shoulders a mass of raw wounds like battlefield craters; she fell across the first two and more caterpillars appeared, busily setting to work like bees gathering pollen.

Ignoring the clamour around her, Mrs Martinson marched directly to the Church Tower Tombola, requisitioned the quart of whisky, and twisted off the metal screw-top. She hadn't been in the army for nothing, she thought grimly. No use standing and screaming when she could do something to help.

She seized the girl's foot, dragged her clear on to the gravel path, rolled her over and proceeded to splash whisky over any caterpillars she could find, hoping it would kill them. Without waiting to see the result, she began to do the same to Mrs Jones but stopped when she realised the woman was dead.

Still, plenty of others needed help too, so she carried on like someone possessed until the bottle was empty. It was only then she became aware that none of the caterpillars had died after all but were still actively chewing into their victims like obscene, hairy maggots. At the sight of them she broke down and cried.

Useless. It had all been useless.

She fell to her knees beside the girl with the halter top,

wanting to fold her in her arms and comfort her. Instead, she began concentratedly to pick the caterpillars off her, two or three at a time.

Their furry bodies stung her fingers as she touched them; their mean little heads swung around to bite through her wrinkled skin: but what else could she do? She couldn't just let the girl die, could she?

Around her – she only vaguely noticed – screams were subsiding into moans. A voice shouted orders. A child sobbed hysterically. Yes, it was war again. It all had a puzzling familiarity. She was not surprised to feel that sharp pain in her upper arm, shooting through her armpit into her chest. Shrapnel, it had been that first time. Now caterpillars, eating a tunnel into her.

It was her voice screaming. Was she going to faint? You stupid cow, Dottie. Never could stand pain, could you?

What a boring husband Henry had turned out to be! If only she'd known in time! Riding on his tank when she first saw him, a modern Lancelot on a charger she'd thought. Angry, too. Yelled at her. As an ATS lieutenant with a signals unit she should never have been anywhere near the front line. Tell that to the Germans, she'd bawled back. Perhaps they don't know the rules!

That sergeant, he'd have been more fun. Slipped a hard hand up her skirt one dark night behind the mess, regardless of rank. Took her by surprise. Wouldn't get far these days, not with tights.

She giggled. Henry had never touched her outside the marital bedroom, and not often there.

'Aa-aaah!'

The shrapnel shifted. Excruciating pain stabbed through her lung like a saw-edged bayonet. Was this it? Was there nothing more to life? After all those years?

Oh God, why did you curse me with Henry?

Why?

*

Ginny had really lost her temper when she heard that woman shouting that there was a caterpillar on one of the little girl's dresses. Of all the stupid jokes! She'd swung around, searching the faces to discover who was responsible. Then she heard the second yell, 'It's on Caroline! The doctor's girl!' It was like a cold, clammy hand clutching her stomach.

'Stay there!' she shouted to Lesley, who had Frankie with her. 'I'll get her!'

'Caroline!' Lesley shrieked simultaneously, rushing forward despite her limp.

'Lesley, let me get her!'

But everyone had the same idea, all wanting to snatch their own children to safety, only that idiot policeman stood in the way trying to stop them, actually holding out his arms as though directing traffic. Before Ginny could prevent it, her sister was caught up in the crowd. She was tripped or pushed – it was impossible to say which – and fell face down under their feet.

Then the rush stopped, everyone paralysed at the sight of the teenage boy cautiously lifting the giant caterpillar from Caroline's dress and bearing it away. The sigh of relief was audible and followed by a sudden round of applause as he reached the wooden fence, then fainted.

'You can stop crying, it's all over now,' she overheard a mother tell her weeping son.

If only it were, she thought grimly. She had a gut feeling it was only just beginning.

While Phuong helped Lesley to her feet again, Ginny elbowed through the crowd to collect Wendy and Caroline who were gazing wide-eyed about them, bewildered and frightened. The moment she reached them Caroline began to cry, but Ginny told her roughly to stop it. That was one complication she just couldn't face.

'We're getting out of here,' Ginny announced when she

got back to Phuong and Lesley. By that time Frankie had joined them, clinging to her mother's skirt. 'Quietly now. No fuss.'

It was like one of those still periods before a storm. A holding of the breath.

'Let's all have a cup of tea!' Lesley announced cheerily, forcing a smile. Her face was strained and there were traces of dirt on her cheek where someone's shoe had grazed her. 'They're probably not serving yet, but I'm sure they'll make an exception. And they've got lovely ice cream.'

Her words calmed the children down a little.

Ginny shepherded them towards the marquee, taking hold of Caroline's hand while Phuong carried little Wendy. Frankie walked with her mother. Following the arrows would have led them past the old oak, but she deliberately made a detour to stay well clear of it.

A sudden fearful screaming started from the direction of the avenue of beeches near the churchyard wall. Lesley stopped and turned, clutching her arm.

'What's that?' asked Frankie innocently.

'Oh, they're probably playing some game,' Ginny answered hurriedly, glancing back. 'Let's find that ice cream before everybody wants some.'

In the marquee the trays of sandwiches they had cut that morning were set out on long trestle tables, ready for the first stream of customers. One of the women serving, someone Ginny didn't recognise, asked what on earth was going on with all that screaming. They made some answer and paused long enough to buy the children an ice cream each to keep them occupied before taking them out into the lane at the back which led directly up the hill to the doctor's house.

It was then that Caroline – backed up by Wendy – demanded to know why they were going home already and when they were going to do their playgroup dance.

Only Frankie seemed to grasp that something was seriously wrong.

Lesley bent down to talk to her. 'You *are* going to be a big girl and help Mummy, aren't you?'

She nodded, tight-lipped. From the field they could hear shrieks of terror, with men shouting and someone moaning gibberish over the loudspeaker.

Leaving Phuong and her sister to get the children back to the safety of the house, Ginny ran back through the marquee, heading for the field. The scene was indescribable, like some Hieronymous Bosch nightmare: a mother piteously clutching her small son whose face and neck were torn open by one long, raw wound; a girl of Ginny's own age lying with her back unnaturally arched over the debris of a broken white elephant stall while fat green caterpillars explored her legs; the barman from the Plough in agonising convulsions on the grass, his face purple as he choked on the caterpillars eating into his throat; oh, and many others, the lucky ones dead already. One thin grey-haired woman was on her knees, holding up her hands clasped together in prayer in the midst of the carnage, her voice penetrating the din from the crazed people dashing about in search of escape: *He hath put down the mighty from their seat and exalted the humble and meek; He hath filled the hungry with* . . . The spot of blood on her blouse grew larger, spreading down her side. Her voice faltered. She sat back on her heels, a look of surprise on her face, then crumpled into death.

'Get some gloves and lend a hand, will you?'

She recognised the woman from the Garden Centre, her thin, harassed face now streaked with blood. Probably she'd had those gardening gloves with her when she'd set up the potted plants stall. Leaning over one of the girl casualties, she plucked the caterpillars off her – two which were already eating into her leg – and killed them.

140

'Here, get her over to the First Aid tent,' she instructed crisply. 'Make yourself useful.'

Ginny picked her up, staggering under her weight though the girl could be no more than twelve years of age, and carried her back to the St John's Ambulance tent, only to find it in a shambles with one of the uniformed men dead and another moaning on the ground among the spilled equipment. She went on to the marquee.

Laying the girl carefully on one of the tables and leaving it to the tea servers to try and staunch the bleeding, she dashed through the back of the marquee to the washing-up area to find some household gloves. She was in luck, spotting two or three new pairs in a helper's shopping bag.

She pulled a pair of them on, then sprinted back to the field praying they'd be strong enough to deter the caterpillars. On the way she passed the local policeman grimly carrying an injured woman over his shoulder, his shirt drenched with sweat and blood.

'In the marquee!' she yelled at him. 'We're putting them in the marquee!'

How many they managed to rescue between them she'd no idea. The work seemed endless, the sun burned fiercely in a pure white sky and for every caterpillar they killed, more appeared from nowhere. At one point, pausing to snatch in some deep breaths, she counted five or six helpers, not including the constable; but the numbers varied. Ginny herself concentrated on the children, even those on the point of death; she knew she'd never be able to carry anyone heavier.

Then she spotted Mrs Martinson lying spreadeagled across a heap of bodies, but still alive. Her face looked almost angelically young. Ginny lifted her bleeding arm, searching for the caterpillars.

'Don't waste your time there!' the Garden Centre person snapped, just behind her. 'She's half-way through

141

the pearly gates already — can't you see? Stick to those we *can* save. That's all we can hope to do.'

But how many were there yet, she thought desperately. Over by the lucky dip lay the vicar, his face distorted into a hideous death mask, his throat torn open. Why did they so often go for the throat, as though they knew that was where humans were vulnerable? Then, a few yards away, she heard the terrible trumpeting voice of a man caught in the very extremes of pain and fear. Reaching him, she almost fainted with shock at what she saw.

The constable lay on his back, his body twisting as though in a fit, caterpillars probing every part of him. Over the groin the blue serge of his uniform trousers was soaked in blood. Two caterpillars had eaten their way through it — from the *inside*, she realised sickeningly. But they were everywhere: around his ankles, poking under his rolled-up sleeves, chewing through his sweated armpits, investigating his eyes . . . his ears . . .

Again he roared out his agony, his whole body shaking, but there was nothing she could do to help him.

A knife?

Perhaps there'd been a knife on one of those stalls. At least she could put him out of his misery . . . spare him some of the pain . . .

The end came of its own accord, worse than anything she'd yet witnessed. One last roar shook him, but the voice died within seconds to become a deep-throated rattle which went on and on, chilling her ice-cold to hear it. When at last it ceased, trickles of blood appeared at the corners of his mouth, as well as from his dead eyes and nostrils.

From overhead came the sound of a helicopter, first circling, then hovering before slowly coming down to land in the neighbouring field. She stood by the policeman's body watching it, unable even to think of what still had to be done. If only, she felt, she could allow

142

herself to collapse into some rescuer's strong grip. Let someone else take it all over.

A caterpillar began lazily to investigate her boot.

'Urgh!'

In alarm she managed to step back, then scraped it off against her other foot and ground it till it burst. Another approached her from the side. And a third. As though they could sense her exhaustion and were marking her out as their next victim. She wanted to cry out, but her words died in her throat. She could hear the woman from the Garden Centre calling something, but didn't know what.

She was next, she could swear to it.

Again she stepped back, almost stumbling and falling over a teenage girl's mangled body. Was it imagination, or did those caterpillars actually stop eating to raise their heads and gaze darkly at her with their nasty little eyes? Was it fear – or were they really moving closer to her from every side?

Her chest tightened. The saliva in her mouth dried, tasting of dust. She wanted to scream. Oh God, she needed help more than these other people, didn't she? Wasn't she still *alive*? With everything still ahead of her?

Send someone to help me, PLEASE!

That whimpering sound puzzled her. Not her own voice, she could swear to it, but nearby. The fear suddenly snapped within her, leaving her cold and rational. It was a child she could hear, somewhere among the remains of a smashed-up stall.

In two steps she was there, defying the threat around her. Scorning it.

She tugged the fallen trestle-board aside to reveal a small boy of about four lying curled up, his thumb in his mouth. Miraculously, the caterpillars had ignored him. Hastily she checked his limbs: not a scratch or a bite anywhere. His mother – wherever she was now – had

143

obviously dressed him up in his best for the All Saints Spring Fête, Ginny noticed with bitterness in her heart.

His big eyes regarded her wonderingly as she swung him to her shoulder and began to pick her way across the field, heading for the marquee.

Two men from the helicopter, masked and in boiler suits, with canisters secured to their backs, were spraying the vegetation along the approach to the marquee. To allow her to pass, one turned off his spray for a couple of seconds. She was uncomfortably aware of his eyes staring at her through the goggles.

It vaguely surprised her to discover how quickly some sort of order was being re-established. A fat, motherly woman took the little boy off her and carried him away between the trestle tables on which the injured were lying. They seemed strangely silent, she thought. A few groans here and there; a man sobbing; heavy, desperate breathing from an old woman fighting for air: but for the most part they lay there inertly, as if already dead.

Bernie, his shirt sleeves rolled up, a syringe in his hand, glanced up and saw her. 'Ginny!' he called across. 'Thank God you're all right!'

She threaded her way between the tables. It looked like some mad butchers' convention, she thought dully as her eyes lingered on those wounds. However much she wanted to turn away she found she couldn't. That exposed flesh and sinew exerted a horrible fascination on her until waves of faintness began to blur her vision.

'Ginny, I need more bandages!' Bernie's voice cut through the mist. 'Get over to the church, will you, and see if you can find some surplices we can tear up. Are you sure you're okay?'

'I'm okay,' she said stubbornly, ashamed of her weakness.

'Get anything you can lay your hands on, providing it's

clean,' he repeated, stooping over his patient again. 'Bring it back here, then try the shop, the pub — you know! And ladies,' he called out impatiently, 'we need more hot water!'

Ginny stumbled out of the marquee, her eyes smarting, her face and neck pouring with sweat. If only she could have been more use to those people, but she knew nothing about nursing or first aid. Her efforts would only make matters worse.

She took the short cut to the church, climbing over the broken wall, then across the treacherously subsiding ground between the untidy clusters of older gravestones to the vestry door which she found unlocked.

No surplices on the pegs though, and the heavy timber cupboard was firmly shut. Nothing in the church itself either. Then she remembered the annual nativity play, and having heard that all the planning and rehearsals were held in the Sunday School room in the Norman crypt. They must have chests full of costumes and drapes down there.

The entrance was through a wide door behind the altar. She ran down the aisle and behind the choir stalls to reach it. Grasping the heavy iron ring she tugged it slowly open, then groped about on the stone wall inside to find the light switch. Unsuccessfully.

It must be down at the bottom, she thought, though that hardly seemed the most logical place to put it. Briefly she searched outside again but could still not find it, so she decided to feel her way down in the semi-darkness. With those people dying there in the marquee, she'd no time to spare hunting for switches.

Keeping close to the wall — there was a hand-rope to guide her — she crept cautiously down the worn, uneven steps. Somewhere, she felt sure, she would come across an electric cable secured to the stonework.

Then she heard the noise: a disturbed breathing sound

which echoed through the still, clammy air.

'Anyone there?' she called out nervously. 'Hello?'

Silence, followed by more eerie sighing. Not human, though; not pronounced enough: more like a faint suspicion of movement in the atmosphere.

One more step she tried; then another. It became darker, the lower she went.

Then suddenly they were all around her – giant, fluttering moths brushing her cheeks with their wings, caressing the back of her neck, landing on her short hair. Her shrieks twisted through that vaulted stairwell, bouncing back at her off the hard stone walls, setting her nerves jarring through her whole body.

She buried her face in the crook of her arm, terrified, trying to press herself into a corner between two stone slabs, and sobbed hysterically. It was then – after her own first screams – that the awful chorus of squeals started, stabbing mercilessly into her brain. She was in the midst of them, shaking with fear as they continued to fly at her, knock into her, crawl over her, probe into her ears with that long, hair-like sensor.

How long she remained there she had no concept. She waited for death – prayed for it, even – convinced there was no possible way of escape. But death did not come to release her and the torture went on.

At last she became conscious of a bright, intense flickering which settled down to become a steady light.

'Oh hell!' she heard a male voice exclaim. 'Bloody hell! Okay, Ginny – keep your eyes covered! Got that? Keep them covered!'

Then came a high-pitched sibilant sound like hissing steam. The pungent smell irritated her nostrils, but gradually she calmed down. The mere knowledge that she was no longer alone helped her get a grip on herself. Gradually the squealing died down and she realised the moths were no longer bothering her.

146

'No, don't uncover your eyes yet, not till we get you away from where I've sprayed.'

'Jeff?'

'That's right. Now I'm going to put my hand on your shoulder and try to guide you back up the steps. Slowly now, one at a time. Careful – there's a corner here.'

Eventually they reached the main body of the church and she opened her eyes again. They felt hot and uncomfortable, but her sight was normal. Jeff Pringle was dolled up like a First World War pilot with goggles, a close-fitting flying helmet and a scarf across his mouth and nostrils which he now removed.

'Lucky you hid your face like that,' he told her, examining her critically. 'Most sensible thing you could do.'

'God, I was scared!'

'Saved your eyes, though. See this white stuff on your clothes? We'll keep some of that to get it analysed, but it's my guess they were aiming for your eyes, probably intending to blind you.'

'The moths, you mean?'

'Spitting it at you, same as they spat at me the other night. Now we'd better find some water and get you washed. What with this stuff, plus the pesticide I was using, the sooner we bathe those eyes the better.'

There was a little washroom which could be reached through the vestry. On the way there, he explained that it was Dr Rendell who had sent him in search of her, fearing something had happened as she was away so long. Everything was well in hand now, he added. The village was riddled with police and the ambulances were running a relay service. Plenty of bandages available too, so there was no need to rip up the vicar's surplices.

'The vicar's dead,' she informed him, glancing around apprehensively. There were too many dark corners high among the tie-beams of the old church. 'Can we really be

147

sure it's over?'

'No,' Jeff said frankly. 'No, we can't be sure about anything.'

9

Bernie insisted on examining Ginny's eyes before agreeing that she could go back to the cottage for a wash and change of clothing. Despite her protests Jeff went with her, taking the keys out of her hand and opening the front door for her. Before allowing her inside he checked the living room and kitchen for caterpillars, but both were clear. The air was suffocatingly hot, but she dared not risk opening a window.

'I'm thirsty.' She made for the sideboard.

'Ginny, you've just come through a double-barrelled shock.'

'Meaning?'

'No alcohol. Let me just take a look upstairs, then I'll put the kettle on.'

'Oh, feel free!' she declared, flopping angrily into her armchair. 'It's only my bedroom!'

Her hand was shaking and she felt totally exhausted. Maybe he was right, but if there was one thing she was *not* going to tolerate, it was being given orders by a domineering male. Listening to him moving about upstairs, she made up her mind.

'All clear!' he announced as he came down, ducking his head. 'Now for the tea.'

'No.'

He grinned at her uncertainly. 'No?'

'I need a bath. I can't have one here, so I'm going to my

sister's place. If you phone me there later we can fix a time to meet, though I've no idea what we can do about this.' She got up unsteadily, but hoped he did not notice. 'I haven't said thank you, have I? You probably saved my life.'

'We're all in danger,' he replied soberly. 'After today, perhaps the authorities will take the threat more seriously.'

Ginny began to go up to the bedroom to fetch a change of clothes, but she paused on the stairs.

'You *do* appreciate what happened?' she asked pointedly. 'This morning we saw no caterpillars at the house nor anywhere else in the village, only at the fête itself. There, they deliberately waited till the field was crowded before attacking *en masse*. How do you interpret that?'

'Assuming the purpose of the attack was simply for food –'

'Well?'

'Some animals hunt alone. Some in packs. Humans do both.'

'As do caterpillars, it seems from today's evidence. But that isn't what I meant.'

'You're saying it was a deliberate ambush?'

'Oh yes. They dropped out of the trees, most of them. What were they doing there in such large numbers? Why concentrate in those trees rather than any others around the village? I think it was planned, don't you?'

'That means an intelligence.'

'Intelligence . . . instinct . . . It's a matter of definition.'

She continued upstairs to the bedroom where she pulled off her stained T-shirt and dropped it into a plastic bag which she could later give to Bernie for the dried moth-saliva to be analysed. On her breasts and over her ribs she noticed traces of a mild rash corresponding to where the saliva had soaked through. Into a canvas grip she put some fresh clothes to change into after her bath, then slipped on a clean T-shirt and went down again into the living room.

'Perhaps you could drive me to my sister's,' she requested. 'I left my car up there.'

'Be my guest!'

Dancing a little in the breeze, the long thin banner high above the road still announced the All Saints Spring Fête. Strung between the trees were the rows of coloured light bulbs which would now not be switched on. Several police cars were parked near the church, together with two undertakers' anonymous black vans, but the last of the ambulances had left. Jeff stopped the Range Rover on the far side and they sat there looking across in silence.

'When I've dropped you I'll go over to see if they still need any help,' he said quietly. 'There might be something I can do.'

'I discovered today that I'm a coward.' Ginny felt a desperate need to confess to somebody. She couldn't have faced telling Bernie; with Jeff still practically a stranger she found it easier. 'I'd never given it any thought before, but when the real test came – well, I was so scared, it was like a kind of mental breakdown.'

'Everyone gets frightened,' Jeff told her.

'This was more than fear. It was . . . I don't know, I just seized up. A kind of paralysis. I didn't function any more. I was . . . oh, so useless!' She was not looking at him as she spoke but still gazing towards the field where it all happened. 'All I can be certain about is that I shall think of myself quite differently now.'

'From what I heard, people were praising your courage.'

'That's sweet of you, but it's a lie.' She turned to face him. 'Anyway, I've got it off my chest now, not that it makes me feel any better.'

'What a strange, complex creature you are!' he

murmured gently, resting the back of his hand briefly against her cheek.

She pulled back from him. 'Drive on, please. That wasn't at all what I intended.'

'Yes, ma'am!' he laughed.

He released the handbrake and the car eased smoothly forward, gathering speed. Within a couple of minutes they had reached the entrance to Lesley's drive. Ginny swung her legs out and retrieved her grip from the back seat.

'Let's be in touch this evening – okay?' she said. She was aching all over and winced as she bent down to say goodbye through the open window. 'Thanks again, Jeff. For the rescue, I mean. The new lease of life!'

He smiled ambiguously, raised a hand, then drove off. Odd man, she thought wearily. Impenetrable. Like an actor in one of those old British war films, playing a part that was all on the surface. She wished now she hadn't made that confession to him.

Ginny trudged up the drive and found Bernie's Rover parked in front of the porch, its boot open. Phuong was on the point of loading a couple of suitcases into it.

'You okay?' she asked Ginny anxiously, stopping the moment she saw her. 'Not hurt?'

'No, I'm fine.' Then she realised she must still have blood smears and God alone knew what else all over her. She'd not even washed at the cottage. 'I'm sorry, Phuong, I must look awful. I came here for a bath. But what's going on? Where's Bernie?'

Before Phuong could answer, Lesley appeared. 'Oh Ginny, I'm glad you've come. We're leaving.' She came down the steps one at a time, supporting herself on her stick. 'I just can't stay here with the children. You've heard the latest news, I suppose? They say forty-nine people died. And who knows where else they'll strike? We can't risk going into our own garden. And look at all

151

the creeper we've got round the windows! They could even get into the bedrooms.'

'Where are you going?' Ginny was beginning to feel faint and longed to get inside out of the sun. '*Is* there anywhere safe?'

'I rang Mary – you remember Mary? We shared a flat when we were students. Well, she's now headmistress of a school in Wiltshire where they've never even heard of caterpillars. So I'm taking Phuong and the children.'

'And Bernie?'

'Oh, Bernie's relieved we're going. He'll have to stay of course because of his patients, and I'll leave him my car. The Mini would be too small for all of us.' Lesley paused, her eyes troubled. 'Oh, I know it seems like deserting the camp, but what else can I do? I can't be much help, not with this foot.'

'Can you manage the driving?'

'Just about. And what about you, Ginny? You look as though you could do with a cup of tea.'

Ginny exploded. 'Oh, for Chrissake, why is everybody going on about tea?' She stared at her sister angrily, yet not really understanding why. A wave of fatigue washed over her and it left her feeling totally isolated and powerless. 'Oh, I'm sorry, Les. I didn't mean to shout.'

How it happened Ginny was not too clear, but she found herself following Lesley into the lounge and sinking gratefully on to the settee, while Phuong disappeared in the direction of the kitchen. Somewhere in the background she could hear the children's voices: Frankie insisting shrilly on something she had to take with her to Auntie Mary's. Then the clink of a cup as Lesley returned.

'Here, I've put a drop of rum in it the way we used to. Bernie wouldn't approve, but he's not here, is he? Have a taste.'

Ginny could smell the rum already as Lesley held the

152

cup towards her. She sipped it. Weak Indian tea with rum, just the way they once drank it during that cold winter together. It brought back memories. Gradually she felt herself begin to relax. That hard edginess slowly dissipated.

'Another drop?'

'Mm. Spoil me.'

When Ginny had finished the second cup, she became vaguely conscious of the children's voices growing even more excited as Phuong took them out to the car. Lesley had already helped take off her boots. She stretched out contentedly, with no desire to move ever again.

'We'll be on our way,' she heard Lesley say. 'It's a long drive. Do anything you want, Gin – you know that. Have a bath, use the spare room, plenty of food in the fridge . . . I'll stop at the church to let Bernie know you're here.'

'How many did you say? Dead?'

'Forty-nine. And about seventy in hospital. You saved a lot of those.'

Ginny shook her head, denying it urgently. 'Not me. Oh God, I've never been so scared in all my life. Yes, you go, Les. Take the children somewhere those caterpillars can't get near them. And phone, will you?'

How long she slept Ginny had no idea. When she woke, she could not remember having heard the car drive off. It was almost dark in the room, though she could just about see the outlines of the furniture. The air was stuffy too, smelling stale; all the windows were shut, firmly secured. Through the open door she could see a strip of light coming from the kitchen. Someone was in there, moving about. She padded over in her bare feet.

'Hello, love! Sleep well?' It was Bernie, crouched in front of the open fridge. With a satisfied grunt he extracted a flat packet of streaky bacon. 'Thought I'd let you sleep. You looked as though you needed it. How are

153

you now?'

'Famished and filthy.'

'I'm doing bacon and eggs for supper. If you're really hungry I could throw in a couple of sausages.'

'Urgh, I couldn't face it! I'll take some muesli if we've enough milk, and then a bath.'

Bernie sat at the table with her as she ate, deferring his cooking – as he said – till she was in the tub. His face was drawn, with deep shadows of tiredness under his eyes. It had been the worst day he had ever experienced, he told her. He'd been called to accidents before, but never anything as horrifying as this. There had been more deaths – two of them in ambulances on the way to Lingford – and more were expected before the night was over.

'I don't know if you've heard already, but ours was not the only incident, though none of the others were as bad.' He rubbed his hand across his forehead, then squeezed the bridge of his nose between thumb and forefinger. 'Isolated encounters, yet several people killed.'

'D'you have a headache, love?' she interrupted him.

'So much pesticide was sprayed around the place, I think we all caught some of it. Make sure you rinse your eyes again. I'll give you something mild and an eyebath.'

Bernie went to the bathroom with her, inspecting it thoroughly before permitting her to turn on the water. The windows were tightly shut with rubber insulation in the gaps, but he was particularly careful about the vents in the floorboards through which the waste pipes led, and also about the bath itself. Before he left she gave him the plastic bag containing her T-shirt.

He was taking no chances, she reflected as she lay back in the soothing water after having soaped herself all over. From now on, that was the way they would have to live. Tapping out shoes before putting them on. Looking out for tell-tale signs in every corner. Wire gauze over the windows. She had even left the bathroom door ajar in

154

case – *just* in case – she needed to scream for help.

The bath water was dirty and she let it run out, using the hand-shower to rinse off the suds. The only shampoo Lesley had left was an unpleasant, highly-perfumed concoction which she'd won in a raffle. Ginny sloshed a generous amount over her matted hair, sticky from the fluid the moths had spat at her. To her relief it washed out easily without taking the hair with it, though the shampoo smell lingered.

Drying herself, she wondered what to do next. Spending the night alone in this house with Bernie had not been what she'd had in mind. There had to be a certain trust between sisters, hadn't there?

She dressed in the fresh clothes she had brought with her – new salmon-coloured jeans, plus a long-sleeved, high-necked cream blouse and different boots – then went downstairs. That was something else they would have to adjust to: keeping well-covered as a protection against these caterpillars.

Bernie was in the lounge, stretched out in one of the armchairs. He stood up as she went in.

'Drink?'

'Whisky. Sorry I took so long. How was the egg and bacon?'

'Fine.' He poured her a generous couple of fingers. 'We haven't seen that outfit before. You look absolutely gorgeous.'

'Bernie, we have to get one thing straight. I'm not spending the night here. I'm going back to the cottage.'

'You're crazy!' He stood stock still, her glass in his hand. 'Have you thought what that means?'

'It means, my love, that you sleep here and I sleep down there.' She took the glass away from him. 'Cheers!'

'If that's all you're worried about you can stay in the spare room and lock the door.'

'If I stayed in the spare room I wouldn't want to lock

the door.'

'Ginny, for God's sake, these things are all around us. For all I know we'd not even get as far as the car. What if they're waiting *in* the car? Let alone the problems of getting into your cottage and checking it's okay.' Looking pale with worry, he poured himself another drink, but remained standing by the sideboard without tasting it. 'D'you really imagine anyone is going to venture out in this village tonight?'

'You would,' she said calmly, sitting down. 'The moment that phone rang and a patient called for you. You'd go through nuclear fall-out to see to some old dear's rheumatism.'

'Half my old dears died today. Those well enough to go to the Spring Fête usually went early.'

They both fell silent, regarding each other sullenly. He was right of course, she knew that much; if only she hadn't fallen in love with him she'd have accepted staying in the spare room with no argument. He suggested phoning around to a few people to find out what was happening in the village – but who? The local constable would have been the obvious man, but he was dead. So was the vicar, and the scout master; and Johnson who ran the garage had lost his wife.

'What about the woman from the Garden Centre?'

'Mrs Agnew? She's one of those in hospital. I don't want to upset people more than necessary, so we have to choose someone fairly level-headed.'

In the end he risked a call to the landlord of the Plough. His two nephews who had been staying with him had both been killed, but at least he was known as a hard, sensible sort of man, not easily upset. As it turned out, no one answered.

'I'm going to the cottage,' Ginny stated firmly, downing the rest of her drink in one gulp. 'A phone call first to Jeff Pringle about tomorrow, then I'm off.'

She found his number in her diary, dialled it and got a recording machine which instructed her to leave her message after the tone. The tone never came. Eventually there was a click, then the line went dead.

'So much for that,' she said, turning back to Bernie. She began to unbutton her blouse. 'Don't get too excited. I'm consulting you now as a doctor. That stuff the moths spat at me seems to have left a bit of a rash. It's patchy, where it soaked through the T-shirt.'

'Does it hurt at all?'

'No.'

'Itchy?'

'It was smarting a little in the bath. Like sunburn.'

'What about your back?'

She slipped out of the blouse. 'Much the same, isn't it?'

'Mm.' He swivelled her around again and she felt her nipples hardening under his gaze, yearning for him to touch them. 'You can get dressed now. I'm going to give you some calamine cream to use when you get home. But I'd like to see you again tomorrow.'

'Any time, doctor,' she murmured ironically.

He was gone for almost five minutes. When he returned he had with him a selection of protective gear to wear during the drive to the cottage: a hat each, with a loose gauze face mask of the type beekeepers use, gauntlet gloves and rubber surgical gloves for underneath them. He helped her put them on.

'Thanks.' With that gauze in front of her face she could not even kiss him goodnight, she thought. It made her feel unusually virtuous. 'Should we go?'

He opened the front door. Before he could object, she had already stepped outside ahead of him. The night was uncannily quiet, as though holding its breath. Gripping an aerosol pesticide spray in one hand, she stepped cautiously on to the driveway. Somewhere in those deep shadows she was convinced the caterpillars must be lurking.

Bernie was only a pace or two behind her. When she got to her car he shone his flashlight inside, searching even under the seats to make certain it was safe. Ginny squirted pesticide into the likely corners, but nothing moved.

'Okay, I'll get in and start the engine,' she decided at last. 'But, Bernie, promise me you'll be careful checking the Mini. Don't skimp it, there's no hurry. Flash your lights when you're ready.'

'You fuss too much, sister-in-law.' As an attempt to make a light remark it failed.

'Lesley doesn't want to lose you,' she retorted.

Nor do I, she added to herself, silently.

It seemed like eternity before the Mini's lights flashed. She breathed a sigh of relief as she engaged first gear and slipped off the handbrake. So far, so good: the caterpillars were leaving them alone. The air was clear in the headlights too, as though every single insect had agreed to desert the village that night, giant moths included. Perhaps with all the pesticide they had used it was not surprising, though she found it hard to believe.

'No, I doubt if that's the reason,' she said aloud, more to keep her courage up than anything. 'They're unpredictable, it's no more than that. Round the next corner – who knows?'

The narrow lane with its overhanging trees was an obvious danger spot. The farther she drove along it, doing no more than 15 mph, the keener became her doubts about the wisdom of returning to the cottage. All that picturesque greenery around it seemed now like a death trap. At every sound she wondered whether those curled up caterpillars weren't dropping on to the car roof.

She drew up on her usual spot, marked by the oil patch,

and turned the engine off but left her headlights on. The Mini arrived almost immediately after her. Getting out, she hurried over to speak to Bernie.

'No, stay in the car, love,' she told him. 'I've worked out exactly what to do. I'm going into the cottage and if everything is okay I'll give you a wave.'

'And if not?'

'Don't even think about it,' she said.

Unlocking the front door, she pushed it partly open and stepped inside, every sense alert. A faint odour of pesticide lingered on the air from Jeff Pringle's spraying; otherwise everything seemed quite normal. Raising her arm slowly, she groped in the dark for the light switch, half-expecting to see giant moths poised on the furniture waiting for her. But no: there was nothing.

She closed the front door again, then turned on the kitchen light, checking all the obvious places. That evening there was not even a cockroach to be seen. And upstairs was the same: no trace of an insect of any kind.

Going to the downstairs window she waved to Bernie in the Mini. He flashed his lights in acknowledgement and slowly drove away.

The sight of her files on the sideboard reminded her that she should really sit down to write her notes on all that had occurred during that terrible day, but she just couldn't face it. Instead, she cleaned her teeth perfunctorily at the kitchen sink, then went up to the bedroom.

Before getting undressed she hesitated for a second. In that flimsy nightdress she knew she'd feel so vulnerable, she'd never be able to sleep. She chose her most sensible pyjamas instead, tucking the top firmly into the elastic waistband, catching the reflection of herself in the dark window as she did so. Perhaps she should draw the curtains, she thought: but then she'd only wonder what was lurking behind them.

159

It was then she saw the giant moth. Brushing against the window from the outside, it fluttered briefly, then landed, flattening its wings against the glass. She recognised those velvety colours again – the browns, and purple, and rich pools of red.

Attracted by the light, obviously – yet did she have the steel nerves it needed to switch off and lie there in the dark? It took all the will-power she could summon up. She arranged her torch and the aerosol can side by side on the bedside table, then stretched out and pressed the switch, plunging the room into darkness.

One thing was certain, Elaine thought as she lay on the bed trying to fan herself with that old copy of the *Daily Mirror* she'd picked up. Wherever he was, Kit had gone for good. Like his father. Like *her* father, come to that.

Like every man she'd ever known. It was something that got into them. They just had to keep on moving. Couldn't settle, least of all with her.

It had caught Kit younger than most. Hardly twelve he'd been when he disappeared. Seven months ago, was it? Well, he'd never get in touch, that was for sure. Of course she'd expected it to happen one day; not so soon though. Kit had always clung to her more than other boys might have done; not many friends in spite of always going on about Lenny and the gang. He'd never really been what you could call popular. He'll stick it at home till he's sixteen, she'd once forecast confidently when talking to the women in the canteen. Sixteen, that's the tricky age.

Twelve.

She no longer worried so much. Whatever he'd gone through had happened by now. Probably living in some hostel under a false name like that boy she'd seen on the telly. Male prostitution, that's what they said went on. What men saw in *that*, she couldn't imagine. Dirty

160

buggers. But the shock would be over, like a road accident. All he had to do now was survive.

Though with any luck, that might not have been it at all. What if he'd been picked up by some woman who fancied little boys? A fat woman, over forty, smelling of powder between her flabby boobs. That sort of thing existed; she'd read about it.

Jesus, it was hot!

She refolded the *Mirror*, trying to make it into a more effective fan, but it fell apart, the sheets slipping on to the floor. Sighing, she heaved herself off the bed and went barefoot down to the kitchen where she held a flannel under the tap, then wiped it over her face and neck to cool down.

It was the fault of that tree outside the bedroom window. Thicker than ever this year. It stopped the breeze getting through so the room got hotter than she'd ever known it. Tapped the glass too when a real wind got up, like some bloody ghost trying to get in.

Bending her head, she squeezed the flannel out over the back of her neck. God, that did her good! She could feel the heat just oozing out of her. Again she soaked the flannel and put it on her neck, closing her eyes at the sheer pleasure of it.

Wet her nightie too, so she drew it off over her head and spread it over the maiden to dry. People laughed at her, having one of those old maidens, but there was nothing more useful.

Going back towards the stairs she became suddenly self-conscious about her nakedness. Not ashamed – no, nothing like that. She straightened her shoulders, stepped proudly, imagining some man playing Peeping Tom at the window. She'd have something to show him!

Who should it be now? Fred, the landlord at the Pigeons, had quite an eye for her, with more than a touch of genuine intent behind his banter. Sense of humour as

161

well; she liked a sense of humour in a man. Then what about the local constable – she'd caught him eyeing her. Those evenings after Kit vanished he'd sat down there night after night supping tea.

Back in the bedroom she stood briefly by the window, almost wishing somebody *would* stare in at her. Make a change after all those years. Here she was, thirty-five getting on for thirty-six, and it was over ten years since any man had touched her. Not that plenty hadn't wanted to – or *said* they did, anyhow – but there'd always been Kit to think of.

She dropped back on to the bed, stretching herself out to stay as cool as she could. Three men was all she'd ever had, she reflected calmly, which must be well below the national average for a woman of her age. The full what's-it, like; not counting the fumbles. The first was Bill out in the shed, only he went to Manchester. Then that soldier after a dance who gave her his mate's name instead of his own, only she didn't let on she knew.

Then Trevor who got her pregnant, so she married him. When he went off without saying, leaving her with a two-year-old kid, she'd sworn that was it – *finito*! No more bloody men were going to meddle in her life.

But now?

She ran her hands down over her smooth skin, enjoying the sensation. Perhaps if she got the doctor to put her on the Pill. Indulge herself, why not? Men did, and she could be just as much a bastard when it suited her.

Her foot was itchy, so she pulled her leg up to rub it. Her fingers touched something unexpected: a thick, hairy lump over her toes. Then the pain sliced into her, aiming with a terrible precision into the soft flesh between the big toe and the rest.

'Shit!' Walking barefoot through the cottage she'd picked up some kind of insect, she realised. But what the hell could it be? '*Oh, Jesus Christ!*'

It bit into her again, whatever it was; as she tried in the

162

gloom to get hold of it, something stung her fingers, piercing through them into her hand. Then she sensed a second one on her ankle; and a third, higher up her leg on the rounded flesh of her calf.

'No . . . ' she sobbed, trying to brush them off, but not succeeding because more were coming. The whole bed was crawling with them. 'Get off! No! *No!*'

It didn't matter what she did, they clung to her like leeches, forcing themselves into her flesh. She could feel their little mouths chewing at her, nibbling their way. Agonisingly pushing herself up to the head of her bed, she groped wildly to take hold of the light cord. At first it escaped her hand, but then it swung back and she managed to catch it.

At the sight of those caterpillars grazing over her body like so many sheep, blood already trickling down over her skin, and yet more caterpillars approaching slowly over the crumpled sheets, she broke down into a bout of insane shrieking.

'Kit? *Kit! KIT!*'

But Kit never came. Nobody came. She was quite alone, lying naked on that bed, living fodder for these vicious slugs. The pain as they chewed into her abdomen was already passing, as though some local anaesthetic were taking effect. She had no legs, of course; they'd gone. She realised that with an odd sort of clarity, quite free from fear or shock. Vaguely she recalled hearing about caterpillars attacking people – on the telly that evening, wasn't it? While she was washing up?

Please, not my neck . . . no . . .

Another scream: it was her own voice, she thought. No more plucking chickens at that place . . . what was it called? No more what was it? Couldn't think.

Couldn't breathe.

Oh, where was Kit, why didn't he come home – her little baby?

10

Ginny woke up the following morning drenched in sweat, wondering why on earth she'd gone to sleep with the window shut. Then her eye fell on the pesticide aerosol on her bedside table and she remembered.

She sat up and looked nervously around the room. Everything was as it should be, and that fact alone made her feel distrustful. Before putting them on she tapped out her slippers; they were clean too. From the window she checked the garden which was bathed in bright sunshine. It all seemed so normal. Several trees had lost a significant proportion of their fresh leaves, but that damage had mostly been done while she was away in London.

Upstairs and down the cottage gave the impression of being totally deserted by all insect life; even the spider among the rafters had gone. Even the midges from around the potted plants, but she had no complaints about that. She opened a couple of windows, then went into the kitchen to ladle pans of cold water over herself to wash off the salty sweat. Drying herself, she noticed how the reddish patches on her skin from the moth-saliva seemed to be clearing up already, but she put some more of Bernie's cream on them before dressing.

The kettle was boiling for coffee when she heard the Mini drive up. Bernie strode in, looking a lot less worried than the previous evening.

'Seems they've all gone!' he informed her after a good-morning peck on her cheek. 'We've already had a party out searching in all the obvious places, but there's no sign of them.'

'I don't like it. They can't just disappear.'

'They can move on.' He took the cup of coffee she offered him and helped himself to toast. 'I've a message for you. The Reverend Davidson phoned to say he's trapped a large moth, if you're still interested.'

'More than ever – aren't you?'

'I'm going into Lingford this morning. They've set up an Emergency Committee and want me there. But the answer's yes, if it's still alive. We've several dead ones already, but no living specimen yet. But be careful with it, won't you?'

She laughed affectionately, running her fingers through his hair. 'Don't worry, Bernie.'

'Not to damage it, I meant.'

'Bastard!'

They drove back to his house where she could use the phone. On the way Ginny was struck by how empty the village seemed. At this time on a Sunday morning people would normally be strolling over to the church and the bells would be ringing. Today she passed only one man walking his dog and the church itself remained locked. The sole traffic was Bernie's Mini just ahead of her, already turning into the drive.

'A service has been arranged for this afternoon,' he said when she mentioned it to him before going into the house. 'They say the bishop is coming over for it. I'll probably go myself if I'm back in time.'

From overhead came the drone of a small plane. At first it was invisible against the brilliant blue sky, but then she caught a slight gleam, like stray tinsel. It must be coming down, she thought, guessing from the sound of the engine.

'Your friend Jeff Pringle,' Bernie commented, shading his eyes as he gazed up at it. 'Another spraying mission, I'd imagine.'

165

'From that height?'

'Oh, he's not all that high. It's deceptive.'

Bernie went off to Lingford almost immediately, leaving Ginny alone in the house. She took the opportunity to make a number of phone calls, first to the Reverend Davidson to arrange to see him after matins, and then to Lesley and Jack. The talk with Jack was the most difficult. He had not found out about the Spring Fête disaster until he'd seen the papers that morning. Being Sundays, they had only managed to squeeze a couple of paragraphs on to the front page of the later editions, but that was sufficient to make him anxious and possessive. He wanted to drive down right away to fetch her, saying she'd be safer in London. In the end her patience snapped.

'Jack, if you don't stop, I'm going to be very angry!' she yelled at him down the phone. 'I can't stand being fussed over by you or anyone. I'm staying down here where I belong.'

'But you don't belong there.'

'I do!'

'But why?'

'Because!' she snapped. 'How the hell do I know why?'

Because of Bernie of course, if she were honest with herself: but she wasn't going to say that to Jack whatever happened. Eventually she put the phone down and looked at her watch in exasperation. She was going to be late getting to St Botolph's. Before leaving she tried Jeff Pringle's number, only to be greeted by the answering machine again. But this time it did produce a recording tone and she left a message to say where she was.

The Reverend Davidson was out on the lawn waiting for her when she at last drove up to his decaying Georgian vicarage. He held the door of her baby Renault as she got out.

'Interesting cars, these. So practical.' He eyed her pink

jeans appreciatively. Indicating his own dark suit and clerical collar, he added: 'I'm in uniform, I'm afraid. Sunday, you know.'

'You're sure you've caught one of our giants?'

'Judge for yourself. It's still in the trap.' His eyes twinkled and he took her arm as he led her round the side of the house to the back garden. 'It fits all the detail you supplied, so your observation was obviously accurate. But I thought I'd wait till you got here before taking it out.'

'And it's alive?'

'Of course.'

'Just one of them?'

'Just one.'

The trap amounted to a deep circular dish made of some dark material together with a Perspex, cone-shaped lid through which a section of the giant moth's wings was visible, revealing the scarlet and purple eye-shaped markings. In the centre of the lid was a hollow in which the mercury vapour bulb was inserted, with an electric cable leading down over the exterior.

'I heard on my radio something of what happened in your village yesterday, and I telephoned a few people to see if I could help, though by then it was too late,' he began to explain before touching the trap. 'Then Dr Rendell this morning was able to fill in a few details. I can hardly tell you how distressed I was.'

'There really was no way you could have helped,' she told him gently.

'Oh, I realise I'm not young any longer, but I think I do understand something about moths. What Dr Rendell described is quite outside my experience. They're normally such harmless creatures. I've never known a moth to hurt anybody.'

'But these do.'

'And we must respect that,' he nodded. 'Which is why

we're going to be particularly careful in taking this one out. If I've understood rightly, they spit a defensive fluid at people.'

'They spit, yes. Whether defensive or offensive depends on your viewpoint.'

'I expect it does, my dear. Either way we must watch our eyes.'

From the garden shed he produced two pairs of safety goggles and an old anorak for her to slip over her blouse. For himself he found a paint-stained overall coat which he changed into, leaving his jacket hanging on a nail, then slung a faded college scarf around his mouth and nose.

'I'd advise you to stand well back while I'm doing this,' he said when they had returned to the trap. 'One can never tell when things go wrong.'

Cautiously he went down on one knee in front of the trap. In his left hand he held a large butterfly net; with his right he removed the transparent Perspex cover. The giant moth remained motionless, gorgeous to look at, while he held the net ready to prevent it flying off. He stretched his hand slowly underneath it ready to grip its tubby body.

Then suddenly the moth set up an alarmed fluttering, attempting to escape, its wings becoming ever more agitated as it felt the net restraining it. And it spat: directly at the Reverend Davidson's face.

'There!' he exclaimed in triumph, pulling off his goggles and stripping the college scarf away from his face. 'Now we've got it!'

He held up the net. The giant moth's struggles were already diminishing as it accepted its fate. Its saliva had been accurately aimed, splashing across the scarf and goggles.

'Won't it spit again?' Ginny asked anxiously, not wishing to get too close to it even now.

'For the time being I imagine it's expended its poison,

168

though it'll be busy making a new lot. That should give us long enough to take a look at it. Let's go into the house.'

Out of curiosity she crouched down for a moment to take a closer look at the trap. Inside the bowl-shaped base he had placed torn sections of supermarket egg-boxes and four or five other moths – small ones mostly, no larger than a couple of postage stamps – were peacefully dozing in the indentations. Other insects were in there too, crawling aimlessly about.

He was waiting for her, so she ran over the grass to catch up. It amazed her, after the hectic days of her television job when there had never been a moment to think, that he could have lived here quietly year after year and actually been paid for doing it.

'Let's go to the work station, my dear,' he said, smiling at her. 'I've prepared a cage for our friend here – something a little larger than usual, though it'll still be a bit cramping. Have you decided what you want to do with him?'

'Is it a "he"?'

'We'll see if we can find out.'

Once in the work station – his name, she remembered, for the large back room he used as a laboratory – he fished inside the net and carefully extracted the giant moth, holding it by the body between fingers and thumb. Ginny's mouth went dry as he invited her to take a closer look at it.

'Nothing to be afraid of, my dear.'

'Don't be so sure!' she said, swallowing.

'I want to show you the antennae. In a butterfly these would be smooth with a slight swelling at the ends, but in this moth you can see they're like feathers. It's a beautiful example, don't you think?'

'Yes,' she tried to agree with him. Yet when they had first met only a few months ago she'd have been so enthusiastic, she thought. Now she wished he'd put the

169

thing away, and quickly.

Instead, gripping the moth with his left hand, he took hold of a slight protuberance with his right and gradually unwound it, showing it to be a slim, thread-like tentacle a couple of inches long.

'Know what this is?'

'No.' Again she swallowed. 'Please – is it safe?'

'Oh yes! I hope.' He grinned at her, an old man's impish grin, knowing he was taking a risk. 'This is the proboscis. He can poke this down inside a flower, or even into a honeycomb, and suck up his food. And I think I told you this is what produces the whistling sound. Now – sex. Mmm.'

Outside, a car drove up and a horn sounded to announce its arrival. The Reverend Davidson glanced at Ginny with a resigned, half-annoyed look on his face. He carried the moth over to a large glass aquarium tank on the laboratory bench and dropped it inside, immediately covering it with a rectangle of double netting held in place by a draw-string.

'Only temporary,' he explained apologetically. 'Now I wonder who our visitor can be? I do hope it's not the men from the County Council again.'

Through the window she caught a glimpse of Jeff Pringle. He obviously knew his way around and had come down the side of the vicarage, thinking to find the Reverend Davidson in the garden.

'You there, padre?' he called out.

'I'm sorry,' Ginny apologised hastily. 'I left a message telling Jeff I was here.'

'We are old acquaintances,' the old man said drily. 'I suppose I'd better let him in. No doubt he will be interested in our prisoner.'

Jeff was brisk and businesslike. He greeted Ginny and stooped to view the giant moth through the glass, remarking how useful it was to have a live one to supply to

170

the university. Then he straightened up and suggested they should go into the living room where he could spread things out on the large table.

'You've heard about the attacks last night?' he asked Ginny as they went through. 'I spent a couple of hours with the Chief Constable – he's a member of the Flying Club, so we see quite a bit of each other – and he's been in touch with both the Min of Ag and the Home Office. We're going to need your cooperation too, padre. As a naturalist you'll be more used to recognising insect behaviour patterns.'

The Reverend Davidson cleared away his books and papers from the living room table to enable Jeff to spread out his map. It showed the whole of Surrey with the edges spreading into neighbouring counties. On it he had drawn crosses and circles in various colours.

'This indicates the distribution of the insects as evidenced in actual attacks and reported sightings. Red crosses are deaths from caterpillar attacks. Thanks to work by Dr Rendell and Dr Sanderson – with of course help from the laboratory staff – it is now reasonable to accept that the cause of death is usually loss of blood due to the severance of an artery. The infection suffered by most survivors appears to come from a parasite.'

'Oh yes, many caterpillars have parasites,' the Reverend Davidson confirmed, studying the map closely. 'These must be moth sightings in blue.'

'That's right.'

'They are fewer.'

'They *were* fewer,' Jeff corrected him. 'Those tiny figures in ink give the dates as far as we know them. They show a marked increase in the past two days.'

'Naturally.'

'I don't understand why!' Ginny joined in vigorously. 'Unless you mean more people are reporting them.'

'When a caterpillar has eaten its fill it ceases to exist as

171

larva but becomes a chrysalis. In that stage, inside the cocoon, its cell structure breaks down and reshapes itself to emerge as an imago – a moth.' He gave his explanation patiently, as though to someone totally ignorant of the subject. 'I'm sorry, my dear. I thought you knew all that.'

'I do!' she retorted, feeling a sudden spurt of anger at his condescension. She tapped her fingers on the map. 'It's you who don't understand. The numbers of caterpillars have increased at the same time! You'd expect them to go down.'

He bent over the map again, then examined the pages listing reported sightings which Jeff produced from his briefcase. 'Yes, you're right,' he admitted, sucking his teeth as he thought about it. 'Absolutely remarkable.'

'The authorities have to decide what to do about it,' Jeff went on. 'As you can see, most of Surrey is affected except the built-up areas. There's some talk of evacuating the population – though keep that to yourselves, will you.'

'The caterpillars would follow them,' Ginny stated her opinion bluntly. 'They'll not stay behind without food.'

'We're thinking along the same lines, Ginny. I favour leaving the food supply where it is. It's the best way to contain the problem.'

'By "food supply",' the Reverend Davidson intervened, his disapproval undisguised, 'you presumably mean human beings.'

'Myself included,' he pointed out. 'However, what in fact they're planning is nothing less than chemical warfare. Large-scale spraying to start at dawn tomorrow. People will be warned to stay indoors and keep their windows closed.'

The old man shook his head sadly.

'That means killing everything!' Ginny exclaimed as the full import of his words sank in. 'Most insects, anyway. Birds will be poisoned, crops will have to be destroyed, and there are bound to be human casualties too, whatever the precautions.'

'Now you understand why I'm telling you,' Jeff said calmly. 'I don't like it any more than you do, but what other solution is there? People are dying. Well over a hundred already.'

The bleeper at his belt began to sound suddenly, cutting into the moment of terrible silence which had followed his words. He asked the Reverend Davidson if he could use his telephone and followed him through to a room at the front of the vicarage, leaving Ginny alone.

She examined the map again, comparing it with the photocopied pages of 'sightings', as the attacks were euphemistically headed. Thank God Lesley had taken Phuong and the girls off to Wiltshire, well from the caterpillars' hunting grounds. Because that's what the map was indicating – *hunting grounds*, with human beings as the prey.

When the Reverend Davidson did not return immediately, she decided to go back into the work station to take another look at their captive moth. Once again – as on the previous night – she found it poised close to the glass with its wings spread out to their full span, as if wishing to dazzle her with their magnificence.

(And hadn't they succeeded on their very first encounter when they had swarmed in her garden to welcome her?)

If only she dared reach inside the tank to grab it and crumple it to fragments in her hand! Or trample on that tubby little body . . . squelch it under her boot . . .

Remembering how it was moths just like this which had actually conned her into admiring them, loving them even, she hated it all the more vehemently.

'Ginny! Ah, there you are!' Jeff came into the room, his face grim. 'Prison visiting, I see.'

'You could call it that.' Obviously he too thought of

173

them as more than mere insects.

'Listen, I must go. There's been another mass attack. On a church this time, during morning service. God knows how many people hurt.'

'I'll come with you!' she blurted out without hesitation. Then a quick picture of yesterday's nightmare flashed into her mind. 'I may not be much use but –'

'Rubbish! Of course you must come. The more experience we both acquire with these things, the better.' He stopped to stare past her in astonishment. 'Maggie Thatcher, look at that!'

Inside the glass tank the moth had become suddenly agitated. It flew up against the net in repeated attempts to get out, emitting a stream of urgent squeaks which sounded like desperate calls for help.

'Oh dear! Excuse me!' the Reverend Davidson exclaimed, pushing between them. He took a rectangle of hardboard from the heap of oddments under the bench and placed it on top of the tank. Almost immediately, the moth calmed down, settling on the bottom. 'That cuts out the light, but unfortunately deprives it of air at the same time. I'll not be able to leave it there too long.'

'As if it understood!' Ginny observed, fascinated.

'Holy, holy, holy . . . ' the congregation of St Michael's sang that Sunday morning, led – for her voice was a half-beat ahead of the rest – by Mrs Thompson, a confident soprano, from her regular pew towards the rear of the church.

'Two full backs and a goalie!' Mark joined in solemnly, nudging his sister Debs.

She giggled.

'Will you two children behave yourselves?' their mother hissed at them, red-faced with annoyance.

Mark put on his most earnest face and took another sideways look at his sister who was pressing her lips together trying not to laugh. Then he raised his eyebrows, imitating the vicar, and the laughter spluttered out of her despite herself.

Their mother looked daggers at them. He felt her hand grip his shoulder and – still singing the hymn – she steered him in front of her until by the *A-a-amen* she had succeeded in placing herself between them. As they sat down he realised the vicar's gaze was on him. He knew what that probably meant – another talking-to, probably about showing respect in the House of God.

'You mean God doesn't want people to laugh?' he'd argued last time, outraged at the idea. 'Funny sort of God if you can't laugh!'

'Mark, you're only eleven years old,' the vicar had informed him patiently, as if he didn't know already. 'You'll understand better when you're older.'

But he had the answer to that one ready. 'The children of this world are in their generation wiser than the children of light,' he'd quoted triumphantly, leaving the vicar flummoxed.

They'd been doing Luke in scripture at school and he'd had to write that bit out a hundred times for talking in class.

He was not a bad old stick, the vicar. At least everyone knew he *was* a vicar, not like that trendy curate they had last year who fancied himself as a lead guitarist and went round in leathers, scaring the old ladies with his motorbike. A real flop, that one. No, if you've got to be a vicar you may as well be a real one, and he talked about those Bible stories as if they genuinely happened, which was good.

Mark stared around the church while the vicar's voice droned on, reading prayers out of a book. Praying is talking to God, the scripture teacher had told them; he hadn't mentioned reading. Last year his class had done a project on this church, how Oliver Cromwell's men had smashed everything up, the bits they hadn't pinched. He'd told Debs about it, adding a dash of gory detail to 'fill out the background' – something his English teacher was always rabbiting on about – and she'd cried, so he'd got into trouble over that as well.

It was the twelfth commandment: Whatever thou shalt do wilt land thee in the shit. Amen.

Above the pulpit was a canopy – Victorian, he'd learned from the project – and something was moving just above it. He nudged Debs to point it out, forgetting for a second that his mother sat next to him now. He pointed all the same, but she pursed her lips, shaking her head in disapproval.

'A bird,' he whispered.

It flew over to the choir stalls, landing on the decorative stone tracery (15th century: he'd got a mark for that) and a sunbeam from the stained glass window fell on its outspread wings.

'Mum, it's a butterfly!' he breathed, nudging her again with his elbow. 'A big one – look!'

His mother saw it and nodded, putting her finger to her lips as a warning to him not to continue chattering, but he noticed her eyes were on the butterfly now.

The next hymn was announced and the congregation stood up, fumbling through their books as the organ played the first few chords. The choir prepared to start, but once again Mrs Thompson beat them to it with a loud vibrato note.

Then she faltered and her note rose in pitch to become a high, raucous scream which brought out gooseflesh all over him. Everyone turned round.

'What's the matter with her?' Mum demanded anxiously, stretching up on her toes to peer over the heads of the other worshippers. 'Can you see?'

Mark scrambled on to the pew but not even Mrs Thompson's hat was visible any longer. 'Maybe she's

176

sitting down, Mum!' he shouted, jumping up and down on the seat for a better view.

'Mark, will you get down!' his mother scolded him in her best I-can-take-no-more manner. He always thought she laid it on a bit thick. 'I don't know what people will think. You're scratching the seat.'

'No, I'm not!' he defended himself cheerfully. Why did she have to make a fuss *now*? 'I've got my trainers on. See? The marks'll come off.'

Over the dark, stained wood of the pew his footprints were clearly visible. He sat down and rubbed his bottom over them, wiping them away with the seat of his jeans.

Meanwhile all attempt to sing the hymn had been abandoned and the vicar had come down to enquire what was wrong. The buzz of conversation was loud, but Mark definitely heard someone say Mrs Thompson was on the floor under a pew.

'Ladies and gentlemen, if you would kindly sit . . .'

The vicar's words were drowned by a terrible, shrill wailing, worse than the banshees in that play the Sixth Form had put on. Then came a shriek from someone else which echoed through the parish church, and echoed again till the sound was coming from every side.

'I'm going to find out what's happening,' Mum said firmly, pushing past him. 'You two children stay here. D'you hear me, Mark?'

They had forgotten the big butterfly, but now there it was again, fluttering close to Mum's hair. Then it flew straight into her face. She tried brushing it away – Mark saw her arm go up defensively – but it was joined by a second, also making deliberately for her eyes.

'Mum!'

Mark climbed over the pews to get to her, knowing somehow he had to reach her before they blinded her. They were everywhere – three of them now . . . no, *FOUR*! It was as if they wanted to peck her eyes out, but

177

butterflies couldn't do that, could they? Not like birds?

'*Mark!*' Her voice didn't sound natural, but was more like a little girl's. A little frightened girl. '*MARK! HELP ME!*'

Before he could get to her he saw one butterfly spit directly at her. The stuff came out in a stream, splashing across her face, and she was yelling with pain. He tried to wipe it away with her hankie, but it was in her eyes which were already bloodshot and bulging. Then another one spat at her, and some of it went on his face too.

Desperately he looked around, but the air was swarming with them. Somewhere he could hear Debs crying for him and he called out, but he couldn't leave his mother now. He pulled off his shirt and wrapped it loosely around her head and face in an attempt to protect her from more attacks. Suddenly he heard a loud squeaking coming at him, like his bike wheel when it needed oiling, and a gob of spittle landed in his eyes.

Oh Jesus Christ, it hurt!

As if it was burning his eyeballs out!

He felt his knees give way . . . the impact of the hard pew against his skull as he fell . . . the softness of his mother's body as he sprawled across her, her shrieks tearing at his heart . . .

A whole chorus of those squeaks was all around him, but Mark was in a grey half-world of his own already. Pain, burning into him like trickling acid, corroding his flesh . . . *Must not give way*: the moment of clarity came and went again. Something was crawling up his leg, gripping his skin with sharp needle-stabs. His face, too: he had a sudden, surreal vision of a cultivator blade cutting into the softness of his cheek.

Screaming, begging for the torturers to stop, he'd give them anything, pay any price . . .

What torturers? He realised it in a flash – hadn't he seen it all on TV – those nature films – that great chain of feeding and being food? It was one second of lucid thought only, then the waves came up inside his head, and his life dissolved into blackening mist.

'. . . are in their generation wiser than . . .'

Before leaving St Botolph's Ginny fetched her own safety gear, such as it was, out of the little Renault and transferred it into Jeff's larger car. While he drove, she struggled into her rainproof blouson jacket which she'd chosen because she could zip it right up to her neck and it had tight elastic around her wrists. Over it she wore the beekeeper's hat and mask from Bernie together with the Reverend Davidson's goggles. Despite it all, she felt far from secure.

'It's the headgear we must do something about,' Jeff commented critically as he swung the Range Rover too fast around a tight bend and narrowly missed ending up with his wheels in a ditch. 'Have you noticed, they go for the head and neck when they can?'

She disagreed. 'I think they attack any exposed skin, it doesn't matter where on the body, so long as they can sense the blood underneath.'

'Feel the pulse, d'you mean?'

'Not necessarily. More like dowsing: water-divining.'

'Let's hope we don't find out,' he said tersely.

They were approaching the village. Already the church spire was visible above the trees. Ginny bit her lip, trying not to betray her nervousness as she wondered what they would find when they arrived. Perhaps they were behaving stupidly even to go anywhere near the place. Neither of them might get out alive.

Rounding the last bend, the sight of two ambulances and a couple of police cars at the roadside, their lights flashing, was reassuring. A policeman flagged them down and seemed to recognise Jeff.

'I've three two-litre cans of pesticide in the boot –

back-packs with hand-sprays,' he called out through the window. 'And Miss Andrewes here also has experience of dealing with these caterpillars.'

'Moths,' the officer said. 'Church is swarmin' with 'em.'

'No caterpillars then?'

'Yes, them too. You'd better have a word with the Chief Inspector.'

They parked just ahead of the police cars and Jeff opened the boot. From a small cardboard carton he extracted a surgical mask which he handed to her.

'Here, put this on under that net thing you're wearing, to cover your nose and mouth,' he instructed. 'And always spray well away from yourself. This is more potent stuff than they were using yesterday.'

'Why's that?'

'Because we want to kill them, not just frighten them off. Or didn't I tell you? Yesterday when it was all over, we discovered one thing was missing – dead caterpillars. Oh, there were a few, but nowhere near the number we'd expected. Same with the moths, too. They may have crawled off to die somewhere else, but no one's certain.'

As it turned out, Ginny was not one of those involved in the spraying. The Chief Inspector chose two of his tallest men, both dressed in overalls, riot helmets and Civil Defence gas masks. Her first impression that everything was under control had been wrong. Most of the victims were still inside the church; only eight or ten had so far been brought out and taken to the village school hall where an emergency centre had been set up.

'It's different from yesterday's attack,' the Chief Inspector said, his voice cool and brisk. 'This time the moths hit first, blinding people. Then the caterpillars followed. So watch out in there, won't you, miss?'

A couple of young ambulance men came running back from the school, preparing to enter the church again.

180

Ginny went with them, silently swearing at herself for not having stayed in safety with the Reverend Davidson. Why did she always have to stick her neck out? Now here she was, scared and probably no use to anyone.

It was like entering some mysterious temple in which an orgy of sacrifice had recently taken place. The sun was soaking through the tall, narrow stained glass windows behind the altar and along the length of one aisle, casting long, straight beams of red, yellow, green, blue . . . Dozens of giant moths fluttered through the air which already carried a musty odour from the first whiffs of pesticide. Among the straight lines of pews their victims lay twisted grotesquely, for the most part silent, their faces and arms a mass of open wounds.

Ginny refused to be sick, however insistently her stomach churned. She must do something to help, she knew – but how? This whole, hellish sight had an enervating effect on her. The two young ambulance men were attempting to ease a woman out from between the pews, managing well enough without her. Two others, older men, dashed past her as they carried someone out on a stretcher. In the transepts on both sides Jeff and the police officers were busy spraying, moving slowly towards the main body of the church. But she merely looked on.

Moths came to investigate her, constantly colliding with her net face mask. She did not even push them aside. But at last she stirred, hearing a whimpering from near the front of the block of pews. Brushing the moths away with her arm, she went to see what it might be. She found a small girl, maybe about eight or nine years of age, hiding her face in her arms and shaking with terror.

'Come on, let's get you out of here!' Ginny said more brusquely than she'd intended.

In response, the child raised her head and screamed violently, leaving her face exposed to the moths which surrounded them both.

181

Ginny picked her up but she wriggled, hitting out with her fists, still screaming. Attempting to hold the girl's face against her own shoulder, she hurried back down the aisle towards the door. A moth spat at them, splattering both with its saliva. The patterned tiles were crawling with caterpillars. Her foot slipped on them as she felt them squash beneath her boots.

But she got the girl outside at last and it was only then in the full glare of the sun that she saw the caterpillar at work on her leg just above the little white ankle sock, already streaked with blood. Ginny grasped it firmly with her gloved hand and killed it.

'Put her down here!'

A policewoman indicated a rough trestle table which had been set up beside the path near the lych-gate. Each of the casualties was placed on it in turn to be checked for caterpillars before going on to the emergency centre. Ginny helped her examine the girl; miraculously, that caterpillar on her leg had been the only one.

'Right, take her into the school now,' the policewoman instructed as the two young ambulance men approached with a badly-wounded man who might have been dead already.

Ginny hoisted the little girl up in her arms again to carry her over to the school hall. Inside, gym mats had been laid out against one wall for the survivors. A policeman with his shirt sleeves rolled up was applying a tourniquet to one man's leg, while a woman helper prepared dressings for another.

The girl's screams had subsided by now, but she was sobbing uncontrollably. Her thin arms clutched at Ginny's neck as she tried to put her down on one of the mats.

'Here, let me have her!' The policewoman had followed her for some reason Ginny could not at first grasp. 'It's all right. The Chief Inspector asks if you can

182

take over at the table while I work in here. He's discovered I did a year's nursing before joining the Force.'

Ginny nodded. 'If that's what you think.'

'That's right, it was my suggestion.' The voice was young and businesslike, with a slight lilt to it. Turning, Ginny recognised Dr Jameela Roy. It was the first time they had met again since that evening in the hospital mortuary. 'If you don't mind, Ginny. The main thing is to make sure no caterpillars get in here.'

The policewoman took the little girl, gently untwining her arms from Ginny's neck.

'Now, let's see who we've got here,' Jameela went on, going over to the line of patients on the mats. 'I understand the local GP was among those in the church?'

Outside, it was clear that the whole operation had entered a new phase. There were more police, and a fire engine had arrived. Its crew in full protective gear were on the point of entering the church. One of the two ambulances had already left but there was a blare of sirens as others approached.

The two young ambulance men had returned with a frail old woman on their stretcher. Her mouth was working busily, trying to say something as they half-lifted, half-tipped her on to the trestle table. The reason for their haste was obvious. At least three caterpillars were visible on her legs and arms, and there were possibly more.

Ginny began to pick them off, making sure each one was dead before throwing it aside, while the younger of the two men attempted to hold her face still as he took out her false teeth. The moth-saliva must have caught her full in the eyes, which stared upwards with a glazed, unseeing look.

They had removed all the caterpillars when Ginny noticed a wave-like movement on her bloodstained blouse. Tearing the flimsy material back, she discovered two more grubbing into her. Horrified, Ginny took a grip

183

on them, one in each hand, and slowly drew them out through her punctured skin. At that very moment, the old woman's body suddenly went limp.

'She's gone,' the younger man said after pulling off his glove to feel for a pulse. 'She wouldn't have made it anyway.'

Ginny destroyed both caterpillars thoroughly, rubbing their tough bloated bodies against the edge of the trestle table until they tore open, spilling out their red-green fluid over her stained gloves. Her concentration was so intense that she didn't at first notice the moths.

'Christ Almighty, look at 'em!' someone exclaimed.

They flew out through the open church door in a dense, fluttering cloud, hundreds of them endlessly streaming into the bright sunshine. Ginny stepped back in a mindless fear that left her shuddering from head to toe, thinking they were coming straight towards her. But – still moving as one – they climbed and wheeled in the direction of the close cluster of houses in the lower village.

There – well, they were hardly more than a smudge in the sky, so she couldn't be too certain, but didn't she see them gradually settling over those rooftops?

11

The Reverend Brian Davidson took the anorak which Ginny had worn and returned it to the garden shed. No doubt she would start preying on his mind again just as she'd done after her first visit, keeping him awake far into the night. His fault of course, not hers: she didn't even realise she was doing it, naturally. Yet she was.

A silly old man, people would call him if they knew.

His parishioners, particularly. Yet there was something in her manner which keyed into his own moods so exactly, it was impossible to deny it. Her face, too – so beautiful, he caught his breath each time he looked at her. The turn of her mouth, that quick warm contact with her eyes . . . oh yes, even her short, untidy blonde hair which betrayed a carelessness about her appearance which he found attractive . . .

In fact, a very stupid old man: though he could not help himself. This was his thorn in the flesh. He was in love. Dazzled by her. Not that she gave him a second thought, but that didn't matter. These modern girls wanted young bodies, not decrepit seventy-year-olds. How long had it been now since his last little adventure? Ten years? With what's-her-name – the one with brown eyes and thick lips at that lepidopterist conference in Dorchester . . . But that was different; that wasn't love.

Humming to himself – a hymn tune, though he couldn't imagine why – he set out a deck chair in the shade at the side of the house, then went inside to fetch Sunday tea: a segment of game pie, salad and a glass of McEwan's Export. He placed the tray on a low garden table beside the deck chair and sat down. The pie was still cold from the fridge, so he left it a moment. In this heat nothing was cold for long.

Perhaps it was the weather, he mused. He'd always been more susceptible to women in the warmer months. Because they wear less, his wife had once told him. Scornfully, he remembered, God rest her soul. Strange to think that even in old age he should miss her bodily. In any case, her explanation was obviously wrong. Any randy male moth could tell her that. No, with moths it was temperature, so why not humans too?

None of which explained why at over seventy he should fall in love again. And go through hell again, no doubt.

He tasted the pie. It was now warmer so he began to eat, chewing carefully as he had to these days. Bodily functions deteriorated until they were an insult to dignity. Yet – he wondered – if Ginny *were* to respond, how would he get on with her? Would that bodily function too let him down?

King David, the Bible reported, was given a new surge of energy by the introduction of a nubile young woman into his bed. Maybe that's what the National Health should prescribe instead of all these pills and injections.

She'd laugh of course, he knew that. Laugh in his face at the first move. Yet if he took it gently . . . perhaps . . .?

In the shade of the house, somewhere among the mass of plant pots, he noticed a quick movement. He put down his glass to watch more closely. Minutes passed without anything happening but he could wait. He kept absolutely still.

Then another quick movement, and the flash of something – brown, was it? Like a long, thin tail. Not a rat . . . no, not a cord-like tail but more . . .

Again, only this time he saw feet.

In all the years he'd lived in Surrey, he'd never once seen a lizard, yet there could be no doubt that was what it was. As always, his field glasses were within reach on the low table. Moving very slowly, he picked them up and brought them to his eyes. About six inches long, he judged, ribbed brown with a long tapering tail. As he watched, its tongue flickered out to catch a housefly which must have been even more surprised by the lizard's presence than he was.

This near-tropical temperature must be responsible, he assumed, although that didn't explain where the lizard had come from. If only he had his camera to hand!

He was so fascinated by the lizard, he didn't at first notice the caterpillar. It was poised on the window sill,

186

about half-way along, the whole front portion of its body raised in the air like a green sphinx. Immediately below it were the plant pots.

It dipped its head again and began to crawl vertically down the brick wall until – more rapidly than he had imagined possible – it reached the nearest pot.

Attracted by the seedlings, he thought as he watched. He focussed the field glasses on it. Those little black eyes seemed so intent on what it was doing as its head turned this way and that, he felt sure it hadn't even noticed him. If Ginny was right about them sensing blood, over what sort of distance would the information carry?

The caterpillar didn't even pause at the seedlings. It made a steady progress around the edge of the pot, then on to the next rim, and from there on to the third which was directly above the spot where the lizard was lurking.

The lizard swung around so quickly, he hardly even saw the movement. In the same instant, the long green caterpillar dropped down, brushing the lizard's back. A rapid twisting and tumbling followed; then they froze, facing each other.

What he saw next was something any naturalist would give ten years of his life to observe. What wouldn't Gilbert White have written about that struggle! The lizard's tongue shot out to seize this new prize, but the caterpillar was far too hefty and had weapons of its own. Recoiling, the lizard seemed on the point of running away; instead, it made a stand.

Why?

Did it instinctively realise this was one enemy which had to be defeated whatever the cost? Or was it merely too greedy to let such a fat, delicious caterpillar escape? If so, that was a mistake.

Darting forward, the lizard renewed its attack only to find the caterpillar suddenly pinning it down, its mandibles working into the loose neck-skin while its two rear

187

claspers held the victim steady.

Through his field glasses he followed every move until the lizard was left dead and mutilated on the stone paving. So absorbed was he by every detail of the fight, he forgot the risk to himself. Even when he realised that one of those giant moths was hovering over his beer glass not a foot away from him he was still oblivious of the danger, despite all Ginny had told him.

Only few moths were visible in daylight, he mused. Until now he'd assumed – from what he'd heard – that this was not one of them. He waited, hoping it would settle on the rim of the glass; instead, it fluttered down to his plate, and then moved off somewhere behind his deck chair.

He twisted in his seat, trying to follow it, only to meet it face on. It seemed as startled as he was himself and began circling his head, uttering a series of piercing squeals. His eyes! He had been so taken up with observing it, he'd quite forgotten about the goggles and scarf which were still in the house.

The burning fluid squirted into his eyes even as he brought up his arm to protect himself. The agony was unendurable. Despite himself he let out a long, broken bellow, clasping his head in both hands, doubling up on the deck chair until he fell forward on to his knees and began rolling on the hard paving.

Other pains attacked him now. On his legs . . . on his wrists . . . But the most intense was that acid corroding his eyes, eating slowly into the nerve ends, freeing his mind through the exquisite torture of his body. Fleeting images came to him now, tumbling madly through his shifting awareness. His wife Alice when they were young, smiling at him with Ginny's eyes; then her older, drawn face against that hospital pillow; twenty years dead, yet her smile was so peaceful, so understanding.

She'd understand about Ginny, wouldn't she?

*

188

The Chief Inspector gave Ginny a lift to St Botolph's vicarage where she had left her car. On her lap she held the gauze mask, stiff in parts with dried moth-saliva. Her salmon jeans, newly bought from the little Lingford boutique, were now stained and filthy, as was the rain-proof blouson. Overalls would have been more sensible, she thought wearily.

'Thank you for your help, Miss Andrewes,' the Chief Inspector said, breaking the silence. They had probably both felt too worn out to want to talk. 'It hasn't been a pleasant experience for any of us, but we are grateful. I'd like you to know that.'

She nodded. What was there to say?

Half of those they had rescued from the church had died before reaching hospital. Of the rest, only two or three seemed likely to survive. One – thank God! – was the little girl she'd found.

'The attacks are spreading, aren't they?' she asked abruptly. 'Almost like a planned campaign.'

'Oh, I doubt if it's planned,' the Chief Inspector disagreed. He was a blunt, businesslike man, probably not yet forty. In some ways he reminded her of Jeff, though he was taller, with boxer's shoulders. 'Think of it like green-fly. They cluster in some trees, not in others. We'll get on top of it, there's no doubt about that.'

'I wonder,' she said.

As if to reinforce her fears, the Lingford Control Room called up the Chief Inspector on the car's radio to report a major incident in South Croydon, the first in a built-up area. She looked at him queryingly as he acknowledged the message and replaced the microphone, but he only shook his head thoughtfully, making no comment.

The old Georgian vicarage came into sight. Her shabby little Renault stood where she had left it, though no longer in the shade. He drew up alongside to let her out.

'You'll excuse me if I rush on,' he said briefly, leaning

across her to open the door. 'I'm sure you understand. And thank you again.'

Ginny unlocked the Renault and tossed the beekeeping hat and mask on to the passenger seat. She was about to get in when she remembered it would be only polite to say hello to the Reverend Davidson. Of course he'd offer her tea or even a drink, so she'd have to make it clear right away that she couldn't stop. There was something rather pathetic about the way he couldn't keep his hands to himself. Thank God she wasn't a choir boy, she thought wickedly, suddenly grinning.

'Hello!' she called cheerfully. 'Mr Davidson?'

She went directly around to the back garden, feeling sure that was where he'd be. Her unexpected vision of him with the choir boys continued to amuse her; she laughed aloud, though it was probably very unfair to him, the poor man. Nor was it very funny, she told herself severely, failing to prevent another laugh bursting out. It was the relief after all those hours spent with the dead and dying. A whiff of hysteria as the spring wound down. She tried to get a grip on herself.

'Mr Davidson? Are you there?'

Rounding the corner, she saw in one glance what had occurred. The Reverend Davidson lay on the paved area nearest the house. Around him were fragments of a smashed glass. A foot or so away stood an empty deck chair with a low garden table next to it.

Ginny still had the goggles in her pocket. She paused long enough to put them on, together with her blood-stained gloves, then hurried over to investigate. Two caterpillars were busy on his legs; their hindquarters protruded, dripping blood, from the bottoms of his black clerical trousers. Opening the clasp knife Jeff had lent her, she ripped open the seams on both legs; then, one by one, she disposed of the caterpillars.

Some blood trickled down his forearm – his sleeves

were rolled up – but that might not have been caused by a caterpillar. There was certainly no sign of one. She tore both sleeves, then checked the legs again, ripping the trousers high above his white, knobbly knees, but found nothing more. His eyes had that terrible bloodshot look she'd noticed on the victims in the church.

Miraculously he was still alive, groaning and muttering to himself in that strange delirium she had first known when Lesley was attacked. Moving the plate away from the low table, she managed to prop him up on it, then catch him when he slumped forward over her shoulder as she half-knelt in front of him.

Gradually she stood up, staggering under his weight, though compared with Lesley he was quite frail and nowhere near as heavy. Holding on to him grimly, praying that she wouldn't drop him, she succeeded in getting him into the house.

As he had explained to her during her first visit, he lived these days mostly on the ground floor, the old vicarage being far too big for him. His bed was in the front room. With relief she let him fall back against the pillows, then stood up to rub her shoulder, wondering if she'd dislocated it.

The wounds on his legs were wet with blood. Using Jeff's clasp knife she tore several strips from one of the sheets and bound them up before telephoning for an ambulance. It took her five minutes to get through, only to be told there would be a long wait and couldn't she bring the patient in herself?

'Ginny . . .'

His voice was weak, the syllables only half-formed, yet she definitely heard him call her name.

'Yes, that's right. I'm here.' She bent over him as he mumbled something else which she couldn't understand. 'I'll get some water. Clean you up a bit.'

She fetched the water in a tall enamel jug which stood

beside the tap. Back in his makeshift bedroom, she removed her blouson top and pushed up her blouse sleeves.

'Now let's get some of this muck off your face,' she said, though she'd no way of telling whether he understood or not. 'Just lie still now and let me do it. There's no need to worry now. You'll be looked after.'

With a piece of sheet as a face flannel she patiently wiped away some of the dried moth-saliva. His skin was inflamed.

'Liz,' he pronounced suddenly, and it sounded terribly urgent. 'Liz . . . liz . . . liz . . .'

'She's someone you know, is she? Liz?'

'Liz . . .' He drew in a deep, uneven breath. '. . . ard . . .'

'Lizard?'

He seemed to relax, his eyelids quivering as though he wanted to close them but couldn't. Should she wash his eyes, she wondered. They were so hideous and she was scared of doing anything wrong. She dabbed them gently and he shuddered violently as though in severe pain, so she desisted, still uncertain. Perhaps she should ring the hospital, or Bernie, and ask advice.

As she leaned over him her forearm brushed against his hand and his fingers immediately closed over her wrist.

'Gin . . .'

'Yes, it's Ginny.'

'Gin . . . liz . . .'

'Is Liz your daughter?'

The suggestion seemed to upset him, but his voice croaked so in his throat; it was difficult to grasp what he wanted.

'I'll get some drinking water,' she told him. 'I'm sorry I'm such a bad nurse forgetting it. I should have given you a drink to start with.'

She eased his fingers away from her wrist, but immediately he started producing a hurried gibberish as though he didn't want her to go.

'I'll be back!' she said tenderly. On an impulse, she stooped to kiss him on the side of the mouth just below the line left by the moth-saliva. 'Shan't be a sec!'

Before she could leave the room the old man began to fight for breath, groaning as he gulped in great draughts of air, one after the other without pause, until suddenly he let go. There was a slight whistling sound to be heard as the air slowly left his lungs, in pitch not unlike the squealing of the moths. She stood by him, unwilling to believe what was happening. She tried to find a pulse. When she didn't succeed she blamed her own clumsiness and hunted for a glass to hold to his lips. No sign of breathing.

He was dead, she repeated to herself, squatting on her heels at the bedside, not knowing what to do next. Having seen what people do in the movies she attempted to close his eyes with her finger and thumb, but the eyelids resisted her, then sprang open again.

There was only one thing she could do. Picking up the phone again from among the clutter on the bedside table, she began to work her way through the four or five numbers where she might find Bernie.

It was late afternoon by the time she got back to her own village. She sensed the unnatural, haunted air as she drove through. There were more people about now, for the most part in small groups of two or three walking away from the church where the Bishop of Lingford had been taking the service of – well, how they had described it she didn't know. Certainly not 'thanksgiving'; and who would wish to remember the events of yesterday?

A service of survival: that would be the best name. She caught a glimpse of the bishop's limousine driving away, but there was none of the usual gossiping among the departing congregation. No one appeared to be talking.

193

They were all lost in their own thoughts, or else watching out for the first signs of another attack.

She had intended driving directly to Bernie's house for a bath. Passing the church she changed her mind and took the road leading to the cottage. She needed to be alone, she realised; at least for the next few hours. Her hands shook on the wheel as she turned into the lane.

In any case, Bernie might not be back yet, she thought illogically. In every way it was better she went to her own cosy home where she could feel secure.

Trying to track him down by telephone from the vicarage had proved abortive. The hospital didn't know where he was but had given her a number for Jameela. She had then called the golf club and a couple of Bernie's friends, still without finding him, so in the end she'd rung Jameela after all who had said she'd take everything in hand and Ginny was to wait at the vicarage until someone turned up. Rather than remain in the same room as the dead man, she had gone into the work station, thinking she might use the time to examine the specimen moth they had caught that morning. She had found the cage empty. The hardboard had been removed, and there was a long tear in the double netting over the top.

At the cottage she sat for a few moments in the car, too exhausted to get out. The thoughts tumbled through her mind. Nothing made any sense.

Before opening the car door she struggled into the stained blouson once more and reached for the hat and mask. Whatever was waiting for her out there, she was going to be ready for it. No way was she going to end up like the Reverend Davidson.

Getting out of the car she was struck by the silence. None of the usual birdsong was to be heard, nor the hum of insects. On the flower bed beneath the cottage window lay a dead thrush, yet no ants or midges swarmed around it as she might have expected. Jeff's spraying must have taken a terrible toll.

In the cottage itself she explored every corner before she felt confident enough to take off her gloves and mask. It was exactly as she'd left it, quite untouched by all that had happened. Unreal, even. She switched on the radio to bring a bit of life into the place, but after the events of that day it all sounded so futile. She preferred silence.

Yet – what next? Eat something, perhaps? Make a start on writing up those notes?

She was much too worn out to do anything. Looked it too, when she caught sight of herself in the mirror. She got some ice out of the fridge, struggling with the plastic tray over the sink to release the cubes. Then she fetched the whisky from the sideboard and poured herself a drink. It did nothing for her; her stomach rebelled against it.

Need some food, she tried insisting to herself, but she had no appetite. Still, she had to keep going so she took a banana from the bowl, peeled it down and bit into it. After the second mouthful, the whisky began to taste better. As she chewed, she washed hastily, feeling very vulnerable to be standing there in the kitchen only partly dressed. It was a relief to get into fresh clothes.

The banana left her hungry. Hunting through the fridge, she decided on toast and scrambled eggs with a couple of tomatoes mixed in. When it was ready she poured herself another whisky to go with it. Ideal, she discovered. It was a wonder none of the good food writers had stumbled across it.

Whisky and scrambled eggs: she'd mention it to Bernie.

'Right! Work, Ginny Andrewes!' she proclaimed aloud, getting up.

From the window, the charm of her secluded garden – once so welcome – had now become a constant reminder that caterpillars might be lurking anywhere among those leaves. She had blocked the gaps beneath both doors, but she knew she'd never be able to concentrate fully downstairs. She rinsed her dishes, leaving them to drip, then took her Caterpillar files up to the bedroom. At least from there she had a better overview of the garden. She also had the advantage of being able to spread out her papers across the bed.

Her first task, as she had discussed with Jeff, was to classify all they had observed about the moths and their caterpillars: their behaviour patterns, rather than the more scientific detail. This was more a job for Lesley, as she'd told him, but Lesley was not available.

'Think of them as actors in one of your plays,' he'd suggested as if that would be any use.

The first paper she picked up was a description she'd written of The Visitation. Fancy calling it *The Visitation* – what an idiot she'd been! She settled down on the bed to read it, but already after the second sentence her mind began to wander, recalling the day she'd moved down to the cottage and how Jack had helped her.

Jack had been one of the first to be attacked by the moths, and she hadn't even believed him!

Hadn't even . . .

She woke up with a start. It was so warm in that room with the window closed, and sleep seemed so inviting. Old Mr Davidson was asleep . . . flat on his back, his red eyes staring up at her . . . winking at her . . . his dead mouth smiling as his hand touched her knee . . . and she wanted to twist away . . . couldn't . . . the grip of the dead held her vice-like and . . .

Again she woke, this time to discover she had fallen back on the pillow. The paper she had been reading had slipped to the floor.

But she was determined to work. She picked up the sheet of paper and took it, together with the rest of the file, over to the window. The hard, upright chair should keep her awake. Again she began to read her own account of that first day, jotting down notes of points that might be useful.

Reaching the bottom of the page, she looked up and stared out of the window, trying to recall her own attitude at that time. She had been so delighted, she remembered; hard to imagine that now. From this same window she'd watched them settling on her garden like a dark veil.

Like . . .

She leaned forward. The sun had already set but there was still enough daylight to see everything quite clearly. That movement on the flower bed was surely not . . . ? No, she could swear it was not green. A darker colour, then: more like an autumn leaf. Brown?

A few inches from it something else shifted slightly. A different shape, she thought at first, straining her eyes to see it; but then she was not so certain. Even as she watched it was changing in contour, and beginning to resemble the first one.

Another dream, her mind insisted. Moths growing out of the ground? It's a nightmare, nothing more. You'll wake up and find it's all nonsense! Pure nonsense! Unadulterated —

She did wake up with a jerk, blinking her eyes to convince herself that she *had* been dreaming, but those shapes were still there. Striding apprehensively across the room, she pressed the light switch, then went back to the window. Had she been deceiving herself? She cupped her hand against the glass pane, but it was difficult to see.

Downstairs by the window in the unlit lean-to kitchen, Ginny was forced to accept the truth of her nightmare. Half-asleep she may have been, but those shapes on the flower beds *were* moths. Others were slowly emerging from the dark soil, gradually unfolding their broad wings, then resting.

197

For a few seconds she could do nothing but stare at them in complete disbelief. She had a confused image of the fully-armed soldiers of Greek legend springing out of the earth where dragon's teeth had been sown. But this was the twentieth century, and these were moths.

They were still not moving, as though waiting for something. A dozen of them, at least; maybe more.

Ginny changed back into the clothes she had discarded earlier – everything: boots, surgical mask, goggles, hat, gloves, the lot. Before opening the door, she checked the food was under cover, then sprayed the kitchen with pesticide, enough to discourage them.

Then she went out, closing the door behind her. The sky was darkening, but the rectangle of light from her bedroom window was bright enough. Against the wall was an old, rusting hoe. It must have been there for years and Ginny had intended to throw it away. She picked it up.

Calmly she went about the task of slaughtering those moths one by one, bringing the hoe blade sharply down on each to sever the wings and crush the body. They made no attempt to fly off, not even the slightest quiver. No regret on her part either as she destroyed those rich, soft, delicate creatures which had so fascinated her when she first saw them.

'Killers, that's all they are.' Her voice was muffled by the surgical mask, but it gave her some satisfaction to speak the words aloud. 'Ruthless killers. Well, humans can be ruthless too.'

She brought the hoe down once again and felt it slice into the emergent moth's tubby body. That seemed to be the last one, yet who could say what lay hidden beneath the topsoil? Starting at the shed, she began to work her way around all the flower beds, hoeing vigorously, determined that not one square inch would escape her.

Bernie arrived just as she was finishing and came into

198

the garden to find her. Save for the light from the cottage windows everything was in darkness.

'Odd time to start gardening!' he greeted her cheerfully. Coming over, he put his arm around her shoulders. As far as she could see he was wearing a motorcyclist's helmet with rubber masking across his face. 'You all right, love?'

She showed him the fragments of wing from the moths she'd killed.

'Came out of the soil,' she explained.

'They what?'

'Oh, let's go inside where we can talk. I've finished out here.'

Leaving the hoe outside in its old position, she led the way in through the kitchen door. There she stripped off her headgear and discarded her stained blouson. Bernie put down his helmet on top of it and took her in his arms. No hesitation about their kissing this time.

'Oh Bernie, I'm so glad you're here,' she murmured, still holding him tight. 'I tried to ring you this afternoon. No one knew where you were.'

'I kept imagining you'd been killed.' He ran his fingers through her short hair. 'Like a recurring nightmare, all the way back from London. They took some of us up to Whitehall to brief the Minister, not that it did much good, I'm afraid. I heard you were involved in that business in the church.'

'That's not all,' she told him, sitting down to pull off her boots. 'The Reverend Davidson's dead. I was with him.'

She tried to explain briefly what had happened, but then stopped in mid-sentence. 'Oh shit!' she exclaimed. 'Not now! Let's get out of these things and have a drink. I don't think I want to go over it all again. Bernie love, the whisky's on the sideboard.'

When she joined him in the living room she wore only

her light housecoat. He had the drinks ready but she merely smiled when he held one out for her, and kissed him instead. It was all she wanted at that moment – a long, savouring kiss to take away her tensions.

'I love you, Ginny,' he told her softly, stroking her back through the housecoat. 'Though I probably shouldn't.'

'Mm-m.' She nuzzled him sensuously, then slowly found his lips again. Breaking away from him, she said: 'I was working upstairs before I saw those moths outside. I've got papers scattered all over the bed.'

'Let's go and clear them up then, shall we?' His eyes laughed as they caressed her face. 'Mustn't interrupt your work.'

No doubts lingered in her mind any longer. At that moment she wanted him more than ever; nothing would make her turn back now. If she was being unfair to Lesley, that was how it crumbled. She couldn't help falling in love, could she? Besides, Lesley need never know. After this business with the moths was over she'd move back to London and that would be the end of it. She'd be the only one to suffer. Not Lesley, if she could help it.

She glanced in the mirror before following Bernie upstairs. A slightly flushed, very guilty face stared back at her. Oh shit, she thought unhappily; if only it could be different.

In his arms, her self-doubts disappeared again. It seemed so right for her to be with him and no one else. He made love gently at first, then with increasing urgency until at last they lay back, completed, yet knowing this was only the start.

She sat up, twisting around to look at his face and run her finger down his chest. 'I'm very much in love with you,' she said quietly, almost as if speaking to herself. 'But if the day comes when this ends, promise me you won't make a fuss.'

'What a depressing thought!'

'Promise?'

'I promise I'll try. D'you intend it to end?'

She shook her head.

'You're very beautiful, Ginny.'

'Rubbish.'

'It isn't rubbish.' His eyes flickered down to her chest. 'That trouble cleared up, then?' He laid his fingertips over the area where the 'sunburn' had been.

'Yes, doctor!' she laughed at him. Taking his hand, she placed it over her breast. 'A small thing, but mine own. You're in a lady's bed, not a consulting room.'

They made love again: a celebration of their new relationship because that was what she was experiencing. They were meeting afresh, as though they had never known each other before, and were conscious of neither past nor future: only an eternal present.

But at last Bernie said he should return home to the house. He wanted her to go with him, but she was reluctant. She sat on the edge of the bed thinking about it. Lesley's house.

'Can't we stay here?'

'I've not been back since morning,' he explained apologetically. His hand lightly touched her thigh, keeping their physical contact. 'There may be messages on the machine. I am the village doctor, don't forget. Please come with me.'

'I'm not sleeping in Lesley's bed.'

'Agreed.'

'I'll get dressed then.'

Had circumstances been different, she'd have chosen that long Indian cotton dress she'd bought last time in London, simply to luxuriate in being feminine. Instead, she pulled on her jeans, then the rest of her protective outfit, making sure not an inch of skin was exposed.

'That's what it was!' she exclaimed suddenly just as

they were ready to leave. She took off her mask and goggles again, then began to hunt among her books. 'I knew I'd read something like it.'

'Like what?' He waited, half-amused.

'Those moths crawled out of the earth as though someone planted them there.'

'Dragon's teeth,' he suggested.

'Too late – I thought of that one first! No, it's here, look!' She found the book and hastily turned over the pages. 'The Death's Head Hawk Moth! The caterpillar burrows into the ground to become a chrysalis, and when the moth emerges it has to wait till its wings dry out before it can fly. Which explains why they didn't try to escape. They couldn't!'

'Know thy enemy!' Bernie quoted approvingly. 'Though it doesn't bring us anywhere near a solution. Come on, love. Let's go.'

12

That night she slept in Lesley's bed after all.

When they got to the house Bernie decided he was hungry. While he checked through the phone calls, she dug some lamb chops out of the freezer and boiled some potatoes. For a vegetable she had a choice of courgettes or a tin of artichoke hearts. The courgettes reminded her of caterpillars, so she chose the artichokes.

'D'you realise it's after eleven?' Bernie announced, entering the kitchen with a bottle of his best claret in his hand. He hunted in the drawer for the corkscrew. 'Lesley left a message to say they're all fine. Send their love. Mrs Blakemore's arthritis is troubling her again and she needs to renew her prescription. Oh, and two messages for you.

Jeff Pringle wants you to ring him. And Jack. You're in demand!'

'Me? I'm tied up here!' she retorted. 'I hope!'

'So do I!' He leaned over to kiss her as she tended the chops. 'Or I shall be jealous!'

He drew out the cork, sniffed it, then put the bottle to one side ready for the meal.

'There've been a couple more incidents, it seems, in –' he started to go on.

'I don't want to know,' she interrupted him firmly. 'Not tonight, Bernie. Please? The meal's almost ready, so I'll just go and change. God, I've been wearing boots all day!'

This was one evening the caterpillars were not going to ruin, she was determined, whatever might happen later. She had brought the full-length Indian cotton with her and went up to the bathroom to change. It felt so good as it slipped over her head and she smoothed it down. It clung to her figure in all the right places. By the time she went downstairs again Bernie was setting out the plates.

What time it was when they went to bed she'd no idea. On the stairs – both of them a bit tipsy from all the wine – she made some suggestion about the spare room, but they found the mattress stripped bare of bedclothes. So narrow, too. The children's beds were out of the question, and it hardly seemed fair to use Phuong's room. Which left Bernie's king-size double bed.

Lesley's bed. Yet it didn't seem to matter so much any longer. That border had been crossed.

Eventually they fell asleep, still naked, with only a light sheet covering them because of the heat. The windows were firmly closed, of course. How long she slept she could only guess, though when she opened her eyes it was still dark in the room. She reached out and touched Bernie's shoulder, but he merely grunted without waking.

Without the caterpillars this would never have happened, she reflected drowsily. Blame them, if anyone. Outside – somewhere – hundreds more must be assembling for their next orgy of human blood. In one village or other, unsuspecting people were quietly sleeping, unaware of the danger they were in. Perhaps she herself would not survive.

She'd been sweating. She ran her hands down over her skin, feeling – oh, so alive, it was unbelievable! Surely Lesley wouldn't begrudge her just a small share of him? Discreetly? It was strange how much better sex could be if you were in love with the person.

Suddenly she thought of the Reverend Davidson – that poor old man, now at peace. Maybe it was the heat reminding her of that holiday in Greece where she'd been so delighted to watch the lizards at play on the wall. Had he really meant *lizards*, she wondered. Or was Liz a person?

Then a particularly horrifying idea struck her. This hot, wet weather had turned everything upside down. Plants flowering out of season, swarms of insects, these vicious caterpillars, previously unheard-of . . . Had it brought lizards too? Was that what he'd been trying to say, that he'd been attacked by a lizard?

After the past few days nothing of that sort would ever surprise her again. She tugged at Bernie's arm, urgently wanting to discuss it with him. He kissed her passionately – still deeply asleep – then turned over.

She would have to wait.

First thing in the morning, while Bernie was holding his surgery, she drove out to St Botolph's. A sober, dark brown Mercedes stood parked before the vicarage. Out of habit, she went around the back and found a thin, dry-looking man established in the living room. As she entered, he looked up from the papers he was studying

204

and removed his glasses.

'It is usual for visitors to ring the front doorbell before coming in,' he remarked tartly, looking at her protective gear with some cynicism. She'd taken Bernie's helmet.

'Not here, it isn't! He never answered. You're the solicitor, are you?' It was only a guess, but too obvious.

'I am *a* solicitor, yes.'

Ginny introduced herself, explaining how she had been there when the Reverend Davidson died. Could she take a look around?

'What exactly do you wish to see?'

'The garden first,' she explained. 'Then his work station.'

'Work station?' His tone was distrustful.

'Laboratory, if you prefer.'

The deck chair had not been moved since the previous afternoon; nor had the low table. Even his plate was still on the grass where she'd left it. Keeping an eye out for caterpillars, she began a slow search of the paved area.

'If you'd tell me what you're hoping to find, I might be in a position to help you,' the solicitor said impatiently.

'I don't know.'

The shed, she thought. She was half-way across the grass towards it when she stopped, uncertain of herself. Of course he must have been sitting down in the deck chair, mustn't he? That meant he'd see everything from a different angle. Turning on her heel she trudged back, tugged the deck chair to where she thought it had been standing when she first saw it, and sat down.

'Really, I do have rather a lot to get through!' the solicitor objected.

But then she spotted it, tucked away between two plant pots. Keeping her gloves on, she took hold of the limp brown tail and drew it out.

'What would you say this is?' she asked the solicitor, holding it up before his face.

He sighed. 'You appear to have found a rather mutilated, dead lizard,' he answered with obvious distaste. 'Is that really so significant?'

'Have you seen one before in this part of the country?'

'I live in London. But I'm told they do exist in England. You're not implying we're about to be eaten by lizards as well as caterpillars, are you?'

'Before he died he was trying to tell me something. I wish I knew what.' She glanced at his dark business suit. 'You've not met the caterpillars yet?'

'Fortunately not.'

'You should wear something to protect your head and hands,' she informed him soberly. 'You're exposing yourself unnecessarily.'

In the work station she found a screwtop specimen jar and dropped the remains of the lizard into it. Perhaps it meant nothing at all, who could tell? The solicitor was hovering around, watching her anxiously and treating her now with rather more respect. He pointed to the rows of round, plastic 'cages' which still held the Reverend Davidson's living specimens.

'I've no idea what to do with these,' he murmured forlornly. 'My brother left no instructions. Perhaps I should give them to a zoo.'

So he was the Reverend Davidson's brother, she thought. There was little likeness.

'Kill them,' she told him bluntly. Weren't they the smaller cousins of the attackers? 'If you can't, then set them free. They'll probably starve to death if you leave them where they are.'

Outside, she heard a light aircraft in the sky above and peered up at it, wondering if it might be Jeff. When she got back to Bernie's house, she phoned him.

His name was painted on a neat little signboard near the gates: Jeff Pringle. The house was a wide-fronted, two-storey villa, obviously thirties-built, painted white with a green tiled roof. As her baby Renault coughed its way up the drive he came out to meet her.

'Had this chariot serviced recently?' he enquired by way of a greeting.

'I keep meaning to.'

Getting her briefcase from the back seat, she followed him inside. The furniture was in a cool modern style. Nothing cheap, though rather too much dark leather for her taste. On the walls were souvenirs from Africa and his other various travels, mostly masks carved in black wood and colourful batik cloths. In one corner stood an electric fan, gently turning. The windows were open, their frames having been fitted with a protective wire mesh to keep out the enemy.

He offered her a drink and she chose lager. When it came, it was deliciously cold in tall, slender glasses. 'Cheers!' he said.

From her briefcase she produced the specimen jar containing the dead lizard and placed it in front of her on the dining table. 'Something new you won't know about yet,' she explained, and told him about the Reverend Davidson.

When she had finished, Jeff opened the jar and shook out its contents on a sheet of white paper.

'It's quite small, as lizards go,' he commented, examining it closely. 'About the size of a gecko. It looks like something has been chewing it up. You don't seriously think this thing attacked the padre?'

'No,' she admitted. She scooped it up into the jar again. 'But the lab will tell us what it's been eating. What's their normal diet?'

'Africa is about the extent of my experience of lizards. Some are vegetarians, but I believe most are carnivorous. That means insects, not people.'

'Caterpillars? Tiny ones perhaps, not like ours?'

207

'You may have a point,' he agreed, making a note. 'I think I know who to ask. Now let's go through everything we've so far learned about these caterpillars, shall we? See if we can't discover something the official committees might miss.'

Their discussion was thorough and businesslike, much to Ginny's relief. They went through the life cycle of the giant moths, at least those stages they had so far observed; then their feeding habits – factually, without sentiment – plus their general behaviour patterns. Jeff took notes as they talked, reading each summary aloud for her approval. She brought up the way the caterpillars and moths seemed able to coordinate their attacks.

'Can we be sure about that?' Jeff pressed her. 'It was not the case at the Spring Fair.'

'But it did happen at the church, and there've been other reported instances too. Perhaps – ' She paused, frowning as she thought it through. 'I was going to say perhaps it's coincidental, but there's more to it. I think their tactics are changing.'

'Which means we're witnessing these moths actually learning from experience.'

'That makes them even more dangerous. And what about the pesticide we're using? Does it kill them, or merely make them sluggish for a time?'

'It's pretty deadly stuff,' he told her. 'A lungful of that would bring the strongest man down.'

'Not relevant. So would nuclear fall-out, yet they say insects could survive it.'

He picked up his pencil and inscribed a big question mark by the side of what he had just written. 'So we need more on the pesticide. There must be some laboratory tests available by now. It seems to be killing everything else.'

'You've heard that we now know where they come from?' she asked.

208

'It has been confirmed?'

'This morning.'

On her return from St Botolph's Bernie had told her that a laboratory technician at Lingford University Research Institute had now definitely identified the caterpillars. They had been bred in the Institute itself, the third generation of a sequence of mutations resulting from advanced experiments in genetic engineering. Work on the project had been stopped the previous year and the people involved were difficult to contact. The research assistant, Adrian Burton, had been appointed to a lectureship in Australia and chosen to travel out by sea. The woman scientist who set the whole thing up was now in America engaged on a US Government contract which, she apparently claimed, did not permit her to comment.

'Sophie Greenberg,' Jeff nodded meaningfully. 'That's Sophie all right. She worries about the wrong things.'

'You obviously know her.'

'I did once. Perhaps they haven't told her what these slugs of hers are getting up to.'

'According to the technician,' Ginny went on, 'they'd an accident in the lab last year. Something to do with a cat. A couple of caterpillars got out and were never seen again. The others died, which was when she scrapped the whole thing. The last straw, he said.'

'What about her notes?'

'Bernie was told she took everything with her.'

'Helpful.' He drained his glass, then stood up. 'Another drink? These are thirsty days.'

Ginny welcomed the break. While Jeff was getting more beer from the fridge she went over to the bow window to look at the louring sky, already illuminated by the first flickers of distant lightning. In a minute it was going to pour down.

The telephone rang and Jeff called to ask her to take it for him. It was an African voice, a man with an unfamiliar accent. She twice had to ask him to repeat what he said before she understood.

'Won't give his name.' She held out the receiver to Jeff when he came back into the room. 'Mystery man – he insists on speaking to you personally.'

'Client, more likely. Caterpillars permitting, I still have a business to run.'

Of course he still flew to Africa, she remembered. Mostly freight, he'd explained to her. He was a bit of a mystery man himself, but he seemed to know quite a few people in key places. Perhaps it was absurdly optimistic to think they could get action on the caterpillars more effectively than the official committees, but someone had to try. At least Jeff might be able to drop words in the right ears. She tried to listen in on his phone conversation, but it was largely one-sided: seldom more than monosyllables from him, and then in French. That accounted for the accent.

'Sorry about the interruption,' he apologised, putting the phone down. 'That man's been on at me for five weeks now but he still can't give me a firm date. Maybe in ten days, he says.'

'Oh?'

'West Africa,' he enlarged. 'A quick return trip, nothing exciting. Now where were we?'

A crash of thunder exploded directly above them like a bomb, almost scaring her out of her skin. She took an involuntary step back and her foot caught on the edge of the carpet. If he hadn't grabbed her arm she might have fallen. In an attempt to cover her fear, she made some joking remark about the Third World War starting, and smiled at him, embarrassed. His face was close to hers. He'd kissed her before she realised what he was up to.

'Sorry!' She twisted away, ducking under his arm. 'That's the last thing I need. I'm involved with someone else, Jeff.'

'I wondered why you were looking so delicious,' he said lightly. 'Then I'll wait. Who knows?'

'I do – so don't bother!'

Before he could reply, the phone rang again. His face darkened as he listened. He glanced towards her, as though implying that the call concerned her too.

'Bloody hell!' he swore softly as the person at the other end went on. 'Of course . . . Yes, I'm sure. What's the name of the road again?'

He wrote it down on a pad, asked for directions, then rang off.

'Lingford – a primary school. I'm afraid there are a hell of a lot of casualties. The children were outside for playtime when the attack happened. Moths first, then caterpillars.' He began putting on a close-fitting zippered jacket as he spoke. 'Normal emergency services are already there, but they're asking for people experienced in handling caterpillars. I said we'd both be along. D'you mind?'

'Of course I'll help.'

Outside, the rain started pouring down as though all the taps had been turned on at once.

During the next few days the attacks multiplied and spread, yet few were as horrifying as the scene they found at that school. The children – none of them older than seven or eight – lay strewn over the hard playground and nearby grass, their blood diluted to a deathlike pink by the heavy rain. Some moaned and writhed in pain; some shrieked for their mothers; many were as pale and still as waxworks. Among them, their teachers had also been struck down, probably having been attacked as they tried to help.

Everywhere Ginny looked she saw green caterpillars, much longer and fatter than that pathetic little lizard, feasting on their helpless victims.

They did what they could. Ginny again concentrated on removing and killing caterpillars before the children were taken for first-aid treatment and then transported to hospital. How many she treated, she had no idea. The sweat ran down her face; her goggles misted up; she longed for each child to be the last, yet more were brought. Eighty altogether had been marked present on the school register; forty-three died before anything could be done for them. Of the rest, only seven were still alive the following morning.

Ginny went to the hospital to visit them. Passing an open door she caught a glimpse of Dr Sanderson sitting at his desk, his frameless glasses on the blotter before him as he wiped his eyes. His son was among those who hadn't survived, Bernie told her later.

By that time the authorities were thoroughly alarmed. The attacks were too numerous to be regarded as merely isolated incidents which would not recur. They extended now across the whole of Kent, Surrey and Sussex. Emergency evacuation plans were instituted for everyone who wanted to get away, particularly families with children, though many preferred to stay put. Their arguments were various: it might never happen to them; they lived in a village which had never seen a caterpillar or moth; or – the most convincing of the lot – they'd be just as much at risk wherever they moved.

In Bernie's living room Ginny cleared one wall of pictures and covered it with Ordnance Survey maps. A special mobile unit had been set up of people trained to handle the caterpillars, with herself as area leader. Every night the maps told the same story: the menace was spreading even farther.

Attacks were reported with increasing frequency from the leafy suburbs of Greater London. Occasional casualties occurred as far west as Reading, including a gardener discovered dead in the grounds of Windsor

Castle. Moths were sighted, though no one hurt, at Pershore in Worcestershire.

Back in Sussex, at Gatwick Airport a major air disaster was only narrowly averted as a jumbo jet coming in to land skidded over thousands of caterpillars on the runway. Passengers were imprisoned on board the plane for more than six hours before it was judged safe enough to allow them to disembark. Among the ground staff the casualty rate was so high that the airport had to remain closed.

Reaction in the press and Parliament was vociferous. If only words alone could defeat the caterpillars, Ginny thought more than once. Government action was demanded, yet it was patently obvious that the Cabinet had not the slightest idea what to do. The tabloids carried blockbuster headlines such as – at their most sober – MANEATING CATERPILLARS HIT SCHOOL. One distinguished itself with FOREIGN CATTIES EAT OUR KIDS, and demanded a tightening of quarantine laws. Meanwhile, *The Times* reported how the caterpillar plague had also spread across northern France and was threatening Paris.

As for television – her own trade, she remembered wryly, though all that now seemed a thousand light years away – at first the news crews merely added a fresh twist to the emergency services' job, though when a cameraman was tragically killed they became more cautious. They also tried an in-depth documentary followed by a studio discussion, roping her in as an expert, no less, but it came up with no solutions. It was after some location filming for that programme that she had dropped in at the cottage and found a postal packet waiting for her. Somehow the post office had managed to deliver it despite the general chaos caused by the caterpillars, and the fact that their own postman was among those killed at the Spring Fête.

213

Opening the packet, she found it contained the manuscript of her proposal for that television drama series. The idea which had seemed so wonderful at the time! A covering letter from the agent commented that it might be rather difficult to place at the present time.

Ginny tossed it on to the little round table, but missed and it fell on the floor. She left it there and went back to Bernie's house.

They saw very little of each other during those days, she and Bernie, except at night in that wide double bed. Any feelings of guilt towards Lesley had long since died. At last she understood what it must have been like in wartime. The normal conventions just didn't apply: how could they when night after night she'd come back splashed with blood after yet another encounter with caterpillars? She didn't even think of it any more.

'I have squatters' rights!' she stated firmly on the one occasion when Bernie tentatively raised the subject. He'd just been speaking to Lesley on the phone and had come into the bedroom, his face troubled, to find her waiting for him. 'Oh Bernie, let's just live for today. What else can we do? When this thing with the caterpillars is over I'll have to go away, you know that.'

In fact, it felt more like camping in the house than living in it. Neither knew when the other would be at home. Bernie attempted to keep up his normal consulting sessions, but there was such a demand for medics, he was also out for long hours at Lingford Hospital. When he did get back, invariably late, he was usually ravenously hungry and hardly human until he'd eaten. She kept the fridge stocked up with food they could cook quickly. First one home started the meal, and good stuff too, not convenience foods. Oddly, she found she no longer felt an antipathy to red meat. As for drink, he insisted on only the best claret and ordered it by the case, joking grimly

214

that — who could tell? — they might both be dead by the time the bill was sent.

The day Jeff rang about the lizard experiment Ginny had already been out twice on emergency calls. For the first she'd arrived too late: a twenty-year-old mother with her baby had taken a short cut to the clinic along a woodland path, despite all warnings. Both dead. The second had been in Lingford in a car park behind the supermarket, a typical double attack with the moths first blinding the victims, leaving them helpless against the caterpillars. What made it even more disgusting, they now knew that if no rescuers arrived in time, the moths would return to hover over the corpses. The proboscis would uncurl and hang dabbling in the wounds, drinking up the plasma. On this occasion they came across another example of it — a young assistant manager lying dead among the shopping trolleys. No one had known he was there.

She got back to the house worn out, hot, sick of the whole mess, only to be greeted by the phone ringing the moment she was inside the door. She picked up the receiver and yelled at it through her helmet: 'Hang on till I'm undressed!' Her mobile unit had been equipped with Army protective suits which were completely secure against caterpillars but a bastard to get on and off. At last she managed to free the upper half of her body. She grabbed the phone. 'Yes?'

What met her ears was a chuckle, followed by some sexist joke about 'can't wait for videophones'.

'Jeff, I'm in no mood!' she snapped. 'What is it?'

'You've been to the supermarket?' he guessed right away. 'I heard about it. Sorry, Ginny, I've obviously caught you at a bad moment. Look, it's about tomorrow. Can you come to London? I've arranged a demonstration of what lizards can do — your idea, Ginny! A couple of

Ministry people will be there. I'd welcome your moral support. More than welcome it – I desperately need it if we're to convince them.'

'Convince them of what?'

'These aren't your tiny lizards. They're two foot long and they chew up caterpillars like they were cocktail sausages. We tried them out today.'

'Where?' she asked doubtfully.

'I've a client who supplies zoos. Didn't I mention him? I must have done. He's got me into trouble often enough. You must remember the famous chimpanzee case when half of them were found dead on landing at Heathrow? Not my fault, I was only the bloody pilot, yet tell the press that! They really put me in the stocks. Anyway, he's the man with the lizards. Keen to help, as well.'

'You think it may be the answer?'

'It's worth trying isn't it? At least it might jolt the Government away from pesticide spraying. Oh, I know it's my bread-and-butter, but on this scale it's mad.'

At eight o'clock they met in the car park behind Lingford Station. To be sure of a seat they took first-class tickets but – blaming caterpillars – British Rail ran a reduced service and they passed the journey standing squashed in the corridor. Two girls near them were talking about a new attack at Oxted during the night; one declared from now on she was going to stay in London where it was safer.

Yet both were dressed in ordinary clothes, Ginny marvelled; as though they were immune from the moths. She herself wore a close-fitting safari costume, with her head and face covered by an improvised Iranian chador, plus sun goggles to protect her eyes. A scattering of other passengers were similarly covered, perhaps a third of them in all. Jeff had equipped himself with a sort of balaclava helmet which made him look like a medieval hangman, and he crowned it with a soft felt hat.

The demonstration was to take place in a rented drill hall near Bryanston Square. An area in the centre of the hall was boxed off. Two lizards were already on display there, drowsing under the heat from the high-powered lamps arranged on stands around them. It was obviously intended to video the event, using three cameramen who were busy setting up their equipment.

A small cheerful man bustled forward to greet them, holding out a muscular hand. Jeff introduced him as Andrew Rossiter, responsible for organising the occasion. The two people from the Ministry had already arrived, it seemed. The woman, in a dark costume, seemed rather tense and did not smile even when shaking hands. The man was fidgety and obviously bothered by the heat. His grey suit had seen better days.

'Right, we're all here now!' Rossiter called out when the introductions were over. He clapped his hands to ensure the attention of the video crew as well. 'This is a private experiment. No press; no outsiders. It'll happen once only, so keep your eyes open everybody, specially the cameramen. No rehearsal, no second chances – right? Now Fred here has ten caterpillars in his box – the big kind that have been causing all the trouble. When I give the word, he's going to empty the box into the confined area where you see the lizards.'

They were a kind of monitor lizard, Ginny had learned, roughly two feet long and not yet fully grown. Their tails tapered until at the tip they were no thicker than a washing line, while their dark, speckled skin had a desiccated look about it.

To one side of the boxed-in area Fred stood waiting, clad in full protective gear and clutching an old biscuit tin in his arms. Rossiter checked that the cameramen were ready, then gave the signal. Fred removed the lid and checked the underside. On discovering a long, curling, green caterpillar clinging to it, he tossed it towards the

217

lizards. It landed with a clatter.

Neither lizard moved.

Slowly the caterpillar began to explore its surroundings.

Fred calmly picked the remaining caterpillars out of the tin one by one and dropped them into the enclosure. Counting them as he did so, Ginny guessed. He wouldn't want to leave any unaccounted for.

Suddenly one of the lizards – without apparently moving – caught the fattest of the caterpillars and swallowed it. It was so quick, Ginny could not be sure she'd actually seen it. She watched more closely, next time just glimpsing the forked tongue as it shot out to seize another.

The second lizard ran forward a few paces, then stopped. In quick succession it took three caterpillars. There was no way they could have escaped.

Within three or four minutes every caterpillar had been gulped down.

'Right! That's it – *cut*!' Rossiter shouted. 'They ate all ten, did they, Fred?'

'Gobbled them up like they hadn't been fed for a week,' came Fred's muffled voice from inside the rubber shield he wore over his face.

'A wonder they don't get indigestion,' the woman civil servant murmured to her colleague. 'How long d'you think they live inside those lizards?'

'A few seconds is my guess,' Rossiter told her confidently. 'Once those digestive juices get working, bob's your uncle! Like to see one of the recordings? Let's have one in slow motion.'

They watched all three recordings. It was obvious to Ginny that the civil servants were impressed, though the woman worried about how dangerous to humans the lizards themselves might be.

'There's a place in Nigeria called Bonny where they

used to think monitor lizards were sacred,' Jeff attempted to calm her fears. 'A hundred years ago, or more, this was. The travellers who went there said they were lying around all over the place – in the doorways, in the road, in the houses themselves. They didn't harm anyone, it seems.'

'Then why did they get rid of them – if they did?'

'Oh, a missionary came along. Attitudes changed. Usual story.'

They coaxed the civil servants into a nearby burger house to discuss the matter further over coffee. If the Government would authorise the shipment of just one plane-load of monitor lizards into Britain they could find out within twenty-four hours whether this was the answer or not. Ginny supported him. It was at least worth trying, wasn't it? Use nature to fight nature; that was better than poisoning the earth.

'Yes, there is the environmental argument of course,' the male civil servant agreed smoothly.

'Oh Jesus!' Ginny swore vehemently. 'Don't you realise the things are killing people?'

She started to describe the scene at the supermarket only the day before, but Jeff stopped her.

'I'm sure they realise,' he said quietly.

It was almost midday when they parted, the civil servants saying that they had to get back to their desks. They would be putting in separate reports, they said, and would try to get a quick response.

Jeff took Ginny and Rossiter into the corner pub and armed them with a large whisky apiece before going off to telephone. Rossiter launched into a self-justificatory monologue about how he truly lived for animals and was not in the business merely for money, oh no, not at all, if it was only that he'd be selling cabbages. It left Ginny feeling that he had now made his own good work look rather cheap. She was relieved when Jeff returned.

She refused a second round, saying she had to get back to Lingford. Jeff was staying on in London, so she went to the station alone, taking a taxi in preference to the tube. Since the caterpillars she felt uneasy in enclosed spaces.

The train was already pulling away from the platform as she arrived and she had to wait three-quarters of an hour for the next. She thought of ringing Jack, but decided against. Had she behaved badly towards him, she wondered? She was no longer sure. Perhaps it was just one of those untidy things that happen when people break up.

But at least the journey back was comfortable. She had plenty of room and passed the time updating the notes which she still conscientiously kept. Occasionally she glanced out at the passing houses, observing how many now had fitted wire-mesh frames over their windows. More, the farther they travelled from London.

An undisturbed day, that's all she longed for now. If only she could get back to the house and find no phone calls on the recording machine, no messages of any kind. And Bernie home early, too. A long, quiet evening together.

At Lingford Station all was peaceful. She went first into the High Street for a bit of shopping, then to the car park. Her Renault ran like a dream since the garage had given it a thorough working over, though she still hadn't recovered from the bill.

The village too was at its most attractive. Few people about, but that was not unusual for mid-afternoon. So far — touch wood — they had been free of both moths and caterpillars since the Spring Fête. In fact, that seemed to be emerging as a pattern. After a mass attack they seldom returned, though she could think right away of two exceptions. It could always happen.

Turning into the drive, she noticed Bernie's Rover parked before the living-room windows. Her first reaction was a flush of pleasure to find him back so early. Then she remembered that Lesley had taken this car. Was she bringing the children home again? But she couldn't!

Ginny sat there shattered, gripping the steering wheel with both hands, unwilling to get out. How could she face her? She'd never be able to carry it off, she knew. But of course she couldn't stay hiding in her car for the rest of the day. Besides, the front door was opening. Lesley was coming out.

Forcing a smile, she swung out of the car and ran forward. Oh God, her voice sounded so false. 'Lesley, how lovely to – !'

Her sister slapped her hard across the face.

'You bitch, Ginny!' she spat at her contemptuously. 'You're sleeping with him, aren't you?'

13

A week passed before Jeff got in touch with Ginny again, one long week of hell.

It had been her own fault Lesley had found out, leaving her clothes scattered about the bedroom as though they had every right to be there. She'd not even bothered to make up the bed in the spare room. No pretence of any kind. Anyone walking into the house would have seen at first glance what was going on – and it had to be Lesley.

She'd made no attempt to defend herself but let the storm break over her, feeling she wanted to sink into the ground and disappear for good. What else could she have done? Lesley was right. Then the phone had started to ring persistently. At last she'd answered it – just to get away from Lesley's bitter fury – and it was an emergency call. A major attack at a comprehensive. Glad to escape,

221

she had changed into her Army suit and gone out right away.

During the following days the attacks never let up and the stream of people fleeing the danger areas now became a flood. Pubs shut their doors permanently, church services were cancelled, and all schools evacuated. Every patient who could be safely moved was transferred to some other hospital, even as far away as Leeds or Newcastle.

Neither she nor Bernie had much time even to think about the mess they found themselves in, though that first night they hardly slept. A dozen times he tried to phone Lesley but first she refused to speak to him, then she left the phone off the hook. Perhaps they should have split up right away but Ginny couldn't face the idea. The worse the caterpillar attacks became, the more she needed Bernie to restore her sanity. But the time would come soon enough, she knew.

When Jeff rang she picked up the phone wearily, dreading yet another emergency call, but brightened the moment she heard his voice. He was leaving for West Africa, he told her; it sounded as though things were moving at last. He planned to return within two or three days with a plane-load of monitor lizards and would be grateful for her help if she was willing.

'The Ministry have agreed?' It was such good news, her exhaustion seemed to fall away from her. 'Oh Jeff, why didn't you tell me?'

'They haven't agreed.' On the phone his voice had a metallic, cynical tinge. 'They sent a letter – second class mail, if you please! – saying they find the idea promising. They're putting it up to their scientific committee for discussion and evaluation.'

'But that could take ages!'

'I'm going ahead without them. Somehow we've got to prove these lizards may be the answer, and I can't think of any other way. Can you come over to talk? Bernie too, if he's free.'

Bernie was not free, so she drove alone to Jeff's house. Since her last visit he had boarded up several of the windows and installed an imposing array of aerials on the roof. Inside the front door she had to pass through a double barrier of overlapping lace curtains designed to keep the moths out.

He led the way to an upstairs room and showed her a bank of radio equipment. Tinkering with it was an earnest-looking, bespectacled boy of about eighteen, wearing a school blazer.

'This is Alan, our local radio ham,' Jeff introduced him. 'He's been organising all this gadgetry and has offered to operate it for us. What you see here is essentially our control room. I'll be flying a 707. Once I'm over northern France, at any rate, we should have radio contact. If possible, I intend to land at Gatwick.'

'Gatwick's closed,' she objected.

In fact, at least one attempt had been made to reopen the airport, but as soon as the personnel started to arrive the caterpillars emerged again. Not even extensive spraying could dislodge them from the nearby fields and woods, it was discovered. As if they were deliberately lying in wait, the Pest Control Officer reported.

'The aim is to release the lizards right in middle of them,' Jeff grinned, tapping one of the charts he had spread out on the table. 'But keep this under your hats, both of you. Top secret, okay? Don't want our Ministry friends interfering. The story for the authorities is that I intend bringing the old 707 into Heathrow – an' I may still have to if conditions aren't right. I'll need to know before I reach the Channel.'

His plan involved Ginny stationing herself at Gatwick in the Range Rover. From there she would report on the situation to Alan by car phone; he of course would be in

223

two-way contact with the plane itself. Jeff had drawn up a checklist of points for her to observe. Clouds, direction of the wind, and so on.

'It's a gamble,' he admitted freely. 'If successful, it'll only prove we need more lizards. One plane-load won't wipe out every caterpillar in the land. But worth a try.'

They left Alan to continue checking over the equipment and went downstairs to the living room where he poured a couple of whiskies.

'I find it hard to visualise Jeff Pringle as a public benefactor,' she commented, adding extra soda to hers. 'Unless you are a millionaire and haven't told me. What are you getting out of this?'

'The same as you,' he retorted. 'Survival. So – long life!'

'Long life!' she repeated, clinking her glass against his. Never had she been more serious about a toast.

'The plane is already in West Africa. I'm being paid to fly it back anyway – well, you know that. You took the phone call yourself.'

She hadn't known it, but she made no comment. 'How many lizards can you bring?' she asked.

'Can't tell till I get there. The locals are already rounding them up and they'll have to be paid. Still, that's part of the game.'

They went over the details a few times. There was plenty that could go wrong and Ginny felt far from sure of herself. Jeff took it all coolly – a routine run, he remarked – yet she suspected a tenseness behind that unruffled front. He had been to recce Gatwick more than once before deciding. When she asked why not bring them in through some other airport still in operation, he fobbed her off with a vague reply about red tape and being refused an import licence.

'Probably true enough,' Bernie grunted when she told

him about it that night. 'After the scandals about zoo animals being found dead in their cages on arrival. About a year ago, wasn't it, he had a run of bad luck?'

'D'you think he has a chance?'

'Darling, I really don't know any better than you. But I desperately hope you're both right about those lizards.'

Next morning Jeff turned up at the house in his Range Rover shortly before Bernie left. While waiting for her to get ready the two men stood in the hall talking. She overheard Bernie speculating on what would happen if a monitor lizard found itself heavily outnumbered by caterpillars: because that, he argued, was the most likely scenario. Wouldn't they kill it? She did not wait for Jeff's answer, but bustled downstairs declaring it was time they got going.

She drove the Range Rover herself to Heathrow just to get the feel of it, dropping Jeff at Terminal Two. He was catching a Paris flight, then transferring at Charles de Gaulle Airport, though he still would not reveal his final destination. Before getting out of the car he leaned across to kiss her. If anything went wrong, she thought, he might easily be killed. Oh God, she'd seen so many deaths since this all started . . .

By the automatic doors he paused for a second to wave, then he was gone. It left her feeling even more apprehensive than usual.

Leaving Heathrow, she was tempted to head into London but decided against it. It was so hot, there was a muggy white sky over the capital and the crowds would be unbearable. At home it was too risky to sit outside, but at least they could open the windows now they had gauze over the frames. They had also had the creeper cut away from the walls, just in case. Perhaps when all this was over – if it ever did end – she could coax Bernie away for a few days to somewhere cool. Iceland, even. One last fling before she surrendered him to Lesley.

If Lesley was prepared to have him back: there was always that.

Ginny had gone over it again and again, but there was no solution: only hard facts. It had happened. Not all her tears – locked in the bathroom to hide them from Bernie – could change a thing.

She swung the Range Rover into a lay-by to wipe her eyes and blow her nose yet again, ignoring the curious glances of the lorry drivers. It was twenty minutes before she felt ready to go on. Then, when she got home, she found a message from Bernie on the tape to say Jameela had been killed the previous night while visiting friends in Kingston. A caterpillar attack.

Ginny sat on the nearest chair and stared at the blank wall, trying to take in what he had told her. Was it even worth going on, she wondered. It all seemed so unfair.

Phuong disentangled herself from four-year-old Caroline who had been climbing over her demanding a story and went into the kitchen to make a start on the meal. Upstairs she could hear Lesley scolding first daughter as she did so often now. Of course Frankie was noisy and often got up to mischief, but that was not the reason, as Lesley herself knew.

In Phuong's opinion she was wrong not to let Bernie speak to her. In her eyes the doctor was a good husband who provided well for his family. A good father, too. If he took another woman – his wife's sister, which perhaps was worse – that could cause much unhappiness but it would pass. To maintain the family should be Lesley's main concern now. For that reason alone she should talk to Bernie. In moments like this families needed the mother's strength if they were not to suffer.

Thinking it over while she cut a few slices of root ginger, she knew she could never speak to Lesley herself

226

on the subject, not unless invited to do so. That was not her place. But she could see danger signals. Mary, as the unmarried headmistress of this large boarding school, naturally had different ideas. She had welcomed them warm-heartedly into her home when they needed to escape from the caterpillars, but she was the first to talk of divorce. Phuong had overheard them together.

The tone of Mary's voice had worried her, she remembered as she picked up the knife and began finely chopping the ginger. No regret that Lesley was unhappy, but a note of satisfaction that made Phuong dislike her. She was actually glad that her view of marriage had been proved right.

As she worked, the music on the kitchen radio gave way to the announcer's voice. She reached out to turn it off but stopped with her fingers on the switch, catching the opening words of a news flash.

'. . . *report having seen the aircraft surrounded by a large swarm of giant moths which may have been sucked into the jet engines, causing them to stall. No figures for casualties have yet been released but the crash is said to be the worst ever experienced at Heathrow and . . .*'

'Phuong, what's "casualty"?' Wendy's voice piped, cutting across the rapid tenor of the announcer.

She flicked the radio off immediately and tried to hide her feelings with a quick laugh. 'Oh, I didn't hear you come in!' she exclaimed, putting the knife down and scooping the little girl up in her arms. 'Have you finished playing with the doll's house?'

'The dolls are asleep,' Wendy informed her. 'What's "casualty"?'

'Oh – that means people who are hurt.' She put her down again and continued working.

'In hospital?'

'Yes, they do go to hospital. Look, I'm doing cabbage today. My way – you like it my way, don't you? Can you bring me the cabbage from the larder?'

'Say please!'

'Please.'

It was one of the games they played when Phuong was cooking. She watched Wendy march off to the larder. English food was the rule, naturally, and usually Lesley was in charge, but everyone liked Phuong's method of preparing cabbage with crushed ginger and garlic. When she could, she tried to divert the children's attention from the news by asking them to help, hoping to ease them away from the nightmares which regularly disturbed their sleep since the Spring Fête.

Her own father had done the same, of course. When she was small, American bombers had flown daily across their patch of sky on their way to kill Vietcong; to calm her fears he'd made up stories about them in which war and death played no part. Later, in that little boat when she'd really needed his strength, he'd been one of the first to die. She'd had to help her mother and brother tip his body over the side.

'Cabbage!'

Wendy returned proudly bearing the spring cabbage in both arms, hugging it like a teddy bear.

Phuong was on the point of asking her to put it on the table when, turning, she caught sight of a green, hairy caterpillar slowly appearing from among the leaves and manoeuvring itself on to Wendy's T-shirt. She stared at it, uncomprehending. Everyone said they were safe here, didn't they? No caterpillars here, surely?

'Wendy!' Lesley appeared in the doorway. Her voice was hardly above a whisper. 'Wendy, stand absolutely still, d'you hear?'

'I'll take the cabbage,' Phuong said, trying to speak normally. She reached out her hands for it. 'You're being a real help today, aren't you?'

'Yes.'

She grasped the cabbage and slowly moved it away, praying the caterpillar would choose to remain on the leaf. Luckily, Wendy still hadn't noticed it.

But it didn't. Its rear end suddenly curled on to the T-shirt which it gripped like a brooch.

Dropping the cabbage, Phuong plucked the caterpillar away from Wendy and stepped back with it between her fingers to deposit it in the sink. Immediately its hairs seemed to bristle and she felt a sharp pain shooting through her hand, causing her to cry out.

She had to get rid of it . . . she had to kill it somehow before it . . . but it clung to her . . . she couldn't shake it off . . .

Her eyes misted and she felt herself staggering back against the draining board. New pains drilled into her wrist as the caterpillar's mandibles set to work. Something hit the back of her head. She was lying on the tiled floor moaning and screaming . . . so much screaming . . . so much burning . . . all over her body . . .

Lesley was shouting something. She could hear the voice faintly. And Frankie? Was Frankie there?

No, it was the ghost whistle of the American jets overhead, and her father swinging her up in his arms, and the hot tangy smell of the sea as it lapped against the side of the boat.

Down through the water he carried her, gripping her tight as they left all sounds far behind.

Lesley had been able to do nothing to save Phuong and blamed herself bitterly for it. Pondering it afterwards while Mary fussed around her, trying to comfort her when all she wanted was to be left alone, she could no longer grasp how quickly it had all happened. She had gone into the kitchen and seen Wendy with the spring cabbage. Even as she was shouting her warning – or that's how it seemed – Phuong had knocked the cabbage

229

out of Wendy's hand and was picking the caterpillar off her T-shirt. Sacrificing herself, because she knew the dangers well enough.

Then suddenly she was rolling on the floor and Frankie dashed into the kitchen, wanting to get the caterpillar off her, grabbing it as she'd grab a handful of sand and screaming hysterically.

Oh God, it was all so confused! Somehow, Lesley remembered, she'd got the caterpillar away from Frankie and crushed it under the rubber tip of her walking stick till its guts squelched out. Frankie, bleeding and unconscious by now, she'd hoisted on to the kitchen table.

Only then had she noticed that two more caterpillars had emerged from the heart of the cabbage and were attacking Phuong's throat. It was too late to prevent them.

The doctor had wanted to keep her in hospital, pointing out – with the medical profession's gift for understatement – that she'd had a shock. Phuong was dead, though Frankie was expected to do all right. But how could she stay in hospital with Wendy and Caroline still at home? She wanted Bernie – the old Bernie from before any of this had happened – but of course he wasn't there. Gone for good.

In a dream the previous night she'd been naked in bed with Bernie and Ginny together, not doing anything, but in a close, warm embrace as they floated with the bed-clothes around them. Then she'd woken up, to lie awake working out how to kill herself without upsetting the children.

Not possible, of course. She had to go on.

Mary went into her own room to telephone, leaving her alone. Wendy and Caroline were in bed, having cried themselves to sleep at last. Then Mary came back to say she intended putting the emergency plans in hand for the transfer of the whole school to Scotland. She had discussed it with the chairman of the governors and she had agreed. Several individual caterpillar attacks had now been reported in the county. It was best to make the move before the panic started.

There was no news. Ginny rang Jeff's house two or three times and at the last attempt Alan answered. All the equipment was in working order, he assured her. No, he'd received no confirmation yet that the plane had left West Africa. The arrangements were vague. Either there would be a telegram delivered directly, or else a phone call from some unnamed office in London. All he knew for certain was that Jeff planned an overnight flight to arrive early in the morning; if there were any delays taking off even that might not happen.

'I'm sleeping here at Jeff's house,' Alan assured her as they discussed all the possibilities. 'If he calls in on the agreed wavelength I'm bound to know.'

'Let's hope it's soon,' Ginny said fervently.

The situation was getting considerably worse and it was only the necessity to wait for Jeff which kept them in the village. Bernie's surgeries had long since been abandoned, and there were few emergency calls any longer simply because most people had already left. Streets were deserted; farms untended. An outbreak of burglaries had resulted in the teenage gang concerned dying horrible deaths. They had been found – three girls and four boys – lying mutilated on what had once been a wealthy stockbroker's well-kept lawn. The caterpillars had been crawling over them as thickly as ants.

From London too the news was not good. The jumbo jet which had crashed on Feltham shopping centre had been bound for New York with a full complement of passengers. Not one survived, and there was a high casualty rate on the ground. It had now been confirmed that moths in the jet engines' air intake had been responsible.

That had been bad enough, but that same evening also saw the first attacks in the London Underground. A Piccadilly Line train arriving at Earl's Court released swarms of giant moths on to the platform as its doors slid open. Waiting passengers ran screaming for the exits as the moths attacked them, but many were blinded. When rescue teams arrived they found more casualties in the centre three cars, though none elsewhere on the train. The following day saw more incidents as hundreds of moths invaded the tunnels. The accumulated filth blackened their wings. Soon not a single station in the central London area was free of them. Their dark forms came fluttering through the tunnels to greet every train and dart into the passengers' eyes. The entire Underground system had to be closed down.

Ginny rang Jack's number more often than she could count, but there was no answer. Had he been hurt, she wondered; or was he simply away somewhere? It was never possible to tell with Jack. But she kept trying, and each time could not help visualising the empty flat where there was no one to pick up the receiver.

These days that happened so often. Bernie too had commented on it. You dialled a number but no one replied. Were they even alive any longer?

14

Jeff glanced out at the white Alpine peaks immediately beneath the Boeing 707, then grinned at Enoch in the co-pilot's seat beside him. On a passenger flight they

232

would be crowding at the windows by now, the more optimistic among them clicking their cameras through the scratched Perspex. It was Perspex they fitted in these rattling old crates, wasn't it?

Not that he disliked 707s; they were first-class planes. He'd flown thousands of miles in them, till the controls felt like natural extensions to his own limbs. Only this old lady creaked with arthritis in every joint. It was lucky her four aged Rolls-Royce Conway 508 engines co-operated so courageously. Perhaps they guessed they were on their way home to the country which created them; or else, with the name Rolls-Royce, they couldn't bear to lose face.

They had stripped out most of the seats to make space for as many crates of monitor lizards as they could squeeze on board. That had caused some delays at Douala, but fortunately their Paying Guest was also late. In fact, this 'flying ark' operation was much better cover for him than their original suggestion. Everyone felt happier about it.

At that first meeting in London a couple of months earlier the idea had been that Jeff would ferry the plane back to the UK for overhaul with the Paying Guest travelling as crew. It had sounded a flimsy way of smuggling the ex-president of a neighbouring country out of Africa, but they assured him the right palms had been crossed with silver, so there should be no trouble.

But this lizard plan, they agreed when he put it to them, was far superior.

He'd also been lucky when it came to recruiting the real crew. Enoch he'd known in Nigeria and would have been quite capable of handling the whole operation alone. Pierre as third pilot, from Senegal, was less experienced but totally reliable. They had been together on several less-than-official runs before. Plus a few that were above board.

233

'I'm going back,' he said, getting out of his seat. 'Need to stretch my legs.'

Enoch nodded.

In the first-class passenger cabin they had left a couple of rows intact. Fred, the expert animal handler who had been sent out ahead by Andrew Rossiter to organise the lizards, lay sprawled in a window seat on the starboard side, fast asleep. On the port side, the Paying Guest sat upright, contentedly turning over the pages of a magazine. Jeff dropped into the seat next to him.

'Everything okay?'

'Oh yes!' He was an unashamedly fat man and his face wrinkled as he smiled. 'I can't tell you what a relief it is to get away! There were two attempts by their agents to kidnap me. To take me back over the border for one of their show trials.'

'Well, that's all behind you now,' Jeff assured him. 'But I need a word about what happens when we land.'

'Don't worry! I'll request political asylum. They won't refuse me. The Prime Minister is one of my dearest friends.'

'I was really talking about the lizards.'

'They smell, my friend. Can't you smell them? I assume I shall disembark first.'

'It may not be that easy,' Jeff told him, and began to explain about the caterpillars.

The old scoundrel, he thought as they talked. If anyone deserved to be put on trial he did, considering the amount of development aid money he probably had tucked away in his Swiss bank accounts. Jeff had known him well in his old West African days. As a young man he'd been in a key position to influence the granting of building contracts and had made a fortune out of backhanders. When he was President that fortune doubled.

'But there's no need to worry,' Jeff explained confidently. 'We've brought safety clothing for you

234

which you'll be wearing, and in any case you stay on board until we've checked everything is clear.'

'I don't like it.' The man's flabby cheeks were actually trembling. 'I prefer to land at Heathrow.'

'The situation at Heathrow is worse,' Jeff lied. 'As I said, I take full responsibility for your safety.'

'You had better, my friend. I'm paying you enough.'

Jeff got up, nodding to Fred who had just woken. He went back to the flight deck. At any rate, he thought, the ex-President was right about one thing. Those lizards in their crates did smell.

'Is he okay?' Enoch asked as he slipped back into his seat and adjusted his headset.

'I guess he is. We'd better call up our private control room to see how things look on the ground.'

At least there would be no trouble with either Enoch or Pierre. With them he'd laid his cards openly on the table, explained what the lizards were expected to do, shown them the safety gear and offered them double the agreed fee. They had accepted.

It was eight a.m. when Alan rang to report he'd established contact with the plane, three days late. The expected call from London had never materialised, nor had the telegram. Ginny had begun to doubt if Jeff would ever return.

In the kitchen she found Bernie had started to tidy up. His face looked strained and tired, not only from overwork. Lesley was still refusing to talk to him, and Mary had been downright aggressive on the phone. It was telling on their own relationship too. Over breakfast they'd picked up last night's argument about how much longer they could put off moving out and had ended by shouting at each other.

'That was Alan,' she told him. 'I have to get over to Gatwick. The plane's coming in this morning.'

235

'I'm coming with you.'

'After all?' She felt a flood of pleasure, and stood on tiptoe to kiss him as he leaned over the sink. 'We'll have to hurry!'

Separate cars, they had agreed. Just in case anything went wrong. Ginny drove the Range Rover, followed by Bernie in a large black BMW he'd rented a few days earlier, wanting something more robust than the Mini in this situation. Ignoring the route signs for the terminal building, they headed for a side gate they had discovered on their first recce. It gave them direct access to the cargo apron. Bernie had used wire cutters on the chain holding the padlock and it still hung there unrepaired.

Adjusting his protective helmet, he went to the gates and pushed them open. Then he came over to the Range Rover and Ginny wound down the window.

'The place seems deserted,' he remarked quietly. 'I've never come across anything so dead. No people, no animals, no insects. I wonder if the airport authorities are right not to have at least a skeleton staff here. Or at least a daily check on what's happening.'

'We'll go where we can see the runway,' she decided. 'Then I'll call Alan.'

Ginny waited until Bernie was safely back in his car before driving slowly into the cargo area. Everything had been abandoned in the middle of a busy work shift. Truck-loads of air freight parcels, containers and lorry trailers stood where they had been left. Only the dead and injured had been moved. She manoeuvred the Range Rover through the obstacle course and across the apron, checking in her rear mirror to make sure Bernie was still behind her.

When she stopped he drove around her, ending with the two cars parked side by side facing opposite directions. He wound down his window. They were only inches apart.

'It's all clear, love.'

With Jeff's field glasses she scanned the airfield but saw nothing on the runway, nor in the untended grass on either side. She reached for the car phone which Alan had doctored to plug into CB equipment, providing a direct radio link with the house.

'Descent check, please,' Jeff requested.

'Roger, descent check, captain,' Pierre responded immediately. 'Window heat?'

'High,' said Enoch.

'Number two auxiliary pump.'

'On.'

'Hydraulics?'

'Checked . . .'

So far it felt good, Jeff reflected as Pierre continued through the checklist. Ginny's report had been precise, closely following the short list of questions he'd supplied. As he'd feared fuel was low; poor maintenance work on the engines meant they were burning more than they should. But there was no doubt they would make Gatwick comfortably. Not that he had any alternative. Alan had passed on the information that both Heathrow and Stansted were out of action; incoming flights were being diverted to Manchester and even Dublin.

'Flying ark. Acknowledge. Over.'

'Go ahead, Alan. Over.'

'Ginny reports caterpillars on runway. I can now put her through to you. One minute.' A hard click cut through the static, hurting his ears. Then came Ginny's voice, recognisable despite the distortion. 'Jeff, this is Ginny. Do you read me? Over.'

'Loud and clear, Ginny. What's this about caterpillars? Over.'

'Caterpillars gathering on runway,' she said slowly. 'Large number. Coming out of the grass. Over.'

237

'Okay, Ginny. I read you. Ask Alan, can he keep this channel open? Over.'

'Wilco, Jeff!' came Alan's young, eager voice.

Ginny put the field glasses to her eyes again. It was an incredible sight. The caterpillars on the runway must now number several hundred, yet their progress was so slow, she was hardly aware of any movement. She was grateful to be sitting inside the Range Rover with the windows up. In the BMW alongside, Bernie gestured to her. She glanced back to see what he was pointing at. It was two giant moths, fluttering around each other near the wide, open hangar entrance. Bernie did a quick mime with his hands and pursed his lips, imitating a kiss – a courtship dance? Was that what he was trying to say?

'Hello, Ginny!' the car phone crackled. 'Come in, Ginny, over.'

'I'm here, Jeff. Over.'

'Request more detail about caterpillars. Are they . . . widely scattered . . . loose pattern . . . close . . . or . . . thick? Over.'

'Jeff, they're close but in patches. Do you read me? Over.'

'I read you, Ginny. Any change, let me know, please. Over.'

Just my bloody luck, Jeff thought. No fire tenders. No foam. No rescue services of any kind. And he only had to put his wheels where the caterpillars were thickest to risk spinning off the runway.

'A bit like landing in slush,' he said with a wink at Enoch. 'Filthy, half-frozen, mucky slush.'

'Landing gear,' Pierre intoned.

'Down,' came Enoch's voice. 'Three greens.'

'Anti-skid.'

(God, we're going to need that!)

238

'On. Four releases.'

'Flaps,' said Pierre.

'Give me forty, please.'

'Forty selected. Moving. Forty checked. Two greens.'

Ginny's voice came urgently through his headset, cutting across Enoch's response. He could sense the fear as she spoke.

'Jeff, I can see moths. A thick swarm of moths just visible in the field glasses. You'll fly into them. Over.'

'Roger, Ginny. Can't spot 'em yet, but . . . ' He glanced at the fuel. There was still enough in the tanks to roast them all alive. Time to speak the unthinkable. 'Ginny — any problems when we land, you and Bernie stay well clear. Okay? Over and out.'

Pringle's luck — it couldn't be anything else! All his life it had dogged him. Everything would go like a dream, then when he least expected it — *Wham!* Dropped in the shit. Like that time he'd dumped a plane-load of holiday makers into a potato field, overshooting the runway for Chrissake! No one hurt save for cuts and bruises, and that stewardess who'd lost the baby she'd told no one she was expecting. Not even his own fault, as the Inquiry established beyond doubt. Could have happened to any-one, but it didn't. Happened to him: Pringle's luck.

They were spot on for a perfect touchdown. There was the runway straight ahead. Then he saw the moths, bloody thousands of them directly in his approach path.

'Oh-oh!' he heard Enoch murmur alertly.

Ginny held her breath. The Boeing was over the end of the runway, its wheels seemingly — from where she was parked — only inches above the ground when the roar of its engines coughed and faltered. Despite this, the great aircraft touched down elegantly and began to race along.

For a second she relaxed, until she realised the Boeing's ground speed was not reducing and its engines still

239

produced desperate choking sounds. Then came silence as they finally cut out. It left the runway, skidding through almost ninety degrees across the grass until at last it did a kind of bellyflop and came to rest on the far side of the airfield.

'Jeff, are you okay? Over.' She shouted into the mouthpiece hysterically. 'Jeff, for God's sake say something. Over.'

'Ginny, what's happened?' Alan's voice broke through. 'Are they okay?'

She examined the Boeing through the field glasses, only too aware that it might blow up at any moment. Jeff had warned them. But nothing was happening. The aircraft was on its belly on the grass, motionless.

'Alan, I'm going over there to take a look. Keep trying him, will you? Over and out.'

Winding down her window just a crack, she briefly told Bernie what she intended before setting out, keeping at first to the taxiway. It was like driving over a carpet of caterpillars, the wheels crunching them to death and slithering over the green juice they extruded. Coming along behind her Bernie seemed to be in even greater difficulty, at one point skidding on to the grass.

He waved to her through the windscreen, trying to indicate that the grass might be the easier option. She joined him and they drove side by side. The ground was soft after all the heavy rain and their tyres left deep muddy ruts. Moths flew against the windows and windscreen; she used her washer and wipers to try and keep them out of her line of vision, but they never let up for a moment. *She* was the intruder, they seemed to be saying; there was no longer any hint of welcome in their interest.

Every few seconds Alan's voice came thinly from the handset, begging for a response from the Boeing. Its radio remained silent, as if the whole plane had died.

Some twenty yards away from the aircraft she stopped

the car and called Alan to describe what she could see. They were not far from the extreme end of the runway. Through the expanse of grass the Boeing had gouged a long, wide causeway of mud before coming to a final stop. She could see no one at the windows; no movement of any kind.

But – just as she was about to finish – the outer skin to the rear of the aircraft began to bulge and shift. She took the field glasses and focussed on it.

'They're opening the doors!' she yelled excitedly. 'I can see them opening the doors. Oh Alan, they're still alive! I'm going over to help. Over and out!'

Bernie too had noticed the plane's doors opening. He was already putting on his safety helmet and fumbling with the press studs of the rubber face mask. He had rejected the offer of an Army suit, saying he found it too restricting. Ginny agreed with him and now preferred heavy overalls, though still using the Army helmet. But nothing they had tried so far was ideal; that was another area where more research was needed.

They clumped over the grass towards the Boeing. The caterpillars were thick on the ground. With every footstep she felt them writhing beneath her boots. By now the moths were whistling again in an eerie concert of high-pitched squeaks which were steadily becoming louder.

Bernie touched her arm, pointing. Something was happening in the plane. In the open doorway, two figures were manhandling what looked like a long, flat crate. Then they tipped it over and seemed to be thumping the bottom.

Out of it fell two of the biggest lizards she had ever seen. Five feet long at least, with whipping tails and stumpy legs which carried them rapidly a short distance away from the plane. They stopped, suddenly motionless; then their heads looked around, as if bewildered.

Watching the nearer of the two, Ginny saw its tongue

241

shoot out. The caterpillars didn't have a chance against it, though some were already beginning to crawl over its back. Lazily, the second lizard picked them off.

One of the men on board came down to join them. He and Bernie together took the weight of the next crate as it was lowered to them and placed it carefully on the ground. Someone tossed down a crowbar which Ginny seized. She levered the lid off, tugging it open to release the next two lizards, almost falling as they tangled with her legs in their eagerness to escape.

Moths came screaming at her as she worked, spitting their venom across her visor and helmet. Caterpillars – some longer and more agile than any she'd ever come across before – crept over the crates and on to her gloves, or clung to the leather of her high boots. Occasionally she paused to pick them off, but more always appeared. She began to feel desperately that they had chosen her out as their special target until she noticed that Bernie and the other man were also covered with them.

She lost count of how many crates she'd opened – more than ten, it must have been – before at last she straightened up, gasping for breath, the sweat pouring over her body beneath the thick overalls. Everywhere she looked she saw these long, slender lizards, dark in colour with pale yellow rib-like patches at intervals down the full length of their bodies. The moths were fewer now; any that ventured too near the ground were soon trapped by those darting tongues.

Muffled grunts came from the two men as yet another crate came down. They staggered under its weight.

'Careful!' Ginny shouted.

Bernie took a blind step backwards in an attempt to keep his balance.

She ran forward to help.

The crate had tilted as it was lowered from the plane

242

and they had gripped it awkwardly. In trying not to drop it they lurched towards the discarded lids with their protruding nails. Before Ginny could do anything, Bernie trod on a loosened board which gave way and he fell heavily with the crate on top of him. A nail ripped through his trouser leg, gashing his calf.

Despite the lizards, caterpillars came out of the grass from all directions, attracted by the blood. They swarmed over him, snuffling into the wound on his leg and searching his safety clothing for more openings.

'Bernie! Oh Bernie!' she sobbed as she went down on her knees to try and pick them off.

There were too many. She wanted to throw them aside but they clung to her gloves. Tearing them apart was more effective but more kept coming. The pesticide aerosol she carried at her belt made no impact on them. Even the lizards were too occupied elsewhere, all but one which darted over to investigate, licked up two or three caterpillars only, then scuttled off in another direction.

Someone took hold of her shoulders and lifted her up, trying to comfort her. Two others had come down to help and were discussing whether or not to get him into the plane, but it was already too late. His fall had knocked his hard helmet awry, snapping open one of the press studs of his face mask. A caterpillar had already found the gap.

It was over, she knew. Blood from his throat slowly dripped on to the grass. One of the would-be rescuers shook his head and stood up. Bernie was dead.

Unable to accept it, Ginny knelt down again amidst the caterpillars to cradle his head on her arm, but it lolled limply to one side and she saw a gash too on the rubber neck-piece below the face mask. From it a caterpillar protruded.

Defeated, she left it to feed; what else could she do? Slowly she got to her feet. From the top of a pile of empty

243

crates a lizard was regarding her philosophically. It began gathering caterpillars off her overalls with its long tongue.

'Come on, then!' she screamed at the others. She retrieved her crowbar and began to tackle the unopened crate which had killed Bernie. 'Let's get these lizards out! Can't stand round all day!'

They had won, though with Bernie's death Ginny was too dazed to take anything in. All meaning had gone.

She returned to the house later that day dreading the prospect of having to tell Lesley what had happened. The first time she rang Mary answered the phone and swore at her angrily when she realised who was speaking. No, she could *not* have a word with Lesley! A click, and the line went dead. She dialled again, only to hear the Number Unobtainable tone.

She was tempted to leave it at that, but it was her duty and she had to go through with it. Somewhere she had a number for the school which she'd looked up days earlier. She found it and rang the school secretary who explained in a great hurry that they were on the point of evacuating everyone to Scotland. Reluctantly she agreed to take a message.

So Ginny dictated the bare facts about Bernie's death and how sorry she was. It seemed so heartless, put like that.

How long she sat there after ringing off she never knew. But at last she stirred herself, collected her clothes from the bedroom, her toothbrush, her pills, her comb, and moved back to the cottage.

The next days were hectic enough to keep her from brooding. They made regular checks at Gatwick and by the end of the week were able to report the airport clear of caterpillars. Their twenty-five monitor lizards had become fat and lazy. With Fred's help she caught a couple and took them back to the cottage to live with her.

Members of the Ministry's scientific committee arrived by Army transport to judge for themselves and pronounced the experiment a success. The attacks in London had brought the Government under considerable pressure to take immediate action regardless of cost. Planes were requisitioned to fly in carnivorous lizards from all over the world. Vast numbers were bought from any country in Africa willing to trade them, although many died when the weather turned cold.

But the caterpillar menace was finally beaten.

Services of thanksgiving were held throughout Britain. The Prime Minister appeared on television to proclaim the success of the Government's policy. At a press conference of his own, the ex-President let it be known that the initial plane-load of lizards had come as his personal gift to the United Kingdom. He modestly suggested that the British Cabinet could have consulted him earlier.

People returning to their homes in the stricken areas were advised to keep monitor lizards as house pets, and many did. But a five-foot lizard can be quite a nuisance in a living room and the majority were given quarters in the garden shed, only to die as winter came on.

Ginny kept her two and was glad of their company during the long empty months that followed. Jeff kept in touch but was usually busy. Alan was in Cardiff doing computer studies. Not even Jack was around. In fact no one knew where he was till he sent her a picture postcard from California.

She was on her own. To fill the days, she put her notes in order and began work on the book her agent was nagging her to write: *The Caterpillar Episode*.

15

'Ginny! I was hoping you'd drop by!'

Jeff strode over to the Renault and opened the door for her. He'd had the house painted, she noticed as she got out; in the warm sunlight it gleamed like a whitewashed Mediterranean villa.

It was a year now since the caterpillar invasion, but it still made her shiver to see his windows standing wide open with no wire mesh to protect them. In fact, all that remained visible from those days were the aerials on the roof. They had actually had the gall to prosecute him in court for operating a wireless transmitter without a licence; luckily, the magistrate had been on his side. He'd fined Jeff one penny, which he had paid himself.

They kissed, then she broke out of his hug to dive back into the car for her shopping bag.

'Strawberries,' she announced, holding it up. 'Thought this time I'd bring something.'

'I have news!'

'What kind of news?'

'Three kinds – good, interesting and indifferent. Which d'you want first?'

'First I want to get out of this sun. It's going to be a scorching summer again. Are you sure you should leave those windows open?'

In the living room she found he had a visitor: a slim, athletic Nigerian dressed in a colourful *agbada*. He stood at the table frowning with hard concentration as he poured himself a beer.

'You remember Enoch?' Jeff introduced him.

'Hi, Ginny! Like a beer? It's all froth. Someone has really been shaking it up.' He put the can down to squeeze her hand. 'No more caterpillars, I hope.'

'I hope so too,' she said soberly, accepting a glass. 'Cheers! Now what's this mysterious news, Jeff? Start with the indifferent.'

'You'd better sit down,' he advised drily. 'It's simply this. The Royal Commission report on the caterpillar invasion comes out tomorrow. For the full details we'll have to wait for the papers in the morning, but I've been up in London having a word with one or two people I know and they've told me the gist of it.'

'Which is?'

'The main conclusion is that the airlift of monitor lizards played only a comparatively small part in the defeat of the caterpillars. According to them, the rapid growth in the numbers of these caterpillars was caused by unusually hot damp weather, combined with the absence in this country of natural enemies. When the weather changed, the caterpillars died off. It's as simple as that.'

'The bastards!' She was appalled. 'Was there anyone on that Commission who actually lived through it? Without the lizards we'd all be dead.'

'As for the experiments which produced the things in the first place, it seems Sophie Greenberg did not give evidence. This kind of genetic engineering – interfering with the sperm or ovum to produce changes in the genetic inheritance – is claimed to be the great white hope for the future. It could stamp out hereditary diseases, so it seems. Or even produce the next generation's crop of Olympic gold medallists. They advise that all experimentation should be brought under Government control.'

'That should be enough to stop it!' Enoch remarked cheerfully. 'Jeff, I'll bring those other cans out of the fridge. Perhaps this beer is too cold.'

Ginny tried to force a smile, but failed. None of this would bring Bernie back to life, nor any of the others either. Government compensation plans had provided some money for widows with dependants and, of course, the disabled. Lesley would get something she supposed. But they were not even taking steps to prevent it happening again.

'You'd think they'd at least keep a stock of lizards in a zoo somewhere.'

'They say too few survived the winter,' Jeff explained.

'Because people didn't look after them, that's why!'

'Oh, I agree.'

Was Lesley keeping any lizards, she wondered. She was sure Mary had been responsible for her sister's silence, particularly about Frankie having been in hospital. It was pure coincidence that she'd heard about it at all. Of course Lesley was bitter, but she'd been the first to acknowledge her guilt, hadn't she? That terrible episode at the house still rankled with her. Told that Lesley was there to supervise the removal men, she'd gone over right away. 'Les – please, can't we make up?' she'd pleaded, desperately needing her sister's arms around her. No response. It had been like talking to someone long since dead inside. Then, as she was on the point of leaving, Les spoke to her. 'You may as well know, Ginny. I hate you, and I always shall.' And those words spun round and round in her mind, never leaving her alone.

'Hey, Ginny!' Jeff called to her across the room. 'Perk up, Ginny! You haven't asked me what the good news is.'

'Tell the interesting news first,' she asked, trying her best to snap out of that mood.

'Ah – the interesting news!' Enoch came back into the room and stood by the door listening, a quiet smile on his face. Darting past him came one of Jeff's domestic lizards. It stopped on the hearth-rug, its eyes fixed on her. 'Yes, well the interesting news is that Enoch has landed a

248

contract for a regular freight run between London and Lagos. I've managed to raise some capital to buy our own plane. We're going into partnership.'

'But that's great, Jeff! A Boeing?'

'707 of course. First of our fleet. We're going to call her Ginny.'

'Thank you, kind sir!' She raised her glass.

'And the *good* news . . . ' He gazed at her, his eyes twinkling and that angular jaw more prominent than ever as he smiled. 'Better fasten your seat belt. You and I are going to Los Angeles the week after next.'

'Oh, are we?' she retorted scornfully. 'Why? And you'd better make it good.'

'Remember that story about moths you tried hawking round the TV companies?'

'Threw it away,' she said. 'It was useless.'

'That copy you lent me to read – well, I had a few extra rolled off to show to a couple of people I know. If you can set the story in the United States we might have a buyer. It's not certain, mind, but I've a feeling a trip there might clinch it.'

Ginny got up, speechless, stepped over the recumbent lizard and put her arms around Jeff, burying her head against his shoulder. 'You really do try, don't you?' she told him when she felt sufficiently recovered from the surprise. 'You old pirate!'

She kissed him.

'Thought you might be pleased,' he said smugly. 'I'll show you the letter. Came this morning. This could be the turning-point for you.'

About an hour later she was sitting in the bow window thinking it over while Jeff was busy in the kitchen preparing a meal and Enoch wandered in and out setting the table. If the American company bought the script, she mused, she might have to stay over there for a few months. But she was ready for that sort of change. Perhaps she'd be able to call on Jack and meet this American girl he'd astonished everyone by marrying. Then something Jeff said caught her attention.

'In really hot weather it seems the life cycle may be no longer than three weeks from egg to fully-grown moth,' he was shouting over the sizzling of the steaks in the frying pan. 'And they multiply rapidly which – according to the experts – is just what happened.'

'But surely they cannot all be dead. Don't they hibernate? So now the warm weather has returned . . .?'

The breeze from the open window was mild against Ginny's cheek. Across the entire width of the sky were broad splashes of red from the setting sun. It was going to be a beautiful day tomorrow.